ULTIMATE DECEIT

Book Two in the Jack Kane series

Dan Stone

ISBN:9798872473718

Cover design by: Erelis Design
Library of Congress Control Number: 2018675309
Printed in the United States of America

ULTIMATE DECEIT

By Dan Stone

PROLOGUE

The road swept around the meander of a babbling river, and Kane drove with his window open so that the fresh summer breeze blew through his hair like a hairdryer. Tidy rows of manicured hedges sprang up from the road's camber in a bright green wall, and above him, gnarled trees leant over both sides of the tarmac to meet in a long-fingered handshake. The sun bathed everything in its warm embrace beneath a pale blue sky, marred only by a hint of wispy clouds.

"Daddy?" said Kim from the back seat. She said the word in a drawn-out drawl, which usually preceded a question from the depths of her sharp, young mind.

"Yes, princess?" Kane responded with the same drawn-out tone.

"What's a haggis?"

"It's a traditional Scottish dish." Kane smiled out of the window, pleased with his diplomacy.

It had been six months since Kane had settled in the Scottish Highlands with his two children, Danny and Kim.

"What's it made of?"

"You don't want to know."

"Just tell her, Dad," huffed Danny. "She's so annoying." Danny was three years older than Kim, and therefore, everything Kim said or did wound him tighter than a spring. They shared the back seat of Kane's Ford Mondeo, which he had bought for cash from a local car dealer.

"Alright, then," said Kane. "It's made from sheep's heart, stomach, liver, and lungs, with oatmeal, suet, and onion, I think."

"Ugh." Kim pulled a strange face and shook her head in disgust. "Why do people eat that?"

Kane laughed and wound his window up as the breeze grew stronger. The road levelled out into a straight run towards the small school at Glencrow Cross. Being in a remote area, the school had less than one hundred pupils and was a fifteen-minute drive from Kane's rented cottage.

"Have a good day, kids. I love you," said Kane as he pulled in at the drop-off point outside the school. They operated a system where parents drove into an area marked with yellow paint and let their children out of the car. Parents then drove away, leaving their kids to be ushered into the school gates by a teacher. Kane waved at a smiling teacher in sunglasses and a bright green T-shirt. "Danny, don't forget to bring your reading book home today."

"OK, Dad," Danny sighed, with his usual sullen, tween boredom. Unless it had something to do with football, Danny wasn't interested.

Kane watched them shuffle into the gates, backpacks heavy with lunches and schoolbooks, and drove off. A black Hyundai Santa Fe pulled out of the line of traffic behind him, and Kane began the three-point turn that would take him back towards home. As he swung the car around, Kane waved at a couple of parents he recognised, and once past the clutter of the drop-off point, he was back to the open roads of Scotland's Highlands. He rounded a bend, and the car climbed a steep hill beside which a grazing pasture fell away to the west, its grass kept short by a dozen sheep with summer-shorn fleeces.

The road levelled out, and Kane noticed the black Hyundai in his rearview mirror. Most families from Danny and Kim's school lived in the opposite direction, where there was a small town. It was more of a village than a town, containing only a pub, a shop and a post office. Out in this direction, there were only hills, farms, and a few remote homes similar to Kane's cottage. Kane, being the cautious man he was, had reconnoitred the surrounding area before moving in, so he knew every car and every person within a five-mile radius. When hunted by assassins and special forces operators, it pays to be on your guard.

Kane made the turn for his cottage. It was a sharp bend, almost a hairpin, and Kane slowed to a crawl as he came through it. The Hyundai Santa Fe followed closely behind him, and the driver abruptly slammed on the brakes to avoid colliding with Kane's vehicle. There were two men in the front seats, big men with beards. The SUV was a seven-seater vehicle, and a shiver ran across Kane's shoulders. Silhouettes of hulking figures in the back seats proved they were not tourists taking in the highland air. The shiver was a warning, the intuition that tingles when someone is watching you out of sight, or the churning sensation in your stomach just before something terrible is about to happen.

Kane slammed his foot down on the accelerator, and his Ford Mondeo sprang along the road. The Hyundai followed at top speed. There was no mistake. They had found him. Kane was a fugitive, a former special forces soldier and a counterintelligence agent. He had, however, fallen foul of his former employers and had previously gone into hiding with his family, assuming new identities to evade capture. Unfortunately, they had been discovered last spring, resulting in the tragic death of Kane's wife and the abduction of his children. Men had died for that, and Kane had thought he had escaped the agency's attention being in so remote a location in Scotland. He lived off the grid, paying for his rent and groceries in cash. The only link to the outside world was via Danny and Kim's iPad connection to the internet.

As the Ford growled beneath him, leaning into turns at top speed, Kane suddenly understood how they had found him. Danny must have connected with his old friends using one of his football games or apps. It was the only way. Leaving their home and friends had been a wrench for the kids, especially for Danny. Losing his mother, combined with the abandonment of his friends, school, and football teammates, had left Kane's son like a hollow shell. So, despite knowing the risks, Kane had allowed Danny internet access to give him some small pleasure, a relief from the hard things in his life. That had been a mistake.

Kane sawed on the steering wheel, causing the car to skid sharply and veer left into the entrance of a farmer's field. The men in the Hyundai had one objective – to eliminate Kane, leaving his children fatherless, taking everything from him. However, they had underestimated Kane's resilience. He was not an easy man to kill. Kane braked hard, and the car's tyres screeched as they slewed into a sprawling spread of bright yellow rapeseed. Kane reached under his seat for the Glock pistol he kept for emergencies and dived out of the car. He rolled in the dirt and ran ten paces to his right. The Hyundai careened into the field, only to find the Mondeo had stopped, its engine still running. Four burly men emerged from the black SUV, all dressed in shirts and smart trousers, each armed with a gun – killers seeking to hunt their prey. Concealed amidst the green crop stems, Kane opened fire. No questions and no hesitation. The wolves had unknowingly cornered a bear, and Kane killed them all with ruthless efficiency.

ONE

Craven ducked his head beneath the water and blew out a chain of bubbles. He re-surfaced from the pool and grinned to himself as cool water droplets streamed down the crag of his face. It was mid-morning, and about now, his old teammates in the Serious and Organised Crime Squad in Manchester would be sitting down to a morning whiteboard meeting to review current investigations and assign tasks for the week ahead. His old boss, Chief Inspector Kirkby, would condescendingly speak to his detectives as though they were children in a geography lesson, and he was the teacher, striding back and forth with his coffee mug in hand, sneering and scowling. Craven, however, was taking a dip in his pool beneath a warm sun rather than listening to that pompous bastard. He couldn't help but smile, content and loving every minute of his new life.

"Bacon sandwich, love?" asked Barb, Craven's

wife. She leaned out of the wide patio window wearing a green vest top and pink shorts. Her face glowed with a suntan beneath a white headscarf.

"Yes, please!" Craven smiled at her and clambered out of the pool, using the silver stepladder at the water's shallowest point. He grabbed a towel and dried himself off before taking a seat on his brand-new patio furniture. Craven chuckled as he listened to Barb singing a Westlife pop song in the kitchen. She was happy, and the Spanish air was working wonders for her chest. Barb had recently gone through a fresh round of chemotherapy for her cancer. When they had lived in the UK's northwest, she had struggled with shortness of breath and coughing that had left her unable to sleep, and she was wheezy throughout the day. Yet, on the southeastern coast of Spain, she had improved, and Craven was delighted.

Barb strolled out of their new villa, clutching a cup of steaming hot tea and a bacon sandwich on white bread. She set it down on the table, and Craven reached out to hold her hand. She grabbed his fingers, her touch warm and comforting. The skin on the back of her hand was dryer and looser than it had been when they had first met decades earlier, but he still got that jolt of excitement whenever he touched her.

"Thanks, love," he smiled. "Are you coming to sit down and enjoy the sun?"

"I'll be back in a tick; I'll just fetch my breakfast."

Craven took a bite out of his bacon sandwich and cuffed a blob of HP brown sauce, which escaped his mouth to rest against his chin. The toasted bread crunched, and the bacon was hot, salty, and beautiful. He washed it down with a swig of his tea. At that moment, life couldn't have gotten much better. However, Craven's relaxed morning and breakfast al aire libre were interrupted when his phone vibrated on the table, and he set down his tea to pick it up. The screen said it was Jim Baldwin, an old friend from the police.

"Jim?" Craven answered with a surprised voice. "Long time no see."

"Craven," Jim said, his Liverpudlian accent just as broad as it had always been. "Rumour has it you've retired to a life of luxury in Spain?"

"The rumours are right, matey. I've got a better suntan than Dale Winton."

"Dale who?"

"Never mind. It's lovely out here. How are you doing?"

"Well, that's why I'm calling. I heard you had

retired and wondered if I could pick your brain about something."

"Go on."

"I'm in private security now. The money's great, and I've been in Dubai for the last four years. Anyway, one of my clients has landed in some serious shit, and it's gone beyond anything me or my guys can handle without help."

"So, what makes you think I can help?"

"This problem involves some seriously dangerous guys and a seriously rich client. He's a stud farm owner from Ireland, money to burn, and someone has kidnapped his daughter."

"Bloody hell."

"Right. There's heavy-duty violence involved, Frank. Guns. You've nicked some serious people in Manchester and Liverpool in your time. I could do with tapping into a bit of your knowledge on this one. I want to help the guy, and the money he's offering is tasty. Do you know anyone with the right skills to help my client? It's a long shot, but the man is desperate. It's his only daughter."

"I know a man with the skills, but I don't know if he'd want to help." Craven instantly thought of Jack Kane. The man who, only the previous spring, had single-handedly brought down one of Manchester's most violent gangs, seizing their ill-gotten gains in the process. Kane had generously given a chunk of that money to Craven, which had funded his new life in Spain. In a turn of events that had brought both men close to death, Craven had helped Kane take down a vast swathe of a government spy agency, and Kane had killed a dozen highly trained agents to get his own children back.

"Can you ask him?"

"I'll ask him, Jim, but I'm not making any promises."

TWO

Kane searched the four bodies for anything of value and clues to identify which agency the dead men worked for. Their pockets were empty, as he knew they would be. But each man carried an MP5 semi-automatic weapon and two spare bullet magazines. The driver had a phone with only one number in its contacts, and as Kane dragged his corpse into the redolent rapeseed plants, he kicked himself for how they had found him. The leak just had to be through Danny and his iPad. There was no other contact with the outside world other than his connectivity through gaming platforms. Kane had been meticulously careful in the past year, avoiding any traces of his existence. He possessed no bank cards, only used disposable burner phones, and paid cash for all his household bills, which were registered in the landlord's name. He was off-grid, as much as anyone could be in the modern world.

He opened his latest burner phone and checked the apps linked to the cameras he had installed at the cottage. Everything seemed quiet – no intruders. He scrolled through the outside camera, then the one in the kitchen, and the place was still and silent. So, either the house was empty, or the people after him were very good.

Kane drove the Hyundai SUV into the crops until the tall stems hid most of its bulk. He put the MP5s and spare ammunition in the boot of his Ford, then reversed out of the field and drove back towards the school, pushing the saloon car to its limits as he leant into corners and sped up hills. If those who hunted him had followed Kane to his children's school, they would also have eyes on his cottage. It was time to leave.

Kane reached the school and told the headmistress that he needed to take Danny and Kim home because of a family emergency. Mrs Fraser was all smiles as she bustled through corridors adorned with certificates and kids' paintings. Her sensible shoes moved silently, and she dug her hands deep into the pockets of a long aran knit cardigan. Mrs Fraser first pulled Danny out of his classroom, and he came without objection. Kim, however, was a ball of questions.

"What's happened, Daddy?" she asked, a frown creasing her round face. "We have gymnastics this afternoon. Will I be back for it?"

"No, princess, I'm afraid not," Kane replied. He placed his hand on her shoulder and thanked Mrs Fraser for her help. They walked out into the car park, and as soon as the children were seated in the back, fussing with their seatbelts, Kane turned from the driver's seat and looked directly at his son.

"Danny, I'm going to ask you an important question, and I want you to answer it honestly. You aren't in trouble; I just need to know. OK?"

"OK, Dad. What is it?" Danny looked at his father with wide eyes, and his cheeks flushed.

"Have you connected with any of your old friends? On anything? Any of your games... FIFA football? What about Snapchat?"

"No, Dad."

"Danny, it's OK. I'm not going to shout. Just tell me the truth. The men who took you and Kim could be back. To protect us, I need to know if you have been in contact with any of your old friends in Warrington or London?"

Danny licked his lips. He swallowed hard and stared down at his trainers. "Sorry, Dad. I have. I found some of the lads on Snapchat, and we have a group." His speech quickened. "But there's only three of us, nobody else. I've been careful, Dad, I promise."

"It's OK, son." Kane turned on the ignition and lurched the Ford into action. Danny's life had been turned upside down twice before. First, when Kane entered a witness protection programme and relocated his family up north, changing their identities. Then, agents from Kane's old counterintelligence agency, Mjolnir, had kidnapped Danny, Kim, and their mother, Sally. The children had witnessed the brutal murder of their mother and had been through hell. So Kane wouldn't scold his son, even though he had disobeyed his instructions.

Sally. Her absence had left a devastating void in all of their hearts. There wasn't a day when Kane didn't miss her or mourn her. She had been the love of his life, and her death cast a haunting shadow over his days and nights.

Returning to the cottage would be risky, given that its location was compromised, and there could be more agents on the way to finish the job the men in the Hyundai had failed to complete. Kane knew he had to take Danny and Kim and leave immediately. While Kane had an emergency bag in the car boot, there were things at the house he couldn't leave behind, particularly those that Kim couldn't live without. One such item was a blanket that Sally used to cuddle Kim with during story time, and

Kim was especially attached to it. It was a small thing, not an item worth dying for, but it was all Kim had left of her mother, and Kane wouldn't let them take that from her.

Kane left the road and turned into a dirt track, little more than two worn ruts in a field of overgrown grass. The track cut through a sloping pasture where it met the gravel driveway at Kane's cottage. Jeff Lowell owned the cottage, just as he owned the farmland for miles around, and he had gladly let the cottage to Kane for cash. The arrangement suited them both. It meant Kane didn't need to use any form of digital payment which those who pursued him could track, and for Lowell, it was an income he could keep without losing half to the taxman. Kane pulled the Ford to a halt twenty paces away from the cottage.

"Stay here," he said, turning to the children. "I'll be back in five minutes. Danny, look after your sister." Danny nodded, and Kim bit her bottom lip. Kane didn't have time to comfort her, and he exited the vehicle, pulling his Glock pistol from the waistband of his jeans. The magazine carried seventeen rounds, and he had fired eight at the men in the Hyundai. One each to drop them, and another to make sure each man was dead. There were nine bullets left.

Kane's shoes crunched on the pathway's tiny

pebbles as he sprinted towards the cottage. He kept low, heart racing, aware there could be a sniper hiding anywhere in the surrounding forest and undergrowth. Back when he was an agent working for the Mjolnir agency, he would not have returned to the house. He would have left immediately if he had even the slightest hint that it was compromised. But times were different now. He wasn't a government agent anymore. He was a man on the run with his children.

The cottage was a two-storey house with three bedrooms. Sprawling ivy covered its front and gable end above a black-painted door. Kane skirted around to the back of the building, just in case a nasty surprise awaited him inside. He slipped in through the back door, treading carefully on the varnished hardwood floors. The place seemed empty, just as the cameras had shown. Kane ran upstairs, grabbed Kim's blanket, and bundled some extra clothes for him and the kids into a sports bag. He retrieved another bag from under his bed, which contained semi-automatic weapons, ammunition, and rolled bundles of cash – all gifts from the gang of human traffickers and drug dealers Kane had taken down in Manchester.

Last of all, Kane retrieved his laptop from the sitting room. It was a clean device with a masked IP address, and just as he was about to close it, he saw an email from Craven. Kane didn't have time to read it properly, but the subject line read: *Work for a man like you.*

Kane closed the laptop and ran back to the car. He bundled the bag containing the clothes, money, blanket, laptop and weapons into the boot of his car and sped off into the sprawling roads of Scotland's highlands.

THREE

McGovern marched along a corridor with ancient high ceilings and grey slate flooring. The rhythmic sound of her heeled shoes echoed off the stone walls, resembling the clip-clop of a shod horse in the vaulted hallway. With each step, her black bobbed hair swayed around the sharp angles of her face. McGovern clutched a smooth laptop case under her left arm.

She was deep within the sprawling corridors of the Palace of Westminster, a building steeped in history and the cornerstone of the British government. First built in the eleventh century, it had borne witness to kings, queens, and Prime Ministers throughout the ages. As she traversed the corridors, McGovern felt the weight of a thousand years of secrets and matters of national security embedded in the storied walls and high ceilings. Sculptures of important men – and faded, ancient paintings – told of historical events and merciless wars. The great spymasters of the late Middle Ages had hatched and foiled plots within its walls, while wars had both ignited and been averted. Powerful men and women had forged careers and reputations within Westminster's vastness, and many had crumbled, suffered, and succumbed to violent ends on the cold stone floors.

McGovern turned into an open door within an archway of perfectly dressed stone. A young man in a dark suit sat behind a desk piled high with paper files. He wore a headset and typed furiously on an old-fashioned black keyboard with chunky keys, staring at the leftmost of two wide computer monitors.

"McGovern," she said in a clipped voice after waiting ten seconds for the man to look up, "here to see Mr Aziz." The man's focus remained on his monitor. McGovern retained her steely composure, yet underneath, she seethed. Soon, they would all know who she was, and soon, they would all respect her.

"Take a seat," replied the man in a broad Essex accent. He flicked his eyes to a set of weathered armchairs against a wall covered with faded green wallpaper. "I'll let him know you're here."

As soon as McGovern's arse touched the chair, a heavy oak door creaked open on iron hinges, and a stout man in a pinstriped suit appeared in the doorway. He removed his clear-rimmed glasses and beckoned McGovern in with a podgy finger. She sighed, rose from her seat, and followed him in.

"Here we are again, Miss McGovern," Aziz remarked in a thick Birmingham accent. He slumped into a leather-backed chair behind a wide desk. Aziz sipped tea from a white china cup and squinted at her through his dark-ringed eyes.

"It's just McGovern," she replied. McGovern refused to call him 'sir', as he was an elected official, not a civil servant.

"Very well, McGovern. Do you have your report?"

"I have it here." She unzipped her laptop case and pulled out a paper file with the words *Top Secret* printed on the outside in large lettering.

"Another paper file? Really?" He sighed and reached out for it. "Your clandestine agencies still insist on living in the past. Just email it to me next time, please."

"With all due respect, Mr Aziz. Your email is not a secure form of communication, and the information in that file is…"

"Let me guess… a matter of national security?"

"Yes." McGovern sighed and pursed her lips.

She sat back and crossed her long legs as though settling in for an arduous, boring seminar or lecture.

"I would remind you, McGovern, that despite your evident disdain towards me, I have been appointed by the Prime Minister himself to examine the operations, funding, and activities of the Mjolnir agency. I have full power and unfettered access. Last spring, Mjolnir agents shot up Warrington with machine guns. People died. Then, a rogue agent, this Jack Kane, went on a killing spree in Manchester. This is unacceptable, and there must be a full and frank investigation into the agency's affairs. I repeat what I said to you last time – I want to know where your funding comes from and who gives the orders. I want to know what activities your agents have conducted on our own soil and abroad. Whether you like it or not, you will tell me who you have killed and why. Do I make myself clear?"

"Crystal. Now, if you turn to page..." McGovern launched into the information she had prepared for Aziz, which she knew would find the ears of the Prime Minister. It was bland, high-level information stating that Mjolnir was an off-the-books agency operated by a rogue commander, a remnant of an old world, the Cold War pre-technology world. The key information conveyed to Aziz was that Mjolnir had been dismantled and disbanded, rendering it non-existent, which should, therefore, alleviate any concerns. Notably, she omitted that she was acting under the orders of MI6 now and that they had fed her the bones of the basic information to relay to Aziz. But, of course, they withheld the truth and instead offered a carefully curated narrative in its place because God forbid any elected official should pry into the affairs and secrets of the state.

Politicians were men and women who had simply won a popularity contest. They were solicitors, teachers, welders and businesspeople. Yet they were not well-versed in the shadow world of espionage and counter-terrorism, which operated behind a gossamer cloak, invisible to the world at large. That hidden world was a place of highest stakes, where elite operatives risked and lost their lives battling against enemy states whose single-minded obsession fixated on the collapse of Western civilisation to subvert its stability and weaken its countries to the point where an attack might succeed. Those enemies were religious zealots, power-hungry dictatorships, and black-hat nations with a burning hatred for any country that had interfered in their pasts.

Mjolnir was one of a handful of secret, black ops, or hidden agencies with arcane connections to senior figures at MI6. It had to be that way. This clandestine approach was essential to combat the ruthlessly wicked people in the world who would destroy Britain and her allies. Using above-the-board transparent tactics didn't stand a chance. There had to be front-facing agencies – MI5 for domestic security and MI6 for international matters. But then there were the agencies who operated using methods the liberal-leaning population would simply not understand. They had to go where the danger was, to the eye of the storm and strike with savage, unflinching force to quash any threat to the British people and their security.

Following the Mjolnir debacle, McGovern had found herself summoned by the higher echelons of MI6, the people who worked in the shadows of the shadows. Under no circumstances could Mjolnir's activity come to light – assassinations, instigated coups, and a litany of activities the British people simply would not and could not understand. They were necessary actions taken by hard-boiled men and women so that the simple folk of Britain could sleep safely in their beds at night.

A phoenix had risen from the ashes of Mjolnir, a new beast of a broader scope with greater access to government resources and international infrastructure. However, this also brought about heightened oversight. But before that phoenix could spread its wings, there were loose ends to tie up, and Jack Kane knew too much. MI6 had made it expressly clear that for McGovern to continue in her existing role, she must succeed. They granted her access to agents and resources, and she had built her own team. Yet what the agency had not explicitly said, but of which she was under no illusion, was that Jack Kane must die. If not, then it would be McGovern's corpse found in the wreckage of a car crash or in her apartment as an apparent suicide. It was him or her.

"So," said Aziz at the end of McGovern's monologue. "You say that you believe Mjolnir is no more and that it is disbanded?"

"Yes, that's exactly what I'm saying."

"Excellent, I'll let the PM know the good news. So, I'll see you back here in a month, and we can decide how to channel Mjolnir's funding into other worthy organisations."

McGovern offered him a wan smile and rose from her seat. Aziz shook her hand, his gold watch gleaming against his dark skin and blue shirt. He held the heavy door open for her, and McGovern strode back out into the ancient corridors. Her stride was longer and more deliberate than it had been on the way in. She passed a painting of Thomas Cromwell and an image of Thomas Cranmer, both ruthless and calculated men in an implacable time. It served her new bosses' agenda for Aziz to believe that Mjolnir was a closed book. It would bring down too much pressure and scrutiny if Aziz knew that there were still loose ends out there, that there were agents still in the wind, and that she had dispatched her most ruthless killer to deal with the Kane problem once and for all.

FOUR

Craven opened his black laptop and waited for it to boot up. He sat at the dining room table overlooking his patio and pool. The Spanish sun shone through the wide glass window to warm his face, and tall trees swayed in a gentle breeze beyond his garden. He punched in his password, and a blue screen whirred into life, the small machine buzzing and clicking. He opened his Gmail to find four new emails in his inbox. The first was from a sports clothing delivery company notifying him of a sale on men's swimwear. He told the email to piss off and then chuckled at his reaction. In the absence of uniformed constables and sergeants, there was nobody in Craven's life left for him to swear at. It was perhaps the one thing he missed about his long career in the police force.

The second email was from an encrypted source, and Craven sat up straight in his chair. It was Kane. They'd kept in touch since they went their separate ways last spring. Craven had visited Kane, and both men often checked in to see how the other was doing. Kane would ask how Barb was adjusting to life in Spain, and Craven would reply by asking about Kane's children. Kane had a secure way of sending emails to a select handful of people he trusted, and Craven was one of the lucky members of that merry band. He did not know who the others were. It worked, though, so Craven had no complaints.

Craven read through the brief email. Kane was in trouble again. Men had come to his new home, and he was on the run. Kane asked if the children could come and stay in Spain with Craven and Barb until things blew over, and he also asked for more details about the job outlined in Craven's initial email.

He stood up from his computer and walked outside. Barb was curled up on a sun lounger, taking a nap. A book lay open on a small table, one of the cosy crime mysteries with the bright covers she loved so much. Her headscarf had ridden up slightly to reveal the stubble beneath, but overall, she was thriving in Spain. The healthcare for her cancer treatment was top-notch, and she had made friends at a local expat centre where she could play bingo. Considering Barb's condition, Craven hesitated, but he couldn't refuse Kane's plea either. Not after what those children had been through. Plus, the kids weren't babies. Their presence might do Barb good, especially the little girl.

Craven went back to his laptop and wrote his reply. His email would go to Kane's untraceable server, so there was no risk of exposing his friend's location or intentions. Craven assured Kane that the children would always be welcome to stay with him and Barb, although he raised concerns about how they would get to Spain. Surely, somebody would be on the lookout for their passports. He gave Kane more details on the job, explaining that it involved an old pal from the police who was trying to help a family in Ireland whose daughter had been kidnapped. The Irish police weren't having much success in locating the missing girl, so the parents wanted to use their considerable means to find other ways of finding their daughter.

Craven hit send on the email and then called Jim Baldwin back to say that he could help with the job in Ireland. The money was good, and if Kane didn't take the job, Craven would do it himself. He still had access to the money Kane had taken from the gang back in Manchester, but it wasn't enough to last forever. And besides, he could do with a bit of excitement – something interesting to get his teeth into. Laying by the pool reading all day was fine for a couple of weeks, but he couldn't do that forever. Barb had her friends now, and she was happy to potter about with the housework, go to the shops and nip to her new girlfriends' houses for coffee. Craven had never been a man who could make friends easily, and he knew he wasn't easy to get along with. His mind was made up – he would help these people in Ireland if he could.

FIVE

The police had found the abandoned SUV and four corpses ridden with bullets in a field of rapeseed crops. A call from London had kept that quiet and out of the local press. In the interests of discretion, a warning was issued, and a payment was made to the farmer, ensuring the matter was sewn up. Condor's commanding officer had assigned her to the case two days prior.

"Get up there and see what the hell's going on. We need to sweep this guy up. No more pissing around. Get rid of him efficiently and quietly," McGovern had ordered, her eyes blazing with fury at the incompetence of the Mjolnir agents. McGovern had dispatched the four men found dead in the crop field, and they were Condor's colleagues. She did not know them, however, because she always worked alone.

Condor could have flown to Scotland, but

she would have still faced a long drive on bad roads to get to where her target was living. So, she had driven instead. She enjoyed driving her latest vehicle, a sleek Range Rover Evoque. The hotel on the Scottish border was serviceable and had afforded her a chance to read the file on Jack Kane. Codenamed Lothbrok, he was an experienced field agent, ex-SAS, and had undertaken heavy-duty operations all over the world, the top secret details of which were redacted from her file with thick black lines. They had addressed the file to her, codename Condor, and she would destroy it once she had committed the crucial details to memory.

Condor pulled up outside Kane's cottage. It was quaint, with ivy on the walls and brightly coloured flowers in deep beds flowing in a warm summer breeze. She had this location in her file and found a thread to pull on, even though she knew Kane would be long gone. There was no other way to find him. He was a ghost, just as she was. Condor stepped out of her car and pulled on a light jacket to cover her shoulder holster. She forced the cottage's front door open and stepped into a small but freshly decorated family home. It smelled of fried mince and family bolognese. Frames containing pressed flowers and pastel paintings of the Scottish countryside adorned the walls. Yet there were no pictures of Kane or his family. She walked cautiously into the sitting room and then the kitchen, just as she would if she were clearing a room with her weapon drawn. The principle of never leaving an uncleared room behind you guided her every step.

The kitchen had pine countertops and whitewashed cupboards. Pans and cooking utensils hung from the walls, along with herbs and clutches of flowers. She breathed it in. Here, at least, was some semblance of family life. There were awful children's paintings of animals pinned to the fridge and a football cards collection album open on one counter. She noticed an unwashed coffee mug and a cereal bowl in the sink. A hasty departure. Condor looked for the junk drawer that existed in every family home. The place where people stuffed electricity bills beside takeaway menus and pens that don't work but are never thrown away. There was nothing like that in Kane's house, just more pictures with hearts and messages to 'Daddy'. Condor screwed up a small heart drawing and tossed it to the floor. Bile rose in her throat, and she cursed Kane for what he had.

Condor's own childhood flashed through her memory like an unwanted movie trailer – scenes of various institutions and foster homes, wicked hands pawing at her young body, and kind smiles for the people who had cared for her but ultimately gave her up. Condor was an orphan of a black single mother who had died from a heroin overdose; she was unwanted, unloved, and tossed around like a scared puppy in a pound. The cottage had no family pictures, but the love inside the place was palpable, and it washed over Condor like a warm blanket. But that warmth fed her hate and bitterness. Nobody had loved her until they realised her exceptional abilities as a student and athlete. Then, everybody wanted a piece of the prodigy. Scholarships and bursaries poured in, along with accommodation, and all that was required in return was a smile and a photo to show how the kind white people had helped the poor little black girl.

"Can I help you, missy?" said a deep Scottish voice behind her.

Condor turned on her heel to find a short man with grey chin whiskers, a checked shirt and corduroy trousers. He took the cap from his head and itched at a frowning brow. Clearly, he must have been the landlord.

"Sorry for barging in," she replied in her friendliest voice, letting a smile split her face. Condor knew she was beautiful, that her smile was wide and beaming with gloriously white teeth below her almond-shaped eyes. "An old friend invited me here. He doesn't seem at home, though?"

"Ah, you mean Ian?"

"Yes, and his darling little cherubs." 'Ian' appeared to be the alias Kane had adopted whilst hiding up in the middle of nowhere.

"They've been living here for about half a year. Seen no visitors, though. Apart from one."

"Who was it? It might be a friend of mine."

"I didn't catch his name. Although we were chatting, and he mentioned he had recently retired from the police force."

"Doesn't ring a bell. Do you know where Ian is?"

"No, sorry. He just upped and left yesterday. I don't know where he is or when he'll be back."

"Then what use are you?" She drew her Sig Sauer pistol and shot the man twice in the chest. His mouth gaped as the bullets tore his chest open and threw him into the back door. He slid down its wooden panels, leaving a scarlet smear like a blood-soaked snail. He stared up at her with wide, horrified eyes, clutching at the holes in his chest. His life blood pumped out of him and pooled on the floor. Condor watched him for a few seconds, the pain in his eyes assuaging her own internal suffering. The fear of death showed in his brown eyes, and a tear rolled down his whiskered cheek. As a girl, she had been afraid once – when wicked men had used her vulnerability to hurt her. Condor raised her gun and shot the old man in his left eye. She had a new thread she could pull to unravel the ball of Kane's whereabouts. A retired policeman.

SIX

Kane knocked on a steel door, and the sound reverberated as though he were in a cave. He frowned at a camera positioned above that door that was staring straight at his face. The alleyway stank of stale piss, and Kane wouldn't want to be found there after dark with his children in tow. The drive to Newcastle had taken hours longer than necessary, mainly because of the frequent toilet breaks for the children and more stops for food along the road. Kane told the children that they were going on a road trip to see an old friend and that if he could, he would take them to see Craven, the nice man they had met earlier in the year.

The alleyway was deep within the vibrant streets of Newcastle city centre but far enough away from the Bigg Market to avoid students and folk enjoying the city's famously raucous nightlife. The door was a large plate of steel with a sliding spy hole at face level, and the building was the bottom floor of what seemed to be a derelict old manufacturing factory. Old business names had once stood proudly high up on the dark brickwork but had now faded into illegible obscurity. The surrounding buildings were a mix of gentrified coffee shops, fashion boutiques, and a spattering of cool-looking bars. The rest of the old structures were empty and dark, their broken window shards jagged in long smashed panes and crumbling brickwork.

Kim hugged Kane's leg, clutching a bag of sweets, and Danny leaned against the wall with his arms folded.

"We won't be long, I promise," said Kane, leaning over to ruffle Danny's hair. Danny rewarded him with a smile. "Listen, kids, when you meet my friend inside, don't be alarmed by how he looks. He sometimes wears a mask because he has some scars on his face. But he's my friend, and the scars make him sad. So, try not to stare. He's a nice man and will try to help us."

"That you, Jack?" came a crackled voice over an intercom. Kane felt relieved as he recognised the voice through the metallic comms system.

"It's me. Thanks, Cameron."

A buzzer made Kim jump, and Kane pulled the heavy door open. It dragged on the concrete pathway, adding more white scrapes to the dozen others. Kane only kept in touch with a handful of people that he deemed worth the risk, and Cameron was one of them.

"Come on," said Kane, holding the door open so Danny could sidle in first. Kane pushed Kim gently through the door and then followed himself. A spindly man in an untied bathrobe emerged from a side door of a dark entrance hall. The man wore an Empire Strikes Back T-shirt over black jogging pants with sliders. He had short red hair, and a pure white mask covered his face. The mask had one eye painted in black and one hole to show his actual remaining eye. The rest of the mask was plain and expressionless, like bright porcelain, with a mouth that neither smiled, smirked, nor grimaced.

"Well, there's a face I never thought I'd see again," said the man. "Still a grim beast, I see? And these must be your sprogs? Come on in."

"It's good to see you too, Cam."

"Who is he, Daddy?" asked Kim.

"An old friend from the army. Come on inside."

"Why is he wearing a mask?" Kane shushed her. The story was too long, and she wasn't old enough to understand.

They followed Cameron through his door,

which he bolted behind them using the sort of locking mechanism you might expect to see in a safe. He shrugged off his bathrobe and hastily tidied away some dirty plates and cans of Coke before leading Danny and Kim to a seating area. The room was a large, open-plan space which could have been an office or a factory before Cam had got his hands on it and turned it into a den of technology and toys.

"Kids, you've come to the right place. There are VR goggles over there, and you can choose from loads of PlayStation, Nintendo, or Xbox games. Take your pick. Be careful with the virtual reality, though. I once broke my nose running into a wall."

Danny's eyes lit up, and he and Kim scrambled for the collection of four flatscreen television screens and multiple game systems in the room's corner.

"Thanks, Cam," said Kane, smiling to see the children happily checking out the wonders of Cameron's collection of games and controllers.

"So, you're in the shit again?"

"I'm afraid so, and I'm sorry to come to you like this. But I don't have many other options."

"You saved my life, even if they left me with this." Cameron gestured towards his face. "So, give me a chance to return the favour. You said passports and credit cards, right?"

"If you can?"

"Of course, I can. I'm sorry to hear about your wife, by the way. The fuckers will get us all in the end." Cam stared into the distance, and his eyes became glassy. "Sometimes I think it's God repaying us for the things we did. Punishing us for our sins. We should be punished, Jack." Cameron dug a hand into his pocket and pulled out a rattling container of pills. He popped the lid without breaking his gaze and stuffed a white tablet beneath his mask and into his mouth.

Kane had thought Cameron was better these days, but that assumption came from infrequent communication via secure email. This was the first time he had seen Cameron in years. They had served together, first in the Parachute Regiment and then in the SAS. Cam was a communications expert, a technical genius who had always been more at home behind a keyboard than a gun. Cameron had become an effective sniper and the team's comms expert. A rocket-propelled grenade had blown up a jingly van in Afghanistan whilst Cam stood next to it. The blast had torn off half of his face and burned his body badly. Kane had dragged him out of the furnace, and Cameron had spent a year in the hospital as doctors tried their best to rebuild the ruin of his face.

"Perhaps we should be punished. Or, instead of causing suffering to others, maybe we should use our skills to help people?" Kane spoke the words before they fully formed in his mind. They just poured out of his mouth like an epiphany. Kane stared at Cameron, whose head twitched a little as though Kane's thoughts amused him.

"We're getting deep, and we haven't even had a drink yet," quipped Cameron. His shoulders relaxed. The tablet was kicking in. "We need to take some photos."

SEVEN

Kim grinned as Cameron took her picture for a fourth time. She was losing her baby teeth, and her tongue poked a gap in her smile. Kane couldn't help but laugh, firstly because she was as cute as hell and secondly because Cam was doing his best to coax Kim into keeping a straight face for her passport photo.

"This one will have to do," Cameron said, staring into the viewer of his expensive-looking black camera with his one eye. "At least she's got her eyes open."

"How long before the passports will be ready?" asked Kane.

"A couple of hours. I need to print them and get the insides up to scratch. I've got two credit cards nearly ready to go."

"Thanks, Cam. How much will all of this cost?"

"Nothing to you. I owe you one, remember?"

Kane remembered. The rest of the team had escaped from the explosion without injury and had even completed their mission – a SAS hit on a high-value target, a picture card in the deck of Isis wanted men. But Cameron had suffered badly after the explosion. Losing his face had torn away Cameron's soul, and he was a changed man. Kane noticed a variety of face masks hanging on the wall, some with coloured patterns, others with smiling or snarling expressions.

"I remember," Kane said. "But you got out, and now this is your life?" He gestured around the ample living space. It had a bed in one corner, and the only separate room was a bathroom. The place boasted black walls, but it was brightly illuminated, adorned with movie posters from the '90s and '00s, such as Pulp Fiction and Event Horizon. Pinball machines and video games were scattered against the walls in random locations, and beside the seating area was a serious computer setup. Desk, keyboard, three huge monitors, and enough hardware to put an electrical shop to shame.

"Yeah, I do a bit of stuff like this. Passports, visas and the like. Mostly, though, I work as a freelancer, writing code and building websites. The money's good, and it allows me to live in peace. Do you think they are still after you, the Government?"

"They found me up in Scotland. I don't think they'll ever stop. But don't worry, I've been careful, and they won't follow me here."

"So, how did they find you up there?"

Kane nodded towards Danny, who was leaning forward in a gamer chair, controller out in front of him as he tapped buttons and stared intently at a screen where Mario jumped across various brightly coloured obstacles.

"Ah," said Cameron. "Where to now then?" As he waited for an answer, Cameron went to his fridge and fished out two bottles of Peroni lager. He opened the bottles and handed one to Kane.

"That reminds me. I brought a bag of weapons with me, but where I'm going, I can't take them. Can I stash them here? I need to leave the kids with a friend for a while whilst the heat's on. Then there's a job I might take on."

"Sure thing. Anyway, what job?"

"Best if you don't know." Kane took a sip of his lager and shrugged as Cameron nodded knowingly.

"I understand. Your business is your own. We should have your documents sorted soon, and you can be on your way. What happened to Sally,

Jack? It's OK if you'd prefer not to say."

Kane sighed and took another drink of his beer. "We've been in touch, on and off, for years, Cam, but I never told you what I did after the regiment."

"I've a fair idea. You and Fowler both went working for MI6, right?"

"Something like that. Anyway, it went sour, and I left on difficult terms and went into hiding. They found me living in the northwest, and all hell broke loose. They killed Sally and took the kids hostage. It was a mess."

"Bastards. I'm really sorry for your loss, Jack."

Kane stared at the floor. People didn't believe it was possible, but Kane had fallen in love with Sally at first sight and had loved her for the entirety of his adult life. Her loss was a crushing blow, and it had been less than a year since she had died. Kane missed her every day, and each night, he would fall asleep thinking of her smile, remembering the times they had spent together and the warmth of her hand in the dark. He couldn't take any risks with Danny and Kim's lives, not after last time. He was their father, and it was his job to protect them at all costs.

EIGHT

Craven took a sip of his coffee and grimaced at its bitterness. He rarely bought the stuff from Spanish cafes; it just wasn't the same as the coffee back home in England. Spanish coffee was bitter and stronger than the stuff he was used to, but he had a good coffee machine in the house and promised himself a nice one when he got home.

Cradling his disappointing coffee, Craven stood waiting in the airport arrivals area at Málaga Airport because Kane's flight was delayed by thirty minutes. The floor tiles were shiny like marble, and the place was heavily air-conditioned to the point where Craven shivered in his shorts and polo T-shirt. People streamed out of the arrivals doors, striding purposefully towards the taxi rank or smiling when they saw a friend or relative waiting for them.

"Fucking horrible," Craven grumbled as he took another sip of his coffee. He marched to the closest bin and threw the cup, contents and all, into its cavernous mouth. The arrivals gate thronged with people in shorts and bright T-shirts as holidaymakers from the UK with pasty skin and suitcases on rollers clogged the exit. The place filled up in no time. Luckily for Craven, he was taller than most men, so he could see over everyone's heads and monitor the exit. He was excited to see Kane and the children. Although their initial meeting occurred briefly amid the carnage of last spring, the shared experience of the searing danger of that time had made them friends for life. The children would be happy playing with Barb by the pool, but Craven was a little apprehensive about whether Kane would take on the job in Ireland. Kane didn't need the money, especially not after the vast sums they had acquired from the Manchester gang, but Craven thought he knew the man by now and might be drawn to the job for the thrill of the action.

Kane strolled through the arrivals gate wearing a pair of navy chinos and a blue Oxford shirt with tan brogues. He was of average height and build, with a plain oval face, brown eyes, and dark hair. Kane was the least distinctive in the crowd, with no flashy clothes, no bright suitcase, or even any distinguishing marks or tattoos. He was the grey man who could blend into any environment. Young Danny wore a red Liverpool football kit, and Kim wore green shorts and a pink T-shirt. Kane dragged one small carry-on suitcase behind him.

Craven raised a hand in greeting, and Kane nodded as he caught Craven's eye.

"Welcome to Spain," Craven grinned, and he ruffled Danny's hair. He softly grabbed Kim's nose between his forefinger and thumb and squeezed it affectionately. The little girl laughed, and Craven pulled a silly face.

"I was expecting a greeting in Spanish," said Kane. He smiled and shook Craven's hand warmly.

"I don't speak Spanish."

"Really?"

"Nah. Everybody speaks English here." Barb had learned some Spanish using an app on her phone and dedicated an hour each day to practice. Craven, on the other hand, was too old a dog to learn any new tricks, and English would suit him just fine.

They made their way to the car park, and Craven put the small suitcase in the boot of his car.

"So, the passports worked alright, then?"

"No problems, and the credit cards worked fine for the booking."

"We'll be at the house in thirty minutes," Craven clapped his hands. "Barb will have a nice lunch ready when we get there, and the kids can play in the pool."

"Thanks for this, Frank," said Kane as they got into the car.

"Anytime. Did you have a think about that job?"

"Kids, put your headphones on." Kane paused whilst Danny and Kim took the headphones for their iPads and put them on. "Someone's taken their daughter?"

"Yes. Ransom demand. The fella is loaded. Horse racing and a stud farm. I don't know much about it, to be honest."

"If men have taken his daughter, then we should help him." Kane turned to look at Craven, and there was a sadness in his dark eyes. Craven had seen Kane kill without hesitation; the man was like a shark. Pitiless eyes and emotionless, a predator who killed without compunction. But there was a sadness there as they spoke in Craven's vehicle. Perhaps it was because Kane's wife had died or because he knew how it felt to have his children taken by wicked men.

"Then we will. But we're up against the clock. The ransom says they must pay the money within seven days or the girl dies."

"Will Barb be OK with the children? She isn't too tired?"

"She's fine. She's on a break from her treatment, and she'll be delighted to have a little girl to spoil for a few days."

"We should go to Ireland, then. See if we can get to the bottom of it."

Craven smiled. "I was hoping you would say that. I've booked us on the last flight out tonight from Málaga to Dublin. We'll be there before midnight."

NINE

Condor sat in a waiting room with chipped yellow paint on the walls. A poster asking people to report violent crime hung on one side of the room, and an aerial picture of Greater Manchester Police Headquarters on the other. She had driven from Scotland to Manchester the day before and had spent the rest of that day checking her laptop for the records of retired police detectives from the Manchester police force. On the drive south, Condor had called the agency's operations team and had them run a search for detectives who had retired over the course of the year. They had cross-referenced that with Kane's location and created a list of male retirees in the northwest.

The carnage surrounding Jack Kane's emergence from witness protection had largely occurred in Warrington and Manchester, and only two Warrington-based detectives had retired at that time. One was a woman, and the other worked in road traffic crimes. There had been twenty-three retirees in the Manchester force. Any detective who had stumbled across Kane must have been a heavy hitter with a decent rank, and from those twenty-three, one name stood out – Frank Craven, former Detective Inspector of the Serious and Organised Crime Squad.

The operations team called ahead and made the appointment for Condor to meet the inspector in charge of the organised crime division under the guise of Condor being an MI5 agent looking to tie up the Jack Kane case. So, Condor waited in a reception area in need of a lick of paint and an air freshener, wearing a visitor lanyard with the name Tina Okocha in large font next to a picture of her taken at the reception desk. She wore a smart black designer suit and a white vest underneath. Condor had left her weapons in the car.

A uniformed policeman with red hair and acne scars across his cheeks opened the door.

"Miss Okocha?" he said in a broad Manchester accent.

"Yes," nodded Condor, standing and brushing down her trousers.

"Follow me, please." He led her through a series of sanitised corridors, his boots squeaking on the shiny floor. The young officer swiped the card inside his lanyard beside a pine door with cross-hatched squares on the window. He opened the door and waved her inside.

"Thank you for seeing me, Inspector Kirkby," Condor said as she entered the room. A man with rolled-up sleeves and transparent-rimmed glasses nodded at her with professional courtesy.

"Please, take a seat," he invited, gesturing to a metal framed chair with a black fuzzy seat pad and backrest. "I was instructed to meet with you, Miss Okocha, and we are always keen to assist our brothers and sisters at MI5. Now, how can I help you?" He looked at his watch and ran his tongue underneath his top lip.

"I'll cut to the chase because I know you are a very busy man," she said. "I'm working on wrapping up the trouble you had last spring with a certain David Langley, a man in a highly sensitive witness protection programme." Langley was the alias given to Jack Kane when he had entered protection for evidence given against the Mjolnir agency and their black-hat operations across the world. Condor's file contained the high-level details of Kane's operational history with Mjolnir. It wasn't a million miles away from her own activities. Only he had ratted on his teammates. An agent was the tip of the spear. At the front of Britain's defence against terrorism and other threats to national security, they knew too much sensitive information to be allowed to provide transcripts of their activities. If such evidence fell into the wrong hands, governments would fall, and powerful people would suffer.

"What a sorry mess that was. Gunfire on the streets of suburban Warrington, of all places."

"Quite. I need some information about a retired member of your team, Frank Craven."

Kirkby sighed and raised his glasses to rub the bridge of his nose. "He was a pain in the arse. Frank was a good copper once upon a time. But his glory days were well and truly behind him. He was dead weight, and to be honest, it was a relief when he left the force."

"How did he get involved with David Langley?"

"As far as I'm aware, he wasn't involved with him. He worked the investigation, but so did every able body in the northwest."

"I see." She smiled, working hard not to patronise the Inspector who had obviously achieved promotion to a rank way beyond his ability. "Do you have Frank's contact details? I'd like to interview him, just to draw a line under the file and close everything off."

"Last I heard, Frank had moved to Spain, and I don't think we have his new address. I'll check with HR. I have his phone number, though, if you want to call him. It might be easier?"

"Yes, perfect. Give me his number, and I will do the rest."

Condor wasted a few more minutes exchanging pleasantries with Kirkby before finding her own way out of the Greater Manchester headquarters. She left her lanyard at reception and strode towards the car park.

Condor took out her phone and called the operations team.

"Name?" said the woman on the other end of the line.

"Condor. Password is nemesis."

"Very well. How can I help?"

"I have a number for you to check. I want to know the current location and locations visited in the last six months." She gave the information and hung up. The results would be with her by the time she had retrieved her gear from the hotel. 'Nemesis' was the password Condor had always used; she liked the word. She was the nemesis of the life laid out for her by her cruel mother and absent father. Condor had dismantled that life and built a new one for herself – one of success, wealth and purpose. She was also the nemesis of her enemies and anyone who stood in her way. She would find Kane and become his nemesis. It was her job, her calling, and she never failed.

TEN

Kane woke up from a fitful sleep on board the flight from Málaga to Dublin. Craven had insisted on buying him a whiskey as soon as the plane was in the air. He had objected at first, not wanting to become dehydrated at altitude, but the alcohol had helped Kane drift off amidst dark thoughts about the future and the challenges of getting Danny and Kim settled if theirs was to be a life on the run.

Craven snored with his head tipped back and his seat reclined. Five empty plastic cups were on the tray in front of him, and five small empty Jameson whiskey miniatures accompanied them. Kane nudged him awake, and the former detective jerked into startled wakefulness.

"What the fuck?" Craven mumbled through half-open eyes.

"Time to wake up, Frank." Kane pointed through the small aeroplane window at the dense flickering lights below them as Dublin came into focus. At night, the city was a sprawling mass of yellow and orange lights beneath them, with roads cutting through and around it, cars like ants crawling along the twisting trails.

Dublin Airport was peculiar in that Kane and Craven had to go through customs upon arrival, even though they had shown their passports at Málaga airport. Despite his trust in the quality of Cameron's work, Kane still felt a stab of nervousness as the immigration officer examined his passport, glanced up at Kane, and then back at the document. Fortunately, he waved Kane through with no problem, and after a heavy queue and much grumbling from Craven, they finally reached the luggage carousels and then exited into the arrivals lounge.

"There he is," said Craven, pointing to a man in a navy gilet. He was tall but didn't quite match Craven's height. Broad at the shoulders, he sported a heavy paunch that stretched the fabric of his clothes. His face was clean-shaven, and his hair was cut close to his skull. The man held up a strip of cardboard with Craven's name written on it in black marker pen.

"Fran Doyle?" Craven approached the man with his hand extended. "I'm Frank Craven, and this is Jack Kane."

"Thanks for taking the trip, lads," replied Fran in a Dublin accent. "You came highly recommended, Frank, and sure, I used to be a copper myself. Jim Baldwin says you're the man to get this mess sorted out. I'm parked just through here."

"Where is Jim?" asked Craven. Kane knew Jim Baldwin was an old colleague of Craven's from the force and that it had been Baldwin who had reached out to Craven for help.

"He's at the stud, working with my team. We brought Baldwin in to help with the case, and he recommended a couple of guys who could also help. You were top of his list."

Doyle led them over a steep walkway, talking about how much better it was to fly into Dublin at this time of night and avoid the traffic on the notoriously busy M50 motorway which encircled Ireland's capital city. They reached his black Land Rover Discovery, and Doyle tossed their luggage into the boot.

"It's a forty-minute drive to Kildare," said Doyle. "We have five days left to pay the ransom and get little Annie back, or the ruthless bastards will kill her. So, I'll fill you in on the details on the way."

"How are the kidnappers making contact?" asked Kane, hoping that the method of communication would present an easy way of tracking them down.

"By phone, but the Guards have already tried to track the numbers. They're always untraceable lines." The 'Guards' referred to An Garda Síochána, the Irish police force. "I'll give you the background first, and then we can get into the details. So, my employer is John Kelleher, a very wealthy man and well-known in the racing world for his horses and breeding studs. John owns a stud farm in Kildare, which you'll see shortly. I work for Mr Kelleher as head of security, and by Jaysus, it's usually a handy enough job."

Kane wondered about that. Doyle seemed like a nice enough guy, but most of the other millionaire businessmen Kane had met in his time usually employed security professionals with a military background, whereas Doyle seemed more like an ex-policeman seeing out the twilight of his career in an easy job which paid good money. Kane had examined the man within seconds of meeting him and could detect no weapons on his person nor sign from the way he held himself that Doyle was any physical threat despite his size.

"Ireland is a safe place, lads," Doyle continued. "You have to understand that, first of all. It's not like it was back in the day with the IRA and all that madness. The only real trouble we have here nowadays is with drug gangs, and the Guards take care of that. So, you can imagine how fucking surprised we were when the bastards snatched little Annie on her way home from school, and we received a ransom demand for ten million euros threatening to kill the girl if it's not paid within a week."

"Does Kelleher have that kind of money?" asked Craven.

"He's a rich bastard, and he has the money. But it's tied up in investments and property. It will take time to turn that into actual cash."

"Sounds like raising the ransom could be a problem. So, who do you suspect has taken the girl?" Kane pressed.

"We haven't got a fucking rashers," said Doyle. Kane assumed 'rashers' meant a clue. "The Guards think it could be a former employee turned sour or gangsters sniffing a chance for a few easy quid. Mr Kelleher also does a lot of racing in the UK and further afield, so the kidnappers could be from anywhere."

"Are the police at Mr Kelleher's home?" asked Craven.

"No, but they're on the case. I know a lot of the lads in the Guards, and they're doing all they can to find Annie."

"Any enemies, rivals, or bad blood we should be aware of?" asked Kane. Solving kidnappings was not his area of expertise. He was the guy you sent in to take down the kidnappers once they had been located, not the one who figured out who and where they were.

"I'll introduce you to a few people tomorrow after breakfast, and then I'll bring you a list of potential bad blood."

That sounded ominous, but then Kane supposed any man who became rich would make a few enemies along the way, especially when competitive professional sport was concerned. Jealousy, rivalry, former partners spurned or cheated. Fran Doyle put his foot down as the car merged with the M50 motorway, and as Kane gazed out of the window at the Irish car registrations, his mind half trying to work out which county the KE, L, or TS letters referred to, and the other half wondering why he had agreed to come to Ireland in the first place.

Kane told himself that his children would be safe with Barb. After all, they'd travelled under new, clean passports and fresh names. The credit card used to book the flight was untraceable, so nobody would track Danny and Kim to Málaga.

The pull on his conscience at the call to help a man who had lost his daughter was simply too much to refuse, especially with Sally's death weighing so heavily on him. If Kane could, he would get Annie Kelleher back. But he only had five days to do it.

ELEVEN

The Kelleher stud farm was a sprawling property of lush grazing fields, paddocks, and a grand house fronted by a fountain and statues of horses in various states of athletic grace. It had been late when Doyle had led Kane and Craven to their rooms inside the house, and Kane had slept deeply.

Kane woke at six the next morning. He showered, shaved, and left his room. The house was an architectural dream of old and new combined. It had thick beams in high ceilings, with lots of glass in each room to let in natural light. Kane followed a polished wood floor into a large kitchen area. The kitchen's centre point was an island with a granite worktop and an old-fashioned range stove. Curling away from the cooking space was a tiled dining area fronted by an extensive set of fold-out patio windows.

The view outside that long strip of glass was breathtaking. Horses ambled about on thick, green grass across rolling meadows set against a rising valley in the hazy distance.

A man sat at the white marble dinner table. He had his head in his hands, and his foot trembled up and down beneath the table. Kane took a few steps closer, and the man's head jerked up. He was of a similar age to Kane, with dark hair swept away from his face. He had a short, clipped beard and eyes as red as hot coals. In front of him, papers scattered the tabletop around an open laptop.

"Sorry to disturb you," said Kane, having that awkward feeling of being caught moving around as a guest in someone else's house. "I'm Jack Kane, here with Frank Craven."

"Ah, the police detective and his friend," replied the man with a wan smile. He rose and rubbed at his heavy eyes, his waxy skin pale above his navy shirt. "I'm John Kelleher." He stuck out his hand, and Kane took it, the grip firm. "Apologies about the mess. I just can't sleep with Annie missing. I have to keep going over every detail. Can I get you a coffee?"

"I'm sorry for the situation you have found yourself in, Mr Kelleher. We'll do all we can to get Annie back safe. I can make the coffee. You sit down, please."

"I insist. How do you take it?"

"I'd prefer tea if you have it? Lots of milk and sugar."

Kelleher nodded and filled the kettle. Kane shuffled closer to the table and cast his eyes over the documents there. There were employee records for the stud, names crossed out or underlined, along with bank statements and a diagram of what looked like a racecourse.

"So, how do you know Jim Baldwin?" asked Kelleher whilst he threw a teabag into a mug and switched on his Nespresso machine to make himself a coffee. He spoke in an Irish accent entirely different from Fran Doyle's. Kane couldn't place it, but Kelleher's was more drawn out, like a slow drawl, rather than Doyle's brisk Dublin accent.

"I don't, actually. My friend Frank is an old colleague of Jim's."

"Ah, OK. And have you worked these kinds of cases before?"

"Not exactly, no. But I have some experience of dealing with what you might call difficult situations."

Kelleher looked Kane up and down, sizing him up like a horse he had purchased, believing it was a thoroughbred, only to discover it was a three-legged nag. Kelleher frowned, and for a moment, Kane thought he was about to ask him what he was doing there if he had no experience, but then Frank Craven strode into the kitchen, filling a doorway with his gigantic frame. At the same time, a tall man with a lantern jaw entered the room from the opposite door, and the two newcomers greeted each other with broad grins.

"Jesus Christ, Frank, you haven't aged well," said the lantern-jawed man.

"Jim Baldwin, you still look like Harold Steptoe, you scrawny bastard," barked Craven, and the two men met in the centre of the kitchen with an enormous bear hug.

Craven expressed his condolences to Kelleher, and the four men gathered around the dinner table with steaming mugs of coffee and tea.

"Four days to go," John Kelleher uttered, meeting the eyes of each man with a steely stare. "Tell me how we're going to get my daughter back." He spoke like a man used to giving orders and used to getting what he wanted.

"Frank is formerly of the Serious and Organised Crime Squad, John. So, let's take him through the details," said Jim.

"Let's hope Mr Craven has more to offer than Mr Kane here, who tells me he knows fuck all about kidnapped children. I hope you won't make a balls-up of this, Jim. If my daughter dies…" Kelleher blew out his cheeks and held up a hand as though the consequences of his anger were beyond explanation. Kane bristled slightly at the insult about his experience but put it down to the man's deep sorrow and concern for his daughter.

"Let's just get one thing straight here," said Craven. "Jack Kane is a former fucking SAS soldier and MI6 agent. So, we aren't here to fuck about."

Kane winced at the disclosure about his past and fixed his eyes on the loose paperwork rather than see the two men eyeballing him with unspoken scrutiny. Kane knew their minds would be awash with doubt, thinking he was too short, not muscly enough. Kane didn't care about that, but he would have preferred to not have his past disclosed if possible. He wondered if he should have used a false name for the job to protect himself from any connected ears with a long reach.

"We have the Americans due to land this morning," piped Jim Baldwin. He met Craven's raised eyebrow with a lifted finger. "Private operators, all ex-military. They do insurance and private work. They've dealt with this kind of thing in South America."

"So how many of us are actually working on

this case?" asked Craven.

"As many as I can get," said Kelleher. "Money is no object here, and I'll pay the ransom if need be. I just want my daughter back. Now, let's get this briefing started. The clock is ticking, and my little girl's life is at stake."

TWELVE

Condor drove her car off the ferry at Dublin Port, following a chain of vehicles loaded up for holidays, with roof racks or bikes strapped to the back and rear windows piled up with luggage. Every flight to Dublin that morning had been booked up, and there were no agency aircraft available to take her on the quick hop to Dublin, nor did she have time to charter an aircraft. So, rather than wait for a later option, Condor took the car ferry from Holyhead to Dublin. She had made the drive from Manchester to Anglesey, North Wales, in little over an hour and a half and was now in Dublin two hours later.

The vehicle chassis rattled on the ferry platforms as her car rolled gently down the sloping exit ramp towards the gaping opening at the ferry's rear. A man in a hi-vis vest waved her on, prompting Condor to drive onto a curving road and past the bored-looking security guards in their tall booths. Bringing her car also meant Condor could bring her weapons. If they stopped her for a random check, one phone call would have her waved through without a problem, but in an airport, it would be a different story.

Her phone rang, and Condor answered on her car's Bluetooth system.

"Condor?" said the officious voice on the other end of the phone. Condor grimaced and checked her makeup in the car's pull-down mirror on the sun visor.

"Yes," replied Condor brusquely, not bothering to hide her disdain. It was McGovern, her new commander. A civil servant with no field experience.

"Progress report, please?"

"I'm in Dublin, tracking a retired policeman and recent associate of Kane's."

"Is Kane there?"

"I don't know yet. I've only just arrived."

"Who is this policeman?"

Condor turned out of the port and into the Dublin Port Tunnel. "We linked him to Kane's activity in Manchester and Warrington last spring, and he visited Kane's place in Scotland."

"Ah, very good agent Condor. Sounds like progress."

"Are you going to call me for an update every day?" Condor was used to being left to operate on her own. Before transitioning to this nascent agency offshoot from MI6, they would give her a job and a detailed briefing, then leave her to do her duty. She had access to help if required, safe houses worldwide, weapons caches hidden in most major cities, and transport. She'd never had an overzealous schoolmarm leaning over her shoulder, observing every move she made.

"No," McGovern's voice bristled. "This mission is pivotal to the success of what we are trying to do here. I can't access the funding for the new agency setup without the Kane issue being put to bed. Millions of pounds in slush funds and offshore accounts are about to be diverted from Mjolnir to our new Medusa agency. So forgive me if I'm a little apprehensive about the mission's success."

"Kane will be dead before the week is up. Now, is there anything else? I'm about to lose you in a tunnel."

"Mind your tone, Condor. You came recommended as the best of the best. If you want a senior agent's position within Medusa, you'd better make sure you know what side your bread's buttered."

Condor hung up the phone. The port tunnel wasn't long, and she hadn't lost the phone signal. She simply didn't want to talk to that haughty bitch any longer. Condor checked her locator for Craven's signal and followed the tunnel exit towards the M50 southbound and Kildare.

THIRTEEN

John Kelleher left his home to meet the American mercenary group, as he had arranged for them to stay in another house on his sprawling property. Craven drank another cup of coffee and listened as Fran Doyle and Jim Baldwin brought him and Kane up to speed with the potential list of suspects.

"So, these aren't necessarily people we suspect of the actual crime. They are simply people who might have an axe to grind, a financial interest in John's business, or are just opportunistic criminals," said Jim Baldwin. He took a piece of A5 white paper and stuck it to the wall with Blu Tack. "There are approximately twenty thousand kidnappings in the world every year, and Interpol claims that's an under-reported figure. They believe that only ten per cent of actual kidnappings end up being reported because people don't notify the police and simply pay the ransom. Interpol also says that only eleven per cent of victims are freed without a ransom payment. On a more positive note, once a ransom has been paid, the kidnappers return forty per cent of all kidnapping victims unharmed and safe."

"Mrs Kelleher and her father shouldn't be on this list for starters," Fran Doyle complained. He stood behind the dinner table with his thumbs tucked into a pair of worn jeans. "There's a shower of shite on that piece of paper, and they have no place on it. If Mrs Kelleher saw her name on that list, she'd cut your bollocks off."

"Mrs Kelleher hasn't always enjoyed the life she has now," said Baldwin. "Let's call a spade a spade here, Fran. She has a drinking and drug problem. I've asked the house cleaner and some of the staff at the stud, and they all said she's always drunk or off her head on cocaine. She came from a rough enough part of Dublin called Tallaght. After she met John, they were married quickly, and she and her father moved into John's estate. The father has a bit of previous, and he's done as well out of John Kelleher as his daughter."

"But the wife would hardly arrange for her own daughter to be kidnapped. As his wife, surely she has access to Kelleher's fortune already?" said Craven, which seemed obvious to him.

"True," Baldwin allowed. "But what about the father? What if he's got greedy? It's worth looking into, anyway. Davey McNamara is his name. Something else you need to be aware of is that Kelleher might not be as flush with cash as we think."

"I'll talk to McNamara today. See what I can get out of him. I've a good nose for a lying bastard," Craven rubbed his hands together.

"Thanks, Frank. Here's a file on his finances and his chequered history." Baldwin took a pink cardboard file from the table and handed it over. Craven opened it and thumbed through recent pictures of Davey McNamara dressed in smart suits and driving a Porsche jeep. There were also photos of him from the '80s with shaggy hair and sideburns. A mug shot and a rap sheet of petty crimes rounded out the file.

"We should start the day with the fucking scumbags," insisted Fran Doyle, his face even redder than its usual red-cheeked state. "Say what you want about Mrs Kelleher, but the family has nothing to do with this. She might like a drink, but she wouldn't stoop to this. There's just no reason for it. Time's against us here, lads."

"Which brings us to the potential criminals," said Baldwin, rewarding Doyle with a scowl for his impatience. "The heaviest Dublin mobs are drug dealers linked with the INLA or the Provisional IRA. Armed paramilitary groups. They control drugs, protection rackets and pretty much every type of nefarious activity you can think of."

"Isn't the IRA supposed to have disbanded?" asked Craven. The mention of the Irish terrorists sent a shiver across Craven's shoulders. He'd been on the force in Manchester at the time of the bombings in the city and remembered vividly the Warrington bombings in which two young kids lost their lives. In his experience, the IRA were ruthless and callous murderers.

"Yes, in 2005. They decommissioned their arsenal back then, handing in over one thousand rifles, two tonnes of Semtex, ninety pistols and a list of other weapons. But they haven't truly disbanded. These days, there are a few active splinter IRA groups, but they are linked more to criminal activity than to the republican movement."

"Careful with the IRA, lads," warned Doyle. "All three of you are Brits. For us in Ireland, the IRA is part of our history. 1916, Michael Collins, independence. There's history there, so don't go running your mouths about that craic, or you'll end up in trouble."

"But how do we reach them?" asked Kane, getting straight to the point. "Presumably, you can't just find an IRA man on the street?"

"Find the drug dealers, and they can lead us to the IRA," Baldwin answered.

"I'll take that then. Give me a list of locations to find these drug gangs, and I'll get to it today."

Craven smirked to himself, knowing full well what that meant. He'd seen first-hand what Kane was capable of in the carnage wrought across England when they first met.

"Then we are down to those with an axe to grind," Baldwin continued. "We have jockeys who used to ride for Kelleher but don't any longer, former employees, and so on. There's a list of four here."

"I'll take those," chimed Fran Doyle. "Sure, I know half of them, anyway."

"Quick question," said Kane. "Why isn't Mrs Kelleher here at the house?"

"She's with her family," Doyle explained. "But Frank will meet her when he talks to her father."

"How did you find out that Annie was taken?" asked Craven, realising that he hadn't yet seen the actual ransom demand. They had been so focused on the race to find those responsible that it had slipped his mind to start with the basics. He needed to do what he did best – think like a detective. "Can we see the ransom demand and also the details of where and how Annie was taken?"

"I have the recording on the laptop," said Doyle. He played the video sent to John Kelleher via a WhatsApp message from his daughter's phone. It showed the girl tied up and a man in a balaclava making the money demand. It lasted for less than a minute. The speaker simply said that they had taken Annie, that they wanted money, and that if it wasn't delivered within seven days, they would kill Annie. The speaker held the phone close to their face so that all that was visible was his black balaclava.

The image showed no surroundings, no buildings, landscapes, or streets. He signed off the video by saying they would be in touch with instructions on how and where to deliver the money.

"They snatched her outside her school, took her right from under the au pair's nose. Before you ask, we did put a trace on Annie's phone. They made the recording within five miles of the school, and then the phone signal died."

"Did any bodyguards or anybody go with the au pair for the daily school drop-off?" asked Craven.

"It's not that type of place," said Doyle, shaking his head. "We don't need guards or security for Annie. It was just the young au pair who dropped her at school. She's a Spanish girl who lives here with the family."

"No offence, Fran," intoned Baldwin. "But it looks like you needed security at the school drop-offs. Annie's gone now, and we need to get her back. I'll talk to the au pair as soon as I can and get a full breakdown of the snatch at the school."

"The American mercs will be here today," said Kane. "And they won't care about subtlety or the gentle approach. They'll come in heavy and bulldoze through these potential leads. Their job is to get paid, and they'll do whatever it takes. I've come across their type before, former special forces. They will be highly trained and very effective. They won't shy away from violence or the risk of arrest. So, we should do any finesse work today before Kelleher fully briefs them."

"So, let's get to it," Baldwin nodded. "The clock's ticking."

FOURTEEN

Kane travelled northbound along the N7 motorway from Kildare towards Dublin. He drove a Ford Ranger pickup truck from the stud, which Doyle had said Kane could use for the day. He followed the directions on the vehicle satnav towards a pub in Tallaght. From the brief description provided by Doyle, Kane understood it to be a large suburb in south Dublin with a mix of both good and bad areas.

As the truck sped along the three-lane carriageway, Kane's mind pondered over the list of potential suspects for the kidnapping. There seemed to be little evidence and little to go off other than hearsay and a few opinions. All they had to work with was the ransom message, footage of the kidnapping, which Kane hadn't seen yet, and a list of tenuous subjects. The thoughts of Annie in the hands of whoever had snatched her whirred around Kane's head continually. He thought of his wife Sally and how she had died at the hands of his enemies and how those enemies had then held his own children hostage. Kane had rescued Danny and Kim in a welter of blood at a remote country house in England, and he would do the same for Annie. A picture of Annie Kelleher hung in the hallway of her family home, and the image of the little girl smiling and wearing her school uniform kept coming to the front of Kane's mind. The kidnappers held that same girl somewhere, terrified and alone, and she needed help.

One of the useful things about Kane's life in the military and subsequent time as a special agent was his set of skills uniquely relevant to this type of situation. As the polite Irish satnav voice told him to exit the motorway, Kane was not going to the pub known as an IRA hangout to make small talk. He was going to shake the trees in the only way he knew how. They were working against the clock, so he either needed to quickly eliminate the paramilitaries as suspects or confirm their involvement. Kane knew little about the IRA. The troubles were over long before his career in the SAS or with the Mjolnir branch of MI6 had begun. From what Doyle and Baldwin had said, it appeared the former republican army was now more intertwined with the criminal world than fighting for a political cause, and that helped Kane. Criminals craved money and were highly sensitive to attacks on their power and reputation.

Kane eased the pickup truck onto a bypass and then turned right at traffic lights into what the green signs in both English and Irish called Tallaght Village. The town comprised housing estates crammed with terraced housing at one end and semi-detached older buildings on the opposite side. A shopping centre dominated the skyline, but next to that, the town centre sprawled across a crossroads, with a bank in one corner and various small retail shops on the other. Kane paused at a red light, and a group of youths in tracksuits, hoodies and caps marched across the road. They reminded him of the gangs he had run into in Manchester. Tracksuits seemed to be the uniform of the street thug, both in the UK and Ireland.

The Lion pub faced him from the corner of a crossroads up ahead. With a bright yellow sign and terracotta paint, it stood out in stark contrast to the drab grey of the surrounding shops and offices. Kane parked the truck at the pub's rear and entered the pub's lounge through the back door. It was dark and reeked of stale lager and old cigarettes, even though a smoking ban had been in place in Ireland for over a decade. It was eleven in the morning, so Kane was alone in the pub save for the barman in a black shirt, busy cleaning glasses.

"What can I get you, bud?" said the barman, looking up from his work. He was shorter than Kane and slightly built, with tattooed forearms under his short shirt sleeves. His face was thin, and his hair was greasily slicked back from his face.

"I'm here looking for some business," replied Kane, coming to stand at the bar. "I understand this is the place to come if you want to arrange some distribution work."

The barman sniffed and held up the pint glass he had polished to a gleam. He closed one eye and examined his handiwork.

"We sell beer, bud. Crisps and peanuts, too, if you want a snack. I don't know about anything else."

"Look, I've travelled here from across the water to make some new connections and open wider distribution channels. I've been told this is the place to come to do that. I'm not here to mess around. Am I in the right place or not?"

"Wait here," the barman said. He carefully put the clean glass away and strutted out the back. Moments later, two men emerged from a back door into the gloomy bar. Their frames filled the doorway, the first man hugely muscled with a shaved head and wearing a vest and tracksuit pants. Tattoos writhed up on his arms and neck, with a giant Irish tricolour at the centre of his broad chest. The second man was just naturally huge, like Craven, with pint-pot hands and a thick neck. He was older than the first man, perhaps fifty years old.

"What the fuck do you want?" the muscle man demanded. He had the round, angry face of a bulldog, and he growled at Kane, showing a flash of gold in his teeth. "You a fucking guard?"

"No, I'm not the police," answered Kane. "I'm trying to find a young girl who was kidnapped a few days ago. Rumour is that the IRA is involved and that this fine establishment is where I can find the IRA in this part of Dublin. I just want to talk to those responsible and see if we can find a peaceful way forward."

"What are you talking about?" said the older man. "Get out before I let Frankie here tear your arms off."

"Tell me what you know about the girl, and there won't be any trouble."

"Alright, bud. I've had enough of you already. Frankie, get this bleedin' eejit out of here."

Frankie grinned and flexed the corded muscle in his chest. He came from behind the bar with a malevolent look on his round face. Kane smiled and went to meet him.

FIFTEEN

Frankie was strong; his arms were as thick as one of Kane's legs. Kane felt the power in the man's frame as he dragged him up from the pub floor by his thumb, and the big man surged to his feet to avoid it snapping. Frankie gurgled, bubbles of blood and snot coming from his nose and torn lips where Kane had first elbowed and then kicked him in the face.

"Do you know anything about the kidnapping or not?" said Kane, pausing with Frankie in his grip but addressing his question to the older man.

"I don't know what you're talking about," he growled in response, and Kane shrugged before grabbing a fistful of Frankie's hair and driving his head forward into the bar. His mouth cannoned into the hard, shining wood, and the muscle man slumped to the floor.

"If you don't know, give me the names of the men above you, and I'll ask them."

"Do you have any idea who you are talking to?"

"A name?"

At that moment, the short barman came hurtling across the space between the bar and Kane with a baseball bat in his fist. He screamed as he ran; the bat held above his head like a sword. Kane sighed and set his feet. The little man was so enraged that he neglected to fully appreciate his surroundings, and as he swung the bat, it smashed into an overhead light, showering his slicked-back hair with broken glass.

The bat slowed, allowing Kane to catch it in his left fist and punch his right into the man's gullet. He twisted the bat free of the little man's hand and cracked it hard across his shins, sending him tumbling to join Frankie on the pub's fetid carpet.

"Alright, alright," said the older man. He came around the bar and sat on a stool with his hands raised to show that he wanted no more trouble. "I don't know nothing about any kidnapping, but I can put the word out and see what I can find out."

"Make the calls now, then. I'll wait here."

"Jaysus," he rubbed the sagging skin around

his eyes and took out an Android phone. "You can't just come in here and rough up my lads like that. There'll need to be a reckoning. Who are you anyway?"

"Just a man trying to find a little girl who is scared out of her mind. Make the calls."

He opened the phone and scrolled through his contacts. "Howya, Cobra. Yeah, I'm good. Come here to me. Have you heard anything about a kidnapping this week?"

Frankie groaned, and Kane helped him to sit up against the bar. He reached over to beside the beer pumps, grabbed a handful of napkins and handed them to Frankie to help stem the bleeding from his face. The barman crawled away and scuttled into the back room without giving Kane a second look.

"I don't know either, some bastard's come into the Lion making a big noise. Says somebody's taken a little girl for a ransom." The older man scowled at Kane and nodded as the voice spoke to him down the phone. "Right, right. He wants to speak to you." He handed the phone to Kane.

"Yes?" uttered Kane.

"Who the fuck are you?" said a voice full of gravel.

"I'm looking for a little girl who has been

kidnapped. Do you know anything about it?"

"We've got you on camera, you cheeky bastard. We're the fucking IRA. You don't just slap our lads around. You'll take a bullet for this."

"Never mind." Kane hung up the phone and turned to the older man. "What's the phone's passcode?" The man shrugged. Kane swung the bat backwards and paused just so the man understood that if he let fly, the timber would make a mess of his pudgy face.

"One nine one six," he said. Kane tried the code, and it worked. He left the pub having earned the ire of the IRA. Kane had discovered little, but he doubted that these men were high enough up the food chain in the paramilitary group to know everything that went on inside their organisation. He returned to the pickup truck and headed towards the shopping centre, dialling Cameron's number as he drove. Kane couldn't give up on the IRA lead just yet. Cameron could trace Cobra's number, and then Kane would pay the man a visit. He assumed Cobra held a higher position in the organisation than the men inside the Lion, and he would work his way up to the top if he had to.

SIXTEEN

Craven sat in the passenger seat of a silver Mercedes E-Class borrowed from the Kelleher stud fleet of vehicles. The morning sun warmed its black leather seats, and manicured trees and flowerbeds lined the driveway to where it joined the main road. Jim Baldwin drove, and they left the stud's plush surroundings to meet John Kelleher's father-in-law.

"What's the wife's name again?" asked Craven. He had taken an empty envelope from the kitchen worktop and wrote the key pieces of information down with a biro.

"Caitriona," said Baldwin. "If she is at the house with the father, go easy on her, Frank."

"If she wants her daughter back, she's going to have to answer some questions."

"She's already been through it fifty times with the Guards, and they're getting nowhere. Also, remember who's paying our fee here. If you piss off the wife, Kelleher might kick us off the job."

"I hear you, don't panic. She's still a suspect, though, until we can rule her out. Which hopefully we can do today. How bad is her drink and drug problem?"

"Bad enough, I think. She's a functioning cokehead and an alcoholic."

"Functioning?"

"She can get about her daily business and look presentable, but she drinks and snorts every day."

"What about her father, then?"

"Dave McNamara. Used to manage a warehouse until his daughter met John Kelleher. Now he runs part of the racing business and has done well out of it."

"He's got previous, right? I didn't have time to read the file properly."

Baldwin shrugged. "Nothing too serious, a bit of ABH back in the early nineties, receiving stolen goods. That kind of thing."

Craven noted the names down on the back of his envelope and tucked it into the jacket pocket of his navy blazer. He looked across at Baldwin with his long face intent on the road ahead. They hadn't caught up since Craven had landed in

Dublin, and they had been good friends once.

"So, do you live here now, Jim, or in the Middle East?" Craven asked. They had been friends as young men on the Manchester Police Force, starting out as uniformed constables and working their way up. They had played football together, and back in those days, the job was a sociable one. They had spent long afternoons and late nights in the pubs and clubs of Manchester city centre.

"I've done a bit of work for the Kellehers recently, but I'm only ever here for a few days at a time. I've only been to Ireland three times. I live in Dubai, Frank. Have done for years. It's tax-free, mate."

"How did you meet John and Caitriona Kelleher, then?"

"A mutual contact. I did some protection work for an Emirati who owns a big stud farm close to Kelleher's land in Kildare. He put me on to them, said they needed extra security."

"Did he say why?"

"What is this, Frank? Fucking twenty questions?"

"Just catching up, Jim. Don't be so sensitive. Have you gone soft with all that sun on your scalp? When did you leave the force, then?"

"About fifteen years ago. Moved out to the Middle East, there was still a lot of trouble out there back then. Lots of security work for ex-coppers like us and former military men. Good money protecting rich folk out there." He still spoke with a thick Liverpool accent. Baldwin wore an Omega watch, and his clothes looked like designer gear. Craven knew little about fashion or watches. But he'd read somewhere that Omega watches were fancy.

"You've done well for yourself, mate. Ever settle down?"

"I was married once. After I left the Manchester force, I moved to Leeds for four years. Met a girl there and was married for two years."

"What happened?"

"She was always fucking moaning, Frank. So, I got rid. You should see the women in Dubai. Plenty to choose from for a man with a few quid."

"Rich bastard then, are you?"

"Doing my best, mate. Let's put it this way. I flew here on a private plane." He flashed a white-toothed smile at Craven and turned the Mercedes into the driveway of a detached house set on an acre of gated, fenced land. "It's not my plane, so don't get carried away. A client let me use his. These are the people I'm dealing with now,

Frank. I've been telling you for years that you should come out to Dubai."

The property was just off the principal thoroughfare of a town called Rathcoole, mid-way between the stud farm and Dublin. The main street of Rathcoole, a commuter belt town, housed a Tesco shop, a bank, a creche, a post office, and three pubs. It had been developed to support the thriving community of new housing estates. Craven had to admit that he liked the cut of the town's jib. Three pubs less than half a mile away from each other on the same street was commendable.

Baldwin gave his name at a silver box intercom, and the steel gates to McNamara's house creaked open. They parked the Mercedes on a curved cobble-locked driveway. A man in his sixties with silver hair in a crisp side part, dark chinos, and a white short-sleeved button-down shirt met them at the front door.

"How are you bearing up, Dave?" said Baldwin, shaking Dave McNamara's hand.

"Ah, sure, you know yourself," sighed Dave. He shrugged and shook his head. They were in the midst of a ransom demand, and McNamara was the kidnapped girl's grandfather.

"This is Frank Craven. He's the man I told you about. Come to help with the case."

"Mr McNamara," said Craven, extending his hand, which Dave took in a floppy handshake. Craven's belly soured; he hated a limp handshake.

"So, you're the bigshot copper from England, then?"

"I don't know about that. But if we can help get your granddaughter back, we will."

"You two had better come in, then. Cait's inside. She's not great, so be gentle if she comes down from the bed to talk to ye."

He led them into a wide hall with a set of carpeted stairs on the left-hand side and wallpapered walls thick with pictures of McNamara with celebrities at various racing events. He was hugging a member of Boyzone in one, drinking a bottle of beer with an Arsenal footballer in another, and then kissing a beautiful girl Craven didn't recognise but who looked like some sort of singer. He'd clearly come a long way from his days managing a warehouse and selling nicked televisions.

"Take a seat," said Dave as he led them into a side room where comfortable armchairs stood on either side of a deep sofa. A bookcase dominated the room, its shelves filled with sporting autobiographies and true crime books. A small desk and a laptop sat in one corner, and opposite the bookcase was a series of framed signed football and rugby shirts.

"So, who's taken little Annie then?" asked Craven as he plonked heavily into an armchair. Baldwin rewarded him with a frown. But Craven had never been a man to beat about the bush.

SEVENTEEN

Condor watched the silver Mercedes drive away from the stud farm, and the blip on her tracker moved with it. The signal from Craven's phone followed the vehicle's path as it drove eastwards along a well-kept road bordered by perfectly trimmed hedges. The signal told her that Craven had spent the night at that address, so she decided to have a closer look inside. Craven was her only link to Jack Kane, and this was a good chance to get an insight into what he was doing in Ireland.

She had built up a picture of the former detective. He was a happily married man who had served for years with no major distinction. Craven had retired to a house in Spain, which seemed to be beyond the means of an average detective's salary. Condor had checked, and there had been no family bereavements and, therefore, no recent inheritance windfall. The operations team at MI6 had checked Craven's bank accounts. There was nothing out of the ordinary there. He had a measly salary, and his wife worked part-time at a local school. They had sold their house in northwest England before leaving for Spain, but the proceeds sat in the Craven's joint bank account, untouched.

There was something amiss. The operations team had pulled Craven's life apart on Condor's instruction, and it had all changed for the detective after the Kane incident. The funding for his new life was untraceable. Craven had paid for the Spanish property using bonds rather than a bank transfer. It stank of Kane, some sort of cooperation or coercion linked to their meeting last spring. Either the former agent had bribed Craven, or the two men were working together. She could have travelled to Spain and waited for Craven to return, but she smelled a rat with this visit to Ireland at precisely the same time that Kane had taken care of a kill team in Scotland. Condor would not be so easy to handle.

She drove her car around the farm's perimeter, which was impressively large. Condor caught glimpses of magnificent horses cantering across lush pastures through gaps in the squared hedgerow. Horses' shining coats and rippling muscles had always fascinated Condor. When she was a little girl, she often imagined galloping away from her foster home on a beautiful pony with the wind in her hair, racing off to a new future as a famous show jumper. She had since learned to ride as part of her training, just as she had learned to drive many vehicles. The brief glimpse of the racehorses caused a smile to creep across her lips. Condor remembered the thrill of the gallop, the power of the animals and the sheer joy of riding. It had been an all too fleeting time of happiness, just her at a stable with a riding instructor. Unfortunately, once she had become proficient at horse riding, she moved on to the next part of her training, which had been withstanding torture, both physical and mental. She did not have such fond memories of that.

Condor parked her car on the grass verge of a lane on the southwest border of the stud farm. She changed her clothes, awkwardly removing her trousers and shirt in the driving seat, and pulled on tactical trousers, a T-shirt and a jumper. She holstered a pistol at her hip and tucked two spare magazines into her pockets. The gun belt also held a small flick knife, a thumb-sized torch and other mission essentials, such as a lock pick and basic battlefield medical supplies.

She left the car and jumped over the low fencing, which ran alongside the shoulder-high hedges. Condor sprinted across a grazing pasture, her boots pounding across the deep green grass as she made her way towards the main building. The main house rose to the north beyond a set of stables, a large barn and various smaller outbuildings. It was midday, and the sun was high in a sky filled with drifting clouds, so Condor ran as fast as she could across the open space until she reached the stable wall. She had crossed the field unseen and crouched with her back against a brick wall. A radio played rock music nearby, and Condor heard the low timbre of male voices coming from inside a building. A horse whinnied, and she skirted around the stable doors, keeping away from voices and moving towards the main house.

A piebald horse's long face peered down at Condor from over its stall. She stood and stroked its soft nose and patted its muscular neck. The horse bobbed his head, and she laughed. The reaction surprised her, an emotion which rarely found its way through her steely shell of implacable focus and managed rage. Condor touched her forehead to the horse's cheek and wished she could stay with the beast. She longed to saddle it and ride through the fields, to brush it down and feed it, to care for and be at one with it. But there was no time for such daydreams or for happiness. She had one man to find and another to kill.

EIGHTEEN

"Did you find an address?" asked Kane. He spoke into his phone as he drove northbound on the Dublin ring road. Kane had bought four burner phones at the shopping centre in Tallaght and used one to send details of the contact number for the IRA man Cobra to his friend Cameron in Newcastle.

"Hey, Jack," said Cameron on the other end of the phone. "Yeah, I found a couple of locations. He sleeps at an address in a place called Crumlin in south Dublin and spends a lot of time at a small casino in Dublin city centre."

"Great, Cameron, thanks. Where is he now?"

"At the casino, I'll send the address to this number. Who is this guy, anyway?"

"You don't want to know. Thanks again for your help." Kane hated to bother his old friend again. Cameron had been through so much, but he was also so capable. Kane knew Cam could use his technological know-how and equipment to track the number he had taken from the phone at the Lion pub. Annie only had four days, and the quickest way to find out if the IRA had any involvement in her capture was to get a location for one of their senior members as soon as he could. That was where Cameron came in.

"Anytime, Jack. If you need anything, just drop me a line."

Kane hung up the call, and a message buzzed straight away. It was a location embedded in a text message from a withheld number. Kane clicked the link, and an address popped up at a place called Collins' Casino on Baggot Street in Dublin. Kane left the ring road and followed the map app on his burner.

The road into Dublin ran parallel to a canal and crossed paths with the Luas, Dublin's tram service. The canal was an old lock-based canal, like the Manchester ship canal in the UK, and would once have been the major trade route into Dublin from the countryside. Horses would have dragged barges along its length to bring goods through the system of locks. However, the waterway was an abandoned relic now, and swans lazed on its still waters as Kane drove by. It was midday, and the canal's edges were bustling with city workers strolling along its banks and eating lunch on benches.

Kane turned the pickup truck onto Baggot Street. He drove through a crossroads and across a bridge over the canal. The street was wide and flanked by Georgian buildings, which once housed the well-to-do of Dublin but were now home to finance brokers, mortgage lenders and other office-based businesses. As the Victorian architecture transitioned into more imposing structures, Kane's map told him that the destination was up ahead. He found a parking space in a small square to the left and parked the truck.

The casino was slotted in between a gentrified pub and a coffee shop. The sign, which had 'Collins' Casino' in white lettering against a green background, nestled above blacked-out windows with a portrait of Michael Collins, the great Irish revolutionary, in one window and a tricolour standing proud in the other. Both windows stood on either side of a black door with an intercom system. Kane went unarmed, wearing trousers and a shirt. He buzzed the intercom system on the casino door.

"Are you open?" Kane said into the metallic box.

"You a member?" answered a voice in the now familiar Dublin accent.

"No, I'm here on holiday and fancied a few games of blackjack."

The door clicked, and Kane pushed it open. He stepped into a musty entrance area flanked on either side by old, heavy oak doors. He tried both handles, and they were locked. Black-painted walls lit with stretches of blinking lights rose along a chipped bannister as stairs led upwards to the gambling hall itself. Kane followed it and entered a small, open space with a red threadbare carpet on the floor. Slot machines covered the four walls, and the inner space held six tables – two with roulette wheels and the rest for poker, blackjack, and other card games.

A bar curled around the wall to Kane's left between the lines of slot machines, and a woman in a white shirt and black waistcoat stared at Kane with nervous eyes. She chewed gum rapidly like she was on amphetamines, and her eyes flicked from Kane to the wall on his right. He turned, and five burly men in a mixture of leather jackets, jeans, and tracksuits emerged from behind the flashing slots.

"I don't want any trouble," said Kane. They advanced. Two of them clutched hurleys, the long, brutal sticks used for playing the Gaelic sport of hurling.

"You fucked with the wrong people, you Brit bastard," sneered a man with a tattoo of a spider on his face. He was young and wore a Kappa tracksuit top zipped up tight around his neck. "You can't just go into a RA pub and fucking attack our men. Do you think we're stupid? That we wouldn't expect you to come here straight after?" He surged at Kane in a flurry of fists, which Kane avoided easily. He front-kicked the man in the groin and moved backwards towards the stairs.

"Not so fast," came a deep voice behind him, and two hands shoved him hard in the back. Kane stumbled forward, and the wooden edge of a hurley came hurtling towards his head. He ducked under the attack, and a fist slammed into the side of his skull. Kane threw himself sideways to escape the press of men closing in on him. He caught a fist and kicked out a man's leg. A hurley connected with Kane's back, and the sharp pain knocked the wind out of him. A man with a scarred face and cauliflower ears headbutted Kane hard. He fell, kicks and punches rained down on his ribs and back, and as he tried to protect his head with his hands, Kane slipped into painful darkness.

NINETEEN

Dave McNamara looked sharp in his shirt and trousers, but his bloodshot eyes and the bags beneath them told a different story. He sat in an armchair with his legs crossed, tapping a finger on one arm, and his foot bobbed up and down constantly.

"We know this is a difficult time," said Craven. "But the more information we can get, the more we can put together a picture of Annie's life and that of the Kellehers. That helps us to find strings to pull on, which might help unravel what's happened to Annie."

"No bother," Dave nodded. "I've already been through all this with the Guards, though. I still don't get why John brought you lads in?"

"John and I are connected through a mutual friend," explained Jim Baldwin. A smile creased his lantern jaw. "I've a bit of experience of these types of situations in the Middle East, and he thought I could help. The kidnappers don't want An Garda Síochána involved, and an attempt to retrieve Annie needs a delicate hand. If the Irish police blunder in heavy-handedly, it could cost Annie her life. I brought in Frank here because we used to work together in the police force back in the UK. Frank had years of experience with the Serious and Organised Crime Squad and dealt with some serious gangs. We don't want the kidnappers to panic and make rash decisions."

"John has an insurance policy for this type of thing. I've seen the premium going on the company bank statements. Kidnap and ransom insurance, it's called. Won't that pay the ransom?"

"It should," said Baldwin.

"Does it also pay your fee?"

"It will contribute to it, yes. It's the insurance company who sent the Americans over to see what's going on."

Craven had heard of that type of insurance cover before. Usually, companies took it out to protect directors or workers travelling to high-risk countries with a history of kidnappings. Wealthy people would also take it out to protect themselves and their family members, but as far as Craven was aware, it was a Latin American or American thing rather than something prevalent in Europe. It was, however, news to him that John Kelleher had taken out such a policy.

"How long has Mr Kelleher had the insurance policy?" Craven asked.

"I've no idea," replied Dave with a shrug. "Best to ask him about that. I know where you're going with this, though, and you can get it right out of your head. John loves little Annie, and he wouldn't hurt a hair on her head. Why would he anyway?"

"We're not saying that," said Baldwin, leaning forward in his chair and smiling. "We just need to explore every avenue, that's all. Can you tell us how you came to work for Mr Kelleher?"

"I went to work for John not long after he and Cait were married," McNamara answered. He spoke with a Dublin accent but with the hard edges polished off. "They made me redundant in my previous job, and John offered me work in his company."

"What did you do before?" asked Craven.

"I was a manager at a factory up in Dublin. We used to package and ship pharmaceuticals. Creams and bottles and such. I ran the floor for years, but in the last recession, they offered me redundancy, and I took it."

"How did those skills relate to the horse racing business?"

Dave laughed under his breath. "Look, the man had a few quid, and he'd just married my daughter. I was out of work, and he offered me a job. These things happen."

"So, what do you do for Mr Kelleher?" Craven supposed Dave was being honest. How many rich people in the world employ their relatives? He didn't know many, but he assumed that most did. It didn't seem too nefarious to him that the newly married John Kelleher would offer his wife's father a job in his lucrative business. Keep the wife happy – the most important part of any marriage.

"I manage his affairs around the estate. You would not believe the hassle of managing the staff, ordering supplies and food for the horses, arranging transport to and from race meets, selling foals, and all the other shite we have to deal with on a daily basis."

"Can you think of any disgruntled former employees or business rivals who might want to get at Mr Kelleher?" asked Baldwin.

Dave scratched his chin and sat back in his chair. "John can be abrasive at times, a bit quick to lose his temper. But that seems to be par for the course for fellas who've made a fortune like he has, right? People are always coming and going from the farm. One jockey recently got into a blazing row with John. I saw it myself. Dickie McHugh is his name, but I don't think he'd do anything to hurt Annie. She's a little sweetheart, and the lads around the farm dote on her."

"What type of man is Dickie? A normal family guy or what?"

"He's a bit of a loner, a drinker. But, like I said, he wouldn't hurt Annie. None of the employees would."

"Anybody else you think we should talk to?" Craven pressed.

"You can ask Cait. I'll call her down in a minute when we're done."

"Thanks, Mr McNamara," said Baldwin, rising from his chair.

"One more question," Craven interjected, a little surprised that Jim Baldwin was ready to conclude the interview after so few questions. "You've been in a bit of trouble in the past. Do you still have any friends from the old days?"

Dave's easy demeanour fell away, and his face hardened like someone had slapped it. "You can fuck off if you think I'm involved in this. Yeah,

I sold some nicked gear years ago, but so did everyone. It was the late eighties, we didn't have a pot to piss in. And yes, I still have friends from when I was younger."

"Any of them involved with the IRA?" Craven's eyes flicked to the faded tattoo of the Irish flag on Dave's forearm.

"Jaysus. You Brits don't have a feckin' clue about Ireland. I got this after Italia '90, the World Cup. I've nothing to do with the bloody IRA, and I've had enough of your stupid questions." He stood and gestured towards the door.

"Can we talk to Mrs Kelleher before we go?" asked Baldwin.

Dave glowered at them both and shook his head. "I'll ask her. She's in a bad way about all of this. Cait's upstairs crying nonstop. She's got her own demons to deal with, and this situation has pushed her to the limits. If I bring her down, don't ask her the sort of questions you just asked me, or she might lose her shit altogether." He left the room and closed the door behind him.

"Why didn't you mention the insurance before?" muttered Craven in a hushed tone, turning to Baldwin.

"I didn't not mention it, Frank. I just assumed you'd know a rich guy like John would have it. But I forget that you're new to dealing with the rich," said Baldwin with a shrug.

"Any other stupendously important facts you haven't mentioned?"

"He hasn't done it for the insurance payout, Frank, so get that out of your head. He's not the type."

"Let's talk to Mrs Kelleher, then. After that, we have this jockey Dickie McHugh to question. I still wouldn't rule out Dave McNamara. We need to look at his finances and those of John Kelleher and build a picture of their circumstances. There must be something here we can't see. Why target Kelleher? There are surely richer people than him in Ireland? So, either he's an easy target, or there's something fishy going on."

TWENTY

A rough hand slapped Kane awake. He grunted as the calloused palm scraped across his cheek and then backhanded him for good measure. As he regained consciousness, a burning sensation stung his wrists and ankles, alerting him to the tight plastic cable ties securing his hands and feet.

"He's awake," said the man who had slapped him. He bent and stared into Kane's face with beady, blue eyes.

The beating Kane had taken left him with a dull ache in his ribs and swelling on the right-hand side of his head. He was sitting on a chair in a room lit dimly by a small window with a cracked pane of old, filthy glass. The floor was dusty and flecked with old rubbish and tangles of lint and grime. The surrounding space was vast and empty. Men's mumbled voices echoed around the high ceilings with hanging, metallic lights. He was in a disused factory or warehouse building, tied and held by the IRA.

A man in a dark suit with a clean-shaven face sneered, addressing Kane, "So, you scrawny bastard, what are you? MI6? Or just a fucking English gangster out of luck?" Behind the suited man, Kane recognised some faces from the casino. Black leather jackets and tracksuits seemed to be the clothing of choice, and his heart sank a little as he noticed the two men from the Lion pub standing to one side. The older man smiled grimly at Kane, and hate pulsed from Frankie like a furnace. The big man had a white plaster cast on his left forearm, and his face was a mess of angry, purple swelling.

"I'm just here looking for someone," said Kane. He ran his tongue over his teeth, two of which felt loose after the beating. "A girl who has been kidnapped. I'm not the police, and I'm not MI6. I'm a friend of the family."

"Bollocks!" shouted Frankie, his voice muffled by the swelling around his jaw. "He's a fucking snake. He's undercover. Put a bullet in the bastard."

"What's your name?" asked the man in the suit.

"Ian Rush," Kane intoned. The former

Liverpool Football Club striker was the first name to pop into his head.

"Alright then, smart arse. We can do this the hard way if you like," the man in the suit hunkered down in front of Kane. "You are going to tell me who you are, what you want with us, and who you work for. You can do that now, or we can beat, burn, and fucking torture it out of you." The man spoke with a Belfast accent, which added a bite to his threats.

"The kidnapped girl is Annie Kelleher. She's the daughter of John Kelleher, the horse trainer. There has been a ransom demand, and I thought your organisation might have something to do with it."

"Do you think we are in the business of taking wee girls prisoner?"

"Well, you have a chequered history of bombing innocent people. So, I wouldn't rule it out."

"Let me have a few minutes with him, Cobra," said a burly man with a gold tooth wearing a wife-beater vest over tracksuit bottoms.

"Alright, go on then." The man in the suit stepped back, and the burly man's shadow filled Kane's vision.

"Frankie over there is my cousin," he growled

into Kane's ear, and his fetid breath washed over Kane's face. "I'm gonna hurt you, little man."

The cable ties around Kane's wrists were so tight that his hands felt swollen from lack of blood flow. His hands were tied behind him while his ankles were bound together in front. Kane squirmed in the chair and noticed he wasn't fastened to it; they'd only placed him on the simple wooden chair with a high back, hooking his arms over the back with his wrists hung below the seat. The long tail of the cable tie's end brushed against his arse, and Kane lifted himself to sit on the loose end.

"Fucking smash him up, Tommy!" called Frankie, and the surrounding men chuckled.

Tommy rolled his shoulders and took a swing at Kane. He threw an overhand punch straight at Kane's face, and Kane dipped his head so that his chin touched his chest. Tommy howled in pain as his knuckles cracked against Kane's forehead. That part of a skull is like an anvil, and Tommy hopped and sucked his teeth, tucking the injured paw under one arm.

The cable tie slipped from underneath Kane, so he twisted his wrists to slip it under his arse cheek again. He pulled his wrists away until the plastic was as tight as possible. The tighter they are, the easier they are to break. Kane forced his wrists apart but couldn't snap the ties.

"I'll make the bastard sing!" shouted a stocky man with a tattoo on his neck. He came at Kane brandishing a hurley. The curved hurling stick was a metre long and flared at one end, making it more like a club than a sporting implement. If it connected with Kane's head, it would cause serious injury.

Kane had undergone extensive counter-interrogation training in the SAS and when he had joined the Mjolnir secret service agency. Fiercer men than these had also captured him in the field. Kane kicked his legs up and pushed himself backwards, tipping the chair over. The hurley whooshed past the space where Kane had been a second earlier, and as the chair hit the ground, Kane forced his arms wide.

The back of the wooden chair cracked under his weight, and the cable ties snapped at their weakest point, the locking mechanism. Kane rolled over, grabbed the hurley-swinging man's legs, and whipped them out from under him. The abandoned factory erupted in shouting as the gathered IRA men sprang into action, each one surging towards Kane. There were six men around him, and he had to act quickly. The hurley clattered on the concrete flooring, and Kane snatched it up. He cracked it across the ankles of the closest attacker and then drove its handle in between the ties at his own ankles. He twisted the hurley, and the cable tie snapped.

A kick cannoned into Kane's back, and he rolled with the blow. He came up with all the speed and agility forced into his body over a lifetime of combat training. Kane lashed out with the hurley, and it smashed into the face of the IRA man who had kicked him, turning his nose into a bloody pulp. Kane spun and blocked a punch aimed at his head before smashing his elbow into another assailant's solar plexus. Bodies dropped around him. The men who had thought to torture Kane for answers now writhed in agony.

"Enough!" shouted the man in the suit. He pulled a Glock 17 from inside his jacket and pointed the weapon at Kane. The IRA men leapt back to get out of the gun's way, and Kane slowly raised his hands. "Get on your fucking knees."

Kane turned away from the man in the suit and continued to raise his hands above his head.

"I said on your knees!"

Kane placed his hands behind his head and moved backwards quickly towards the armed man. Kane was used to using a gun. It had been a tool of his livelihood for most of his adult life. He had shot, wounded, and killed many men in his career. The first few kills had haunted him, made him feel sick, and forced Kane to question his morality. But after that, it was just work. Shooting another human being is not easy. Even though the man in the suit carried the weapon and was clearly a high-ranking member of the Irish Republican Army, Kane doubted that there was much cause to use the gun in modern Ireland.

Back when the IRA were actively fighting for the unification of their country, they were a highly trained and dangerous organisation. But not anymore. So Kane quickly backed into the gunman, hoping that he would hesitate before pulling the trigger.

"Stop, now!" the gunman bellowed.

The cold, hard barrel of the gun jabbed between Kane's shoulder blades, and he swiftly spun around. He used his raised elbow to knock the gun aside, and he grabbed the man's hand, forcing the weapon high. It all happened in the blink of an eye. Kane whipped his right hand up, twisted the weapon free of the suited man's grip and pointed it at his face.

"Now, I think it's time for you to answer my questions," Kane said with a smile. He shot Tommy in the kneecap just to show them he was serious. The sound of the gun was like thunder in the old factory. The bang caused every man but Kane to cover his ears and close his eyes in shock. Tommy fell to the concrete, screaming in agony. Kane was tired of wasting time with the IRA. He just needed answers, and he needed them fast.

TWENTY-ONE

"He's shot Tommy," mumbled Frankie, his eyes filled with terror. The IRA men stared at Tommy, whose shattered kneecap pulsed blood onto the cold concrete. He ground his teeth and reached towards the wound with shaking fingers, not quite touching his ruined knee.

It had been an explosion of immediate, visceral violence. Kane had acted without hesitation, knowing that the sound of the gunshot would frighten the band of rough men and the terrible wound would shock them. They backed away, mouths open in disbelief, wide eyes flitting from Tommy to Kane.

"Did your organisation have anything to do with the kidnap and ransom of Annie Kelleher?" said Kane. He spoke slowly and clearly, the gun held low and pointed at the suited man's stomach.

"No, we did not," uttered the suited man. He glared at Kane with unbridled fury in his brown eyes.

"I want your names, your wallets and your phones. Take off your clothes and put the phones and wallets inside one shirt."

They looked at one another incredulously.

"Our fucking clothes?" exclaimed the man in the suit.

"What's your name?"

"Fuck you, that's my name."

Kane lowered the gun so that the barrel pointed at the suited man's legs. "Your name, or I'll blow your kneecap out just like his."

"Martin Byrne. We have nothing to do with taking the girl. But you won't get away with this. We are everywhere, we…"

"That's enough," Kane interjected before turning his attention to Frankie. "You can leave your underwear on." The big man blushed as he pulled his boxer shorts back on.

They stripped down and left their items in a black tracksuit top.

"Now you can all go," said Kane. The six men looked at him with dumbfounded faces. "Go," Kane repeated and waved the gun towards a red door at the far end of the factory. Byrne led them out, turning once to glare back at Kane, who waved at him and smiled. Two men assisted Tommy and helped him limp away. The IRA men had nothing to do with Annie's disappearance. They were simply enraged at his brazen attack on the Lion pub and looking for vengeance.

The IRA lead had been a dead end. Kane looked at his watch, and it was three in the afternoon. He had wasted the best part of the day ruling them out of the investigation. Kane checked the Glock's magazine, and only five rounds were remaining. He clicked his tongue and tucked the gun into the rear waistband of his trousers.

Kane took up the phones and wallets and marched out of the warehouse, going in the opposite direction of Byrne and his men. He pushed open a warped steel door, which scraped on the pavement and left a chalky mark on the old flagstone. Kane edged out and into a Dublin backstreet. He winced as his eyes adjusted to the sunlight and walked up a lane of uneven cobblestones. A blue sign on the wall above him said Back Lane in white writing with the same words repeated in the Irish language.

Kane exited the cobbled lane and found himself back on Baggot Street. The gang had moved him less than half a kilometre from the casino to the disused factory, and he picked up the pace, knowing that he had to get as much distance between him and the IRA as possible. Kane had escaped them, for now. At one time, they were a force feared worldwide, highly trained and utterly committed to their cause. Some of that old determination would remain, and Kane knew that news of his confrontation in Dublin would reach more serious members of the paramilitary force. He didn't want to be around when they came looking for him. The IRA had nothing on him, however, other than his face. No name, no phone, no location. So, he hurried to the pickup truck, drove back towards the canal, and followed the road out of Dublin.

Kane called Barb using the hands-free Bluetooth setting on the vehicle's dashboard.

"Hello?" she answered in a cheerful voice.

"Hello, Barbara, it's Jack."

"Oh, hold on. Kids, it's your dad," she shouted, and Kane smiled because he could hear Danny and Kim laughing in the background. "They're just playing in the pool."

"So, they are both OK?"

"We are having a great time. The sun is shining, and we might do a barbeque later. How's Frank?"

"He's fine. Still helping an old friend. I'll ask

him to call you."

"How much longer will you be gone?"

"Perhaps as long as a week, Barbara. But hopefully not that long."

"Alright then. You two be careful. Say hi to Daddy."

"Hello, Daddy," Kim chimed. Kane's heart clenched. He had only left his children a short time ago, but he thought about Kim and Danny constantly.

"Are you looking after Auntie Barbara?"

"Yes, Daddy. Come back soon."

"I will, princess."

Kane heard Danny shouting hello in the background, and he hung up the phone, reassured they were both safe, unlike Annie Kelleher, who was still in the hands of her kidnappers. Kane had wasted a chunk of his first day chasing after the IRA, and he needed to move onto a new line of inquiry – fast. Kane reached the N7 motorway and sped the truck towards the stud farm. He hoped Craven had got somewhere with the father-in-law because time was running out for Annie.

TWENTY-TWO

Caitriona Kelleher was distraught. Her face was a swollen mess of red, tear-stained cheeks, a nose snotty from crying and bleary-eyed terror. She came down the stairs of her father's house wearing grey jogging bottoms and a plain white shirt, her hair scraped back into a ponytail. A wash of potent perfume partially masked the smell of old wine. Even beneath the fear and sorrow for her daughter's kidnap, her green eyes shone like emeralds, and her high cheekbones protruded alluringly.

"We are here to help, Mrs Kelleher," said Baldwin. Dave McNamara helped Caitriona sit on a high-backed chair in the kitchen and clicked the kettle to make her a cup of coffee.

"Has there been any news?" she asked, wiping her running nose with a tissue.

"John brought these men to help find Annie," explained Dave. "They're specialists."

"Find her? Men have taken her for money. They said in the video that if we try to find them, they will kill her. Why are we trying to find them? Just pay the money and get my daughter back." Caitriona's bottom lip trembled, and she looked from her father to Craven and Baldwin with disbelieving eyes.

"It's important that we try to find these men, Mrs Kelleher," said Baldwin.

"Why? Just pay them and get my daughter back. Has John got the money together?" she asked, turning to her father.

"He's getting it, love," soothed Dave. "It's a lot of money, and they want it in cash and cryptocurrency."

"We are compiling a list of people who would want to do this to you and John," said Craven, trying to speak as gently as possible. His usual bull-in-a-china-shop approach wasn't suitable for a woman on the edge of a nervous breakdown over the disappearance of her daughter. "The people who have taken Annie must know your wealth, your lack of security, and perhaps have an axe to grind."

"Who could it be? We have done nothing to anyone. Should we have had more security? This is Ireland, not bloody Syria," she sniffed, dabbing a tear at the corner of her eye.

"Is there anybody you think we should look into?" asked Baldwin.

"I'm staying here to be close to my dad and away from the police at the stud. I don't know anything, and you have come here to question me, even though I want to be alone. I don't want you to go after these men. Just leave them. You are putting my daughter's life in danger. Please, just leave. Go back to wherever you came from and leave us alone."

"Mrs Kelleher," intoned Craven, realising that perhaps his usual bluntness was required after all. "You assume the kidnappers will release Annie once they have the money? What if they don't? What if the money drop is late, and they kill your daughter? What if they kill her, anyway? How do you know she is not being harmed as we speak? Any information you can give us will help. We must find these men and get your daughter back."

Caitriona stared at Craven, her mouth slack and her left eyebrow twitching. Maybe he had overdone it a bit, but she had to be aware of the risks. She burst out crying and ran out of the kitchen straight back up the stairs.

"Fuck's sake," snapped Dave McNamara. "Get

out, lads."

Craven followed Baldwin back to the car. He didn't get any sort of gut feeling about McNamara's involvement in the case. In all of his years as a detective, Craven had done hundreds of interviews and developed a sixth sense, or gut feeling, whenever he spoke to a guilty party. It was a thing he couldn't put his finger on or explain, just a feeling. And he didn't get it about Dave McNamara or his daughter. All they wanted was to get Annie back unharmed. Craven swore under his breath because the case was running into a dead end. They needed to shake more trees because somebody somewhere had to know something.

TWENTY-THREE

The broad iron gates to Kelleher's stud creaked open, and Kane drove the pickup truck along the winding pathway towards the main house. It had taken him over an hour to drive from the city back to the heart of County Kildare, with the traffic already building ahead of rush hour. A Mercedes followed him along the driveway, and as he parked up, Craven and Jim Baldwin stepped out of the shining silver car.

"Well," said Craven after raising his hand in greeting. "Did you manage to uncover and question a secretive and highly dangerous band of ultra-violent paramilitaries?" Baldwin chuckled at the sarcasm in Craven's voice.

"I did, as it happens," replied Kane. "I took a bit of a kicking, though. But we can rule them out as suspects. They would have told me if their men had anything to do with this or if anyone connected with their organisation was involved."

The three men strode towards the main house, shoes crunching on the tiny grey driveway stones.

"How can you be so sure?" asked Baldwin.

"Trust me, they'd have talked."

"I don't even want to know the details," muttered Craven with a sly grin. He rang the doorbell, and after a long pause, John Kelleher opened the sizeable black door and walked away without greeting, just leaving it open for them to enter. "What's in the bag?" Craven asked.

"It's not a bag. It's just a jacket with some wallets and phones of the IRA men I had the pleasure of spending the afternoon with. They might come in useful."

Craven just shook his head in disbelief, and Kane followed John Kelleher's lead into the vast kitchen. John rested one arm on the large marble-topped island and kneaded the bridge of his nose with the other hand.

"Well?" he asked, "Any leads?"

"It's been a busy day," said Baldwin. "We've followed up on all the leads we had. But nothing solid to go on."

"Well, then, it's a good job Mr Franchetti and

his team have arrived." Kelleher waved towards the dining area, where a man in combat fatigues sat with sunglasses perched atop a shaved head. Fran Doyle sat across the table from the American, drinking a steaming mug of coffee.

"Leo Franchetti. Founder and owner of the Black Eagle Agency," piped the American in what Craven thought was a Texan or similar-sounding accent. "Pleased to meet you, fellas."

"Mr Franchetti came highly recommended by my insurance company, so please apprise him of all the information we have gathered to date. His assessment of the situation will determine if the insurance policy will pay out or not, so share every scrap of information with him."

"Insurance company?" queried Kane.

"Mr Kelleher has kidnap and ransom insurance," said Craven. "The policy will cover the ransom payment and his costs."

Kelleher held eye contact with Kane as if challenging him to ask how long the policy had been in force. The insurance policy added an extra dimension to the kidnapping. If Kane was going to think like an investigator rather than a blunt instrument, he had to look at the case from all angles. If Kelleher's father-in-law was a suspect, then surely so was John Kelleher, no matter how unlikely it seemed. They had to look at every single person connected to Annie and her family.

"Good to meet you," smiled Craven, and he shook Franchetti's hand warmly when the American strode over from the dinner table. Kane followed, and Franchetti's handshake was firm and confident. Franchetti was a big man, taller and broader than Kane. He was heavily muscled, tanned, and sported a black moustache.

"My boys and I are all ex-special forces, SEALS, Delta, or Rangers. We provide security, extraction, recon, and target retrieval all over the world. Every operator on my team was trained by the greatest fighting force the world has ever seen – the US Army and Navy," Leo Franchetti beamed. His muscled arms folded across his chest, and he grinned with pearl-white Hollywood teeth. "So, what are your backgrounds?"

"I'm Jim Baldwin, and this is Frank Craven. We are both former detectives in the UK police, and I've worked private security in the Middle East for longer than I care to remember," said Jim.

"OK, so investigative experience. Nice. What about you?" Franchetti raised his eyebrows in Kane's direction.

"Jack Kane, former British Army soldier." It irked Kane to provide his real name to the

American mercenary. With the problems he had with the British government, Kane would have preferred to use a pseudonym, but Craven had already given Kane's name to Baldwin, Kelleher and Fran Doyle, so there seemed little point in secrecy.

"What unit did you serve in, friend?"

"Paras, then the Special Air Service." Kane left out his subsequent role with the Mjolnir agency. Its function as a black ops wing of MI6 was too hard to explain and inappropriate to share.

"Alright then. So, we have a genuine soldier here, fellas. Great to meet you, Mr Kane. Going by your age, you must have seen action in the Middle East?"

"A bit, yeah."

"Well, I've brought ten soldiers with me on this mission. And we're here to help. So, brief us with the intel, and we can get started. We will get your daughter back, Mr Kelleher, you can rest easy now that Black Eagle is here."

"Take him through the details, Fran," said John Kelleher. Fran Doyle bustled about with his laptop, and Franchetti resumed his seat at the table with Kelleher and Jim Baldwin.

Craven and Kane excused themselves and went to make a drink. They had been through the briefing already, and sitting through it again would run down Annie's clock even further.

"How did it go with the father-in-law?" asked Kane. He searched the cupboards and found a red box of tea bags.

"I don't think he's involved," said Craven. "I met Mrs Kelleher as well. She's distraught, and she's definitely got addiction issues. So, I don't think she's tied up in this either."

"What else do we have to go on, then?"

"There are a couple of former employees we can try. A jockey who was fired, people like that. Fuck all, really."

"Whoever is behind this is confident and experienced. So, it can't just be local gangsters. If it isn't the IRA, then men must have come in from abroad. Operatives who would need to bring in equipment, just like our friend Mr Franchetti there."

"OK, so what are you saying?"

"That someone has employed professionals to come in and kidnap Annie. Their employer has identified that she's an easy target and that the Kellehers have enough money to pay millions in ransom. If this team has flown in privately, there will be a record of them somewhere. I'll investigate that and see what I can dig up."

"This insurance policy thing is a bit fishy. I think it's about time we had a proper look at Kelleher's finances. We should be able to access his bank accounts, and I'll look at this policy. Fran should be able to let me poke around a bit."

"Good, let's try to do that this afternoon so that we don't lose another day chasing cold leads."

"Are they really the greatest fighting force the world has ever seen?" asked Craven, stirring his coffee and annoyingly using the same spoon to fish out the tea bag from Kane's mug.

"I think the Romans, Alexander the Great, Genghis Khan, and Napoleon might have something to say about that. They're the best in our day and age, that's for sure. The British Army has the SAS and SBS, which are as good as anything the Americans have, but they are on a different scale in terms of size and equipment."

John Kelleher sprang up from his seat, sending his chair crashing to the tiled floor. He held his phone out in front of him as though the thing would explode.

"It's them," stammered Kelleher. "It's the kidnappers calling."

TWENTY-FOUR

Fran Doyle answered the WhatsApp video call on his Apple MacBook laptop. The green screen turned to deepest black, with shades of fizzing grey pixels.

"Mr Kelleher," said a voice. Some sort of technology muffled it so that it came in a robotic American voice devoid of accent.

"I'm here," John Kelleher answered. He set his jaw, and a frown creased his forehead.

"Time is ticking, so you will need to have our money ready, or your daughter will die." The screen suddenly switched from black to a white background. The picture wobbled and jerked as though whoever took the video was using a mobile phone. Kane peered at the screen, focusing on every centimetre, hoping to uncover any clue as to the kidnapper's location. A balaclava-covered head filled the white background, eyes covered with sunglasses, and a wide slash of a mouth grinned through the laptop screen. "We know you are searching for us. That is a mistake. We will soon send you instructions on where to deliver our money. You should be ready to travel, Mr Kelleher. We want our ten million euros split, fifty per cent cash in unmarked large denominations and fifty per cent in Monero cryptocurrency. Now, just to keep you focused and to warn you to keep your hounds away from us, I have a little video to play."

The screen crackled again and cut to show a small girl with long black hair sitting against the white screen. She wore a red school blazer, and her wet eyes gleamed with the profound fear Kane had seen so many times on the faces of children in war zones. It was sheer terror, encompassing the fear of death, pain and suffering. Anger surged inside Kane like a fire kindling on dry timber.

"Please help me, Daddy," Annie Kelleher pleaded in a small, frightened voice. John Kelleher broke down then, his entire body racked with shuddering sobs of pain. Annie's pale face stared into the camera, and her bottom lip trembled. Kane thought of his own daughter, and he forced down a lump in his throat.

"That should sharpen your resolve, Mr Kelleher," said the robotic voice as the balaclava appeared once more. "Will you have our money ready?"

"Yes, yes I will," whimpered John Kelleher, leaning towards the screen, a trail of snot and tears looping from his face to his pleading hands.

"The cam's off on our side," whispered Fran Doyle, placing a hand on his employer's shoulder.

"Very well," said the kidnapper. "More instructions to follow. Have your passport ready."

The call ended, and John Kelleher ran from the kitchen, unable to control his sorrow.

"I recorded that," said Doyle, and he and Leo Franchetti dissolved into discussing how they could analyse the call for clues. Kane listened as they delved into the intricacies of the untraceable Monero cryptocurrency and its prevalent use in illicit activities on the dark web and with ransomware.

"Fucking hell, that was hard to watch," sighed Craven, puffing his cheeks out. "I'm going to freshen up in my room for five minutes, and then I'll get working on the accounts."

The big detective stalked out of the kitchen, and Kane wiped a hand across his face. It had been hard to watch. Annie was alone and afraid, held by men who would kill her if they didn't get what they wanted. They weren't amateurs – arranging the kidnap exchange abroad would cause the Irish police jurisdictional problems, as well as making it difficult for the men Kelleher had brought in to travel undetected. Facing an imminent deadline and the additional demand to adhere to the kidnapper's travel instructions, the window of time to find the kidnappers and ensure Annie's safe release was narrow. Of course, they could simply let John Kelleher pay the ransom, especially if he had insurance to cover it. Kane wondered why Annie's father would not just pay the sum and get his daughter back. The risk, of course, was that they would kill her anyway.

Kane followed Craven to freshen up. His next step was to check the flights in and out of Ireland over the last week. Whatever kidnapping team had snatched Annie must have entered the country somehow.

TWENTY-FIVE

Craven opened the door to his bedroom and stepped inside. Shutting it behind him, he leant against it, taking a moment to exhale and close his eyes. Craven took his mobile phone from his pocket and pressed his wife Barb's contact. The number rang out, and he sighed.

The bathroom was large and tiled, with a mosaic of copper and silver tiles set into spirals of varying sizes. The mirror was long, just like you would expect to find in a fancy hotel, and the taps were Victorian with white handles. Craven ran the cold water tap and splashed it on his face. He stared at himself in the mirror, stretching the wrinkles and sagging skin around his eyes and mouth.

What am I doing here?

Craven had thought this would be a simple

favour for his old pal Jim Baldwin, but it was turning into much more. Kane had been in some sort of violent exchange with the IRA, and God only knew how that had gone. Some bastards had kidnapped a girl with millions of euros demanded as ransom. Craven had no clue who was responsible, whether it was something to do with the insurance, organised crime, or anything else for that matter. He felt out of his depth. He had retired from the police and had not expected to get drawn into another serious investigation.

The problem with this whole mess was that he couldn't stop. Not with a little girl's life hanging in the balance. Craven stared at his paunch and his thinning hair. He had never been a stellar copper in his prime, never mind now that they had put him out to pasture. Of all the people gathered to help John Kelleher retrieve his daughter, Craven felt he could help the least. He splashed more water on his face and ran through the tenuous leads they had pulled together on the case, but his mind was blank. The accounts could yield something, but it wouldn't be a good thing if they did. It would be some sort of financial irregularity and cast the spotlight on the Kelleher family. Craven wasn't sure he wanted to turn over that stone.

"Hello, Detective Inspector Craven," came a woman's voice, startling Craven so badly that he jumped away from the sink. He turned to find a woman standing in the bathroom doorway. She was tall and black, with her hair scraped away from her face into a tight bun. She had a silenced handgun in her right hand, held low and confidently aimed at Craven's midriff.

"What the fuck?" Craven gasped, his heart thumping in his chest from the surprise.

"I hear you are a friend of Jack Kane?"

"Jack, who?" Craven swallowed hard. Who was this woman, and how had she found him here? He thought of the Mjolnir agents he and Kane had tangled with last spring. All of them were armed, ruthless, and deadly. Craven saw that same steely look in the woman's almond eyes. She was after Kane, which meant she was an assassin or secret agent or whatever title government agents called themselves.

"Don't play games, Frank. I know you got close to Jack Kane, and I also know you visited him in Scotland recently. I don't want to hurt him, just to bring him in for questioning."

"I don't know what…"

She raised the gun so that the shining, cold metal pointed at Craven's eye. "I can make you suffer if you prefer. Just tell me where to find him, and I'll be on my way."

"Alright. I know Kane. He's my friend. But I

don't know where he is."

"Come on then, out of the bathroom." She took a step back and waved the gun to show him which way to go. Craven stepped slowly out of the bathroom and moved towards the bedroom. A double bed filled most of the space, with two bedside tables, a small side table, and one narrow armchair. The woman stayed in the open space before the bathroom door, and Craven beside the bed.

"I saw him in Scotland ages ago. Haven't seen him since."

"Why were you with a wanted criminal in Scotland? Kane is a rogue agent, wanted for murder and many other charges by the police. Why would a former detective, who has just retired and bought a luxurious Spanish villa, befriend such a man? Shouldn't you have turned him in?"

Craven stared at her. She knew all about him, which meant that whatever branch of MI6 she worked for also had their beady eyes on his business. She knew about the money they had seized from the Manchester gang and that he and Kane were friends. Craven's only experience with these agent types was extreme violence. He could see in her eyes that she was losing patience with him, and it was surely only a matter of seconds before she used other methods of making him talk.

"OK. Kane and I became friends last year. He has a family and…" Craven leapt to his right and grabbed a lamp from the small table. He threw the lamp at the woman and charged at her. She snarled, batting the lamp aside with her gun so that it smashed against the wall. Craven barged into her, his size and weight driving her into the wall, his shoes crushing the lamp's porcelain remnants.

The woman drove her knee into Craven's groin, and he groaned with pain, doubling over involuntarily. She grabbed a fistful of his hair and yanked his head away from her before smashing the butt of her gun into his face. Craven stumbled backwards and fell on the floor with a thud.

"Frank, what's going on in there?" came a familiar voice from outside his door. It was Kane, and Craven smiled through the blood in his mouth.

"Help, Jack!" he called, and moments later, the door crashed in as though a battering ram came through it.

TWENTY-SIX

Kane had returned to his room to hide the Glock pistol he had taken from the IRA. He didn't want to be walking around John Kelleher's house with a gun on him, but the weapon might come in useful. As he was about to stow the weapon in his suitcase, he heard a loud thud and something smashing against his wall.

Craven was in the next room, and Kane paused, listening carefully. Another thud and a groan resounded. Kane kept hold of the gun and walked outside of his room. Knocking on Craven's door, he heard more sounds of a scuffle coming from inside.

He leant towards the door and shouted to Craven to ask if everything was alright. The reply was a frightened cry for help. Kane took a step back and kicked the solid pine door off its hinges without hesitation. A woman turned to face him, holding a silenced gun. There was no shock on her face, just a look of fierce recognition.

"Jack Kane," she uttered impassively and fired a shot from her weapon. Kane anticipated it just in time and threw himself to the ground, narrowly avoiding the silenced bullet that embedded itself into the wall behind him. Kane dived towards her and fired his own pistol. Gunfire shook the room, and the bullet missed her head by a fraction.

She lunged at him, teeth gritted in a rictus of determination, aiming a kick at Kane's face. Reacting swiftly blocked it. She brought her gun around to shoot him at close range, but Kane manoeuvered inside her reach and batted it aside.

They exchanged a flurry of punches and kicks in the small space, neither able to land a decisive blow. A perfect match in skill and strength, they grappled for control, grasping for holds, and Kane slammed her backwards into a mirror that smashed onto the hardwood floor. She slid down the wall, dazed from the impact.

"Who sent you?" he demanded, pointing his gun at her head.

She blinked three times and refocused, smiling up at Kane mirthlessly. "Did you think you could just run? You almost took out the entire Mjolnir agency. They want you dead."

"Who does?" Kane had hoped that the threat to his life had ended with the deaths of his former employers and that there was nobody left to hunt him. But life was never that simple. Deep in his heart, he had known they would come for him again, and they would never stop coming.

The woman raised her gun, prompting Kane to rapidly kick it out of her grasp. Undeterred, she rolled with the blow and came at Kane like a cornered lion. She beat him backwards, her fists connecting with his head and her knee driving into his ribs. He fired two shots from his Glock, but she drove his hand upwards so the shots cannoned into the ceiling. He wrestled with the woman, their eyes meeting amid the struggle, and then Kane heard boots running along towards them and the clamour of American voices shouting. He had fired three shots since entering Craven's room, and the sound of the gunfire would have undoubtedly reverberated throughout the Kelleher home.

Franchetti came barrelling into the bedroom wielding a shotgun and flanked by two equally hulking members of his team.

"That's enough now, miss," Franchetti said in his Texan drawl. "Drop your weapon and raise your hands."

The woman rolled across the carpet and snatched up her silenced weapon. She fired a shot at the Americans before dashing towards the bedroom window. In response, Franchetti and his men unleashed a deafening barrage of gunfire. Kane aimed carefully and squeezed the trigger, but the bullet intended for her back slashed through the meat of the woman's thigh as she crashed through the windowpane, leaving only a fog of misted blood in the air.

Kane ran to the window and peered between the jagged shards of glass. They were on the first floor, and below them was a flowerbed of neatly tended shrubs running the length of the house, surrounded by a mix of patio stones and stained wooden decking. Yet there was no sign of the woman.

"Where the hell did she go?" Franchetti exclaimed, appearing next to Kane at the window. The American searched the garden, peering down the sight of his shotgun as he turned it in wide sweeps.

"Gone," said Kane, out of breath from the struggle.

"Lucky we came when we did; looked to me like she had the drop on you boys. Anybody want to tell me who she was and what's going on here?"

"It's a long story," muttered Kane.

"Well, sir, we don't got much time. So, give me the short version."

Kane glanced at Craven, who sat on the edge of the bed with his head in his hands. The past had caught up with Kane again, and now an agent had come to John Kelleher's house armed and ready to kill. The man was already up to his neck in trouble with a kidnapped daughter to worry about, and now Kane was adding to the weight of that most terrifying situation. Franchetti deserved an explanation, and so would John Kelleher. So, Kane opened up about his experience with the Mjolnir agency and its operatives. He spoke about the black op in desert tunnels where most of his team died and then how he had been persuaded to testify against Mjolnir in return for a new life. He told Franchetti how the agency had found him and killed his wife, and the American listened patiently.

As Kane spoke, every man in the room listened intently. It was a story that was hard to believe; Kane knew that. However, a formidable killer had set her sights on the Kelleher stud, and she would remain relentless in her quest to eliminate the former Mjolnir agent. The inevitable conclusion was stark – either she would meet her demise at Kane's hands, or Kane himself would fall. The kidnap investigation had suddenly become infinitely more complicated because Kane had unwittingly compromised everything.

TWENTY-SEVEN

Condor limped through the undergrowth. Thorns and briars tore at her face and hands, and her blood streaked across leaves and branches. The bullet had gone straight through the flesh of her left thigh, and there were no broken bones. Her face stung and throbbed from the shards of broken glass which had sliced her flesh as she leapt from the window. She paused momentarily, slumping against the branch of a silver birch tree to calm herself.

The building swarmed like a kicked hornet's nest. Men in black tactical gear patrolled the perimeter, armed and searching the grounds with controlled sweeps of their rifles. There was an armed military-trained team in that building, and she had not expected that. Kane was there. Her target had been located. That, at least, was a win. The ex-policeman was strong but unskilled, and Condor probably should have put a bullet in his head.

She looked at the backs of her hands. A dozen cuts oozed blood like red pearls, and she dared not feel the wounds on her face. She took off again, scrambling through the undergrowth until she came to the edges of the farm. Condor clambered over the hedges and dragged her injured leg across the road. The sound of a vehicle approaching at high speed made her pick up the pace, and she threw her tired body into a farmer's field, rolling in a cabbage furrow. She lay there until the vehicle passed, just in case it was the men from the house searching for her.

Condor pushed herself up and kept moving, keeping low and heading toward her car. She came upon the lane where she had left it and slumped into the driving seat. The leg wound pulsed, and Condor allowed herself a stifled scream of pain. She flipped down the sun visor and slipped open the mirror. Condor gasped. Her face was a web of scrapes and cuts. Blood smeared and leaked across her cheeks and lips, and the bottom of her left earlobe was torn open, dripping blood onto the car seat.

She slammed her fist into the steering wheel and counted to ten, taking deep breaths at each number. She was Akachi Akinyemi, an unwanted child who had risen to become Condor, a lethal assassin and unbeatable warrior.

I am Akachi Akinyemi, and I will kill you, Jack Kane.

She repeated those words in her head over and over, slamming the car into gear and taking off at full speed. She had a medical kit in the boot, along with weapons and everything she needed to turn that house into a burning pit of hell.

Her phone rang, but she ignored it. It was McGovern, and Condor did not want to talk to her until the job was done. Akachi Akinyemi never failed, and she wasn't about to start now.

TWENTY-EIGHT

"Seems to me like this entire operation is one big clusterfuck," remarked Leo Franchetti. He leant back in his chair, crossing his hands behind his shaved head. "If we want to get Annie home safe, we need to lock this thing down and get on with the investigation. No cops, keep it quiet, do it our way."

"Why did you bring this man here if you know he is a wanted man and could be a threat to Mr Kelleher and his family?" asked Fran Doyle. He paced the kitchen with his hands balled into fists and his shoulders hunched.

"Because Jim asked me to come, and he asked if I knew anyone who could help," said Craven. "If I was in trouble, I don't know anyone better equipped to help than this man. Especially if there's going to be trouble." He gestured with his thumb towards Kane, who stood away from the table, talking to some of Franchetti's men. Craven looked at Jim Baldwin and raised an eyebrow, looking for support.

"You brought a fucking lunatic into my house at this time. When my daughter is missing!" John Kelleher shouted. He roared so loud that everybody in the room looked away, casting their eyes at the floor or ceiling to avoid his gaze. Not because they were afraid of him. He was perhaps the least physically capable man in the room, but because he was a suffering father whose rage was justified. "Guns were fired. It's fucking insane. I want you and him gone now."

"Maybe it was a mistake bringing you here, Frank," Jim Baldwin intoned. He stood, the legs of his chair scraping on the tiled floor. "We can take it from here. Why don't you and Mr Kane leave us to it?"

Craven opened his mouth to protest but snapped it closed again. Kelleher was right, and so was Jim. "We only wanted to help. But we'll leave now. Apologies, and best of luck finding your daughter."

"Just get out," barked Kelleher.

Craven left the table and grabbed Kane by the arm, leading him towards the bedroom.

"What's going on?" asked Kane, looking down at Craven's grip on his forearm.

"They want us gone. And we should go. I don't know why we came in the first place." They climbed the stairs and reached the bedrooms. The room to Craven's door was destroyed after Kane had smashed through it.

"We can still help with this thing, Frank," said Kane, pausing before entering his room.

"Best if we just leave them to it. I'm sorry I dragged you into this. Look, we can be on a plane back to Spain today. There's no way that fucking mad assassin woman can follow you with your new passport. Let's just go home and put this behind us." Craven smiled wanly. He was tired and felt foolish for accepting Baldwin's request to help. Baldwin probably thought he was going to get the Frank Craven from twenty years ago, not a washed-up retired copper without a serious collar for longer than he could remember.

"That woman will come back. She won't give up. She's a secret service assassin, probably from a similar agency to the one I worked for. If I'm not around when she comes…"

"The Yanks are here. Let them deal with it. Let's get back to Barb, Danny, and Kim. Get your gear, and I'll meet you outside in ten minutes."

Kane opened his door and disappeared into his room. Craven picked his way between the broken glass and wooden splinters which littered his bedroom floor. He threw his clothes and toiletries into his bag and sat on the end of the bed to check his phone. Still no reply from Barb. She was probably having too much fun with the kids, he thought. An unread email notification caught his attention, a message from Fran Doyle, sent earlier that day before the woman had attacked.

Craven opened the email. There were six spreadsheet attachments, and the subject line read 'Kelleher Accounts'. The body of the email was blank. Craven closed his phone, picked up his bag, and left the room. He had the accounts, but there seemed little point going over them now. Craven would return to his life of sun and relaxation with Barb, yet he sincerely hoped John Kelleher would get his daughter back safely. He had let Jim Baldwin down and didn't expect to be paid for his work in Ireland. Craven had incurred the costs of the flights, but other than that, he wasn't too badly out of pocket. It was a small price for a lesson learned. Craven's days investigating and solving crimes were well and truly behind him.

TWENTY-NINE

Dublin Airport was like a scene from an apocalypse movie. People in brightly coloured shorts and T-shirts milled about the outside area of terminals one and two with faces strained by weary disappointment. Queues stretched from inside the terminals to wind and weave their way between cones and bollards, stretching back into the car park areas. Airport workers in hi-vis jackets strode purposefully between the mass of people, trying not to make eye contact with frustrated holidaymakers and annoyed business travellers. Kane watched two women through the car window. They shouted at each other with wide eyes as accusations of queue jumping flew between them. The whole thing had descended into chaos.

"What's going on?" asked Kane as the taxi ground to a halt in the traffic leading up a ramp towards departures.

"I think the bloody French airport workers are on strike again," tutted the taxi driver. He was a small, wiry man with an African accent mixed with a hint of Irishness.

"He's right," nodded Craven, staring at his phone. "Just googled it, and the strike has had knock-on effects. It's the air traffic controllers and the baggage handlers in France. Flights out of Dublin are at a standstill."

"Doesn't look like we'll be going anywhere today, then," said Kane. He had resigned himself to leaving Annie Kelleher's plight in the hands of the Garda and John Kelleher's team. Undoubtedly, the Americans were competent to handle any action if an opportunity arose for a rescue attempt. Kane was looking forward to seeing Danny and Kim again, but he had no plans for what to do next or where to go. They had started to build a new life in Scotland – a new school and new friends. Kane had hoped they could remain hidden there, under the radar and out of sight of those who hunted him.

It had all been so perfect – a rented home he could pay for in cash, bills paid for by the landlord and included in his rent. He was completely off-grid. But in the modern world, expecting a teenager to maintain a secure online profile was a tall order. Their world was now online. Danny rarely watched television unless there was a football match on, and even then, he would watch it with his iPad open next to him. It was all YouTube, games, and Snapchat. Which, unfortunately, was how Kane's idyllic new life had turned to ashes.

Kane would need to be vigilant about Danny and Kim's digital footprint wherever he went next, considering the potential risk of hunters lurking in the shadows, waiting for any sign of Jack Kane and his family. Kane watched an overweight woman hobble over to an airport worker and then plonk into a wheelchair. He wheeled her inside, to the front of whatever queue she was in. The surrounding people sneered and pointed at her. The world was a different place than when Kane had been a boy. It had changed beyond recognition. His childhood home had one television, and the children's shows were on for a few hours in the morning and again in the early evening. That was it, no twenty-four-seven access to entertainment. Kids then had to go outside and play with their friends if they wanted to have fun.

Outside of Kane's window, two children played a game of clapping hands. They slapped hands with each other in fast, complex actions, mirroring each other in time with their singing. They laughed, and their parent smiled down at them. A pang of guilt snagged at Kane. Much like his life in Warrington in the protection programme, he had been bored in Scotland. He told himself that it was a wholesome thing to take care of his children, to live a quiet life. He owed it to them to provide a safe environment for them to thrive and grow healthily. But Kane loved the action of his old life. Combat and the challenge of fieldwork, danger. He hadn't realised it when he was in the SAS or as a Mjolnir agent, but that was who he was. Whilst in the field, he had told himself that he yearned for home and to be with his family, but it just wasn't true. He loved Sally and the children, but he was happiest when he spent a few days with them and then returned to the dangers of his job.

The notion that he preferred his work to his family life was not a comfortable realisation to behold. No man should think or feel like that, but Kane did. That was a burden he had to carry and deal with. Danny and Kim were safe with Barbara, and Annie Kelleher was in danger of losing her life. But Kane was happy. He had a problem to solve and enemies to fight. It was selfish and counterintuitive, but it was the truth.

The taxi driver leant out of his window and shouted something to the driver in front, who stuck his hand out his window in a thumb-down gesture. Kane's mind buzzed with the dilemma of where to go with his children like an impossible puzzle. It intertwined and flowed around his thoughts, merging with the other problems he faced. The assassin at Kelleher's stud hadn't known he was there; Kane was sure of that. She had gone to Craven's room and must have followed a breadcrumb trail to find him, not Kane.

"What did that woman at the stud say to you before I got there?" Kane asked.

"She asked me if I knew you," said Craven. "I said no, of course. But she knew I had visited you in Scotland, and she had put two and two together."

"So, she tracked you to Ireland to question you about me?"

"That's what she said, yes."

"She must have tracked your mobile phone. Interesting that she didn't go to Spain, where your phone records would show that you had spent most of your time recently. She was in a rush and gambled that she could find me faster by coming here."

"She wants you badly then, mate."

"She is only acting upon orders. But we took down Mjolnir last spring. So, who sent her? Who gave the order?"

"Didn't your old agency have links to MI6, the Secret Service, or something like that?"

"Yes, kind of. Similar source of funding and oversight, but the black-ops agencies, the teams who do the dirty work, fly under the radar out of necessity. A lot of what they do can never find its way into the newspapers or the mainstream news. People would be outraged. They have no idea what must be done to protect their way of life."

Craven suddenly turned pale. "Wait a minute," he gasped and grabbed Kane's arm. "So that fucking assassin woman knows where my place in Spain is? She could go for Barb and the kids to get at you."

Kane nodded. They would all need to move again, Craven and Barb included. It was such a mess. The decision to give evidence against the Mjolnir agency had ruined Kane's life. His wife Sally was dead, and he and his children were on the run once more. What sort of education and life would they have if their childhood was spent constantly on the run from people who wanted to kill their father? He had to build something better for them, something more secure and permanent. There had to be a way to free Danny and Kim, and he simply had to find it.

"If that killer tracked my phone, I should throw the bloody thing away," Craven grumbled. He rolled down the car window as though he would toss it into the road.

"The assassin doesn't know we are returning to Spain," said Kane. "She thinks we are still here." He pointed to Craven's phone.

"We are still here," Craven raised an eyebrow. "Look at the state of this place. There's more chance of us winning the fucking lottery than getting a flight to Spain today."

"If the assassin thinks we are still here, then we can bring her to us. Let us be the hunters for a change. Get to her before she can travel to your house in Spain."

"Ah," said Craven, beginning to catch on.

"And whilst we are here, we need to move around. If she's tracking your phone, we can't keep it static. It's too suspicious."

"Well, if we are hanging around, then why not follow up on the remaining leads we've got on the Kelleher case? Anything we come up with, I can just turn over to Jim Baldwin."

"What's left to do? We have the disgruntled employee, the former jockey. I wanted to check the recent private and charter flights into Ireland to see if a team has come into the country for this job."

"And I've got Kelleher's financials on my computer, so we can go through those."

"She'll come for me again, the assassin. It's in

her nature. She's a wolf who won't stop until she eliminates her target. And when she comes, she will find more than sheep waiting for her." Kane leaned forward and placed a hand on the taxi driver's shoulder. "Change of plans, mate. Can you get us out of here and take us to a hotel in Dublin city centre?"

"Yes, boss, no worries," said the taxi driver, turning around to smile at Kane and Craven. "I know a few places."

"None of them rip-off hotels, though," said Craven, shaking his head. "It's fucking daylight robbery in Dublin. I'm not paying five hundred quid for a hotel and a tenner for a pint of beer. Somewhere cheap and cheerful will do for us."

THIRTY

Condor's jaw muscles worked beneath her face. They rippled and shifted her dark skin, and her teeth ground like millstones. The sanitised wipe from her first aid kit had changed from pure white to dark crimson as she dabbed the clotted blood from her scratched and sliced face. She threw the wipe into the sink to join the other half dozen piled at the plughole, leaking her blood into the basin.

The City West Hotel was a golf course hotel twenty minutes from the Kelleher stud farm in County Kildare. The hotel must have been grand once but had since fallen into disrepair. Despite the impressive drive into its grounds marked by bold gates and lush green hedging, the interior was jaded, with faded carpets and tarnished furniture. Men with sallow skin and sad expressions loitered around the grounds and reception area. It seemed the place was surely a refuge for asylum seekers. Condor had booked herself in and met the withering stare of the hotel receptionist as he took in her bedraggled appearance.

"Horse riding incident," Condor had said and flashed a poignantly fake smile.

The bullet wound in her leg was the worst injury. The first thing she had done after sliding her hotel room key card into the door was limp into the shower. Hot water was like heaven as it pounded against her aching muscles and rinsed the dark blood from her leg. The bullet had passed through the outer flesh of her thigh, not going through the muscle but slicing it like a thick-bladed knife. It ached and stung like hell when she cleaned the ragged flaps of skin with antiseptic from her medical kit.

Condor finished cleaning the wounds on her face. Jumping out of the window had been her only option. To hesitate would have meant death or capture – which would have been just as bad. Based on what she had read in Jack Kane's files, he was clearly not squeamish. Falling into his hands would have subjected her to brutal questioning, agonising torture, and then death. So, the window and its clawing, lacerating shards of glass had proven to be the preferable outcome.

She should have killed Kane at the stud and

the big detective with him. Condor felt she had gotten the better of the fight. Kane was skilled, without question, but there was no denying he fell short of her expertise. As an expert in karate, jiu-jitsu, judo, and aikido, she rarely faced defeat on the training mat. Next time, she would eliminate Kane and then report to McGovern, enabling Condor to assume her new role as a senior agent in McGovern's newly formed agency. Condor would have pride of place, travelling the world doing what she loved. She would be at the tip of the spear, taking down terrorists and evil men whilst enjoying the perks of her position – flying on private planes and enjoying the best hotels and luxury the world had to offer.

First, however, she had to kill Jack Kane. Condor sat on the closed toilet seat and picked up the needle from her first aid kit. She reached up to the shelf behind her to grab the bottle of Jameson whiskey she had bought in the hotel bar and took a long drink. It burned her chest on the way down but steeled her resolve to do what must be done. Condor passed the needle through her flesh and pulled the stitching tight. Blood pulsed from the wound, and she patched herself up piece by piece.

Condor would give herself the night to sleep and recover. Then, she would be back on Kane's trail. He was a washed-up ex-agent, over the hill, out of shape and out of practice. He would not come between Condor and her goal. She never failed.

THIRTY-ONE

The taxi driver took Craven and Kane to the Mespil Hotel in the heart of Dublin's city centre. This contemporary and spacious hotel, adorned with numerous windows, overlooked the historic Grand Canal. Craven had baulked at the price for two rooms but comforted himself knowing that it was, in fact, the Deli-Boys' ill-gotten gains that paid the bill. The Deli-Boys were the vicious Manchester gang Kane had brought down last spring.

Craven, somewhat absentmindedly, paid for two single rooms on his credit card. It dawned on him that Kane never used cards and paid for everything in cash. After he paid the bill and took the lift to his room on the third floor, Craven pondered the implications of being too easily traceable through his financial and digital activities and wondered whether he should be more careful. If the assassin at the stud had his name, could track his phone, and had linked him to Kane, then perhaps he was compromised. Craven didn't fancy living a life on the run, especially not when Barb was still recovering from cancer and required regular check-ups and treatment.

The light and airy room featured many home comforts and was well-equipped with ample furniture and a large Samsung Smart TV mounted on the wall. Kane was in the adjacent room, and the two men had agreed to meet in Craven's room in ten minutes' time to go through Kelleher's accounts. It was after five o'clock in the evening, and looking for flights to Spain could wait until the morning.

Craven washed his face and unpacked his clothes from his small suitcase. He had three spare shirts, two pairs of trousers, and clean underwear. Craven grumbled at the espresso machine on the side table, wondering what was wrong with a bog standard kettle. As the little machine hummed and sprang to life, he took out his laptop and set it up on the desk. From his window, Craven saw people in suits and smart office wear marching along the canal pathway, streaming out of the city like worker bees.

The espresso machine switched off, and Craven tentatively set about making a drink for himself and Kane. His phone rumbled with a notification, a text message from Barb. She apologised for missing his call and told him that she'd been to a water park with the children and then taken them out for dinner. Craven smiled to himself. She was enjoying looking after Danny and Kim. Barb would have made a brilliant mother, so kind and caring. It was the tragedy of their love that they could not have children. They had tried so many times until they eventually discovered Craven was the problem. He fired blanks. Frank loved Barb with all his heart, and it cut him to his very core that he could not fulfil her greatest desire – to have a child.

Craven replied, telling her he loved her and that he and Kane were OK. At that moment, there was a knock at the door, and Craven opened it to find Kane waiting for him.

"As punctual as always," noted Craven, checking his watch. "It's only been eight minutes."

"Better to be early than late," said Kane, sliding past Craven's bulk into the bedroom.

"Not too early, though. It's just as rude to be very early as it is to be late."

"It's two minutes, Frank. Shall I come back?"

"No need to get your knickers in a twist. Calm

down."

"What's that smell?" Kane wrinkled his nose and frowned at Craven.

"I haven't farted, if that's what you're thinking. It's the fucking coffee. I would have made you tea, but there's no pissing kettle, and I don't know how to work the bloody machine properly!" He angrily jabbed his finger towards the espresso maker and two cups on the side table. "It smells like weasel shit."

"How do you know what weasel shit smells like?"

"Oh, fuck off. What's with the jokes all of a sudden? You've normally got a face like a slapped arse."

"Sorry, Craven. Shall we look at these accounts?"

They took a chair each, and Craven opened the first spreadsheet.

"Alright then," said Craven. "This looks like Kelleher's personal account."

The provided spreadsheet was exported from a Bank of Ireland online account. It showed credits and debits going back six months and opening and closing balances for each month. Craven followed the screen with his finger and sipped at the weasel shit coffee.

"He's running close to the bone every month," remarked Kane. "Most months, it looks like he has to transfer money in from other accounts just to cover bills."

"Yeah, he's spending a fucking fortune. There's at least two grand a month here on hairdressers and nail bars. His wife is living some life. There's also a shitload of cash going out every month. Probably Mrs Kelleher's coke and wine habit."

"He's got at least three loans coming out as well as his mortgage."

"Right. So, based on this account, it doesn't take a forensic accountant to see that John Kelleher is fucked."

"What else do we have? Are the stud business accounts there?"

Craven minimised the personal account file and opened the one titled Kelleher Stud. It opened in a similar format to the first, a simple export from a Bank of Ireland business account. Doyle had gone back six months, and the sheet was again broken down into credits, debits and opening balances.

"Jesus," Craven blurted. "How can you make so much money off fucking horses?" He pushed the poorly made coffee aside and marvelled at the sums coming into the account for stud services. There were transactions for hundreds of thousands of pounds from other racing businesses across the globe. But despite the sums of money coming in, more dripped out of the accounts like an open tap. Bills for horse feed, the mortgage for the land on which they had built the stud, wages for employees, travel costs, car purchases and upkeep, monstrous insurance bills.

"Literally," said Kane.

"You really are in a good mood. What's wrong?"

"Nothing. I'm always like this."

Craven curled his lip because Kane was most certainly not always in good form. Most of the time, he was a surly bastard and hard to talk to.

"Anyway, I think it's safe to say that our Mr Kelleher is in financial difficulty," said Craven. "I don't know much about accounting, but I don't see any provision for income tax in any of these accounts."

"We can see the man is losing money, and clearly, the payout from a kidnap and ransom insurance policy would come in handy right about now. But is it enough debt to make a man put his daughter through this ordeal?"

"Well, if Kelleher is behind it, at least he knows Annie isn't in any real danger. She is being treated harshly, yes, and is probably terrified. Maybe he thinks her suffering is worth it for the money?"

"I don't see it," said Kane, shaking his head. "I don't particularly like John Kelleher, but I didn't get any inkling that he could be this ruthless. Whilst we're online, take a look at flightchecker.com. It'll list any private or chartered flights coming in and out of Ireland's airports. Let's see if we can see anything that might look like a team flying in for the kidnapping. We can cross reference destination points with numbers of passengers and see what comes up."

Craven pushed the laptop towards Kane. He understood what Kane wanted to do but did not know how to go about it. Tech had never been his strong point.

Craven sat back and finished his horrible coffee. They now knew that John Kelleher had the motive to stage his daughter's kidnapping and an insurance policy rich enough to get him out of his money problems. But it felt like a stretch. There had to be someone responsible. It just didn't feel like a setup to Craven. He resolved to follow up with the disgruntled employee jockey in the morning whilst Kane chased down the flight records. Flying back to Spain could wait.

If the kidnappers were going to make John Kelleher travel with the ransom, Craven had very little time to figure this thing out. Otherwise, they would have to pray it was a setup or that the kidnappers let Annie go.

THIRTY-TWO

Kane woke early the following day after a restless night of sporadic sleep. He rarely slept well in hotels. The rooms were always too hot, and Kane often felt he was being watched. In the regiment, he had learned to sleep in the most uncomfortable of situations, but for some bizarre reason, he had never been able to apply that to hotels.

He showered and shaved, yet it was too early for breakfast, so he walked along the canal, thinking over the Kelleher case. A cycle and walking path ran between the waterway and the road, and already, people were making their way into the city for work. It was six-thirty in the morning, and a sickly pallid sun crept over the distant chimney stacks and slated roofs. Heavy iron-coloured clouds hung low in the sky, oppressive and close, and a drizzling rain spat in intermittent gusts to patter the canal water.

The guilt of enjoyment in his work still plagued Kane, and he had spent much of the night twisting and turning. He wondered if Sally knew it too, deep down. Perhaps it was a thing they both recognised but left unsaid. After all, what sort of monster would rather fight, shoot, kill, and out-think his enemies than spend time with his family?

Kane reached an old lock, freshly painted black with white tips on the long balance beams. The lock chamber was low, and the uphill gate served as a pathway across the water from a nearby housing estate to this side of the river. Reflecting on the inevitable passage of time and how all things change, he wondered what the canal must have been like a century ago when barges would have thronged its waters. He imagined barrel loads of Guinness and sacks of grain coming back and forth with robust draught horses tirelessly pulling the boats from the riverbank. Now, the canal was used for simple pleasure boating, and its banks were for the endless train of people heading into the city for work.

All things change, but him, that is. Kane was still the man he had always been. The only difference now was that he didn't have to follow orders. For too long, he had followed orders blindly, never questioning the right or wrong in it, rarely understanding or caring why he was in a particular place or what relevance his target had on world affairs. Now, he acted for himself and his family and would always try to be on the right side. That included making sure Annie Kelleher came home safely to her family. Kane turned and headed back to the hotel, ready for his breakfast. A final thought fought its way into his brain. It had been hanging around since he left Spain, loitering, trying to enter his conscious train of thought but pushed back and left to fester. Were Danny and Kim better off without him? Didn't they deserve a settled, safe life out of harm's way?

Kane reached the hotel's glass doors before he chewed over that most unthinkable of questions. He entered the hotel restaurant and spotted Craven sitting at a double table, drinking a cup of hot coffee.

"Tea, please," Kane said to a waiter, who nodded and hurried off to fetch the drink.

"We need to get stuck into this case today," stressed Craven, popping a forkful of bacon and fried tomatoes into his mouth. His plate was piled high with an Irish breakfast.

"First job is to get out to Casement Aerodrome," nodded Kane. "I want to check all flights in and out of there for the last month. We already checked the ones from the major airports like Dublin and Cork last night and didn't turn up anything interesting. I've landed at Casement before, on a job once. It's on the outskirts of Dublin. If there's a plane coming into the county quietly, then it will have landed there."

"Why there and not at Dublin or one of the others?"

"Because there will be a log of the arrival there. An immigration record, use of landing facilities and such. Casement is a semi-military airport. It's the only airfield used by the Irish Air Corps. The CIA has used it before, and it's where visiting Prime Ministers and Presidents might land. Or a team of special operators with enough money to buy a silent entry into the country."

"What if that mad woman attacks us again?" Craven picked up his phone and shook it at Kane, illustrating the point that she could track them down at any time.

"Let's hope she does."

Craven shrugged at the logic in that and poured himself a fresh cup from his pot of coffee. Kane helped himself to a breakfast of fruit and yoghurt from the buffet and washed it down with a pot of tea. After breakfast, they walked up Mespil Road and hired a car at a local Hertz. It was still only eight in the morning, and Kane was determined to make progress towards finding Annie Kelleher.

THIRTY-THREE

Casement Aerodrome was twenty minutes south of Dublin city. It sat roughly halfway between the city centre and County Kildare. Craven had wanted to hire a bottom-of-the-range vehicle, grumbling as always about the cost, but Kane had convinced him to hire a BMW 5 Series. Casement was a secure facility used by the Irish Air Corps and An Garda Síochána, so they couldn't simply stroll in and ask questions. Kane needed a car with gravitas if his plan was going to work.

They turned off the N7 motorway and approached Casement Aerodrome slowly. Kane gestured to the gateway across the entrance. It wasn't heavily fortified or protected. A wire fence ran the perimeter, and a guard hut and single barrier blocked vehicular entry from the road.

"Let me do the talking," said Kane.

"Whatever you say," agreed Craven. "I hope you know what you are doing."

Kane had no proper plan of infiltrating the airfield, but he didn't fancy scaling the fence and trying to sneak his way in. There had been no time to study the airfield or its buildings, and he wouldn't know where to look for flight records. As far as Kane could tell, the airfield contained at least five buildings, comprising a mixture of hangars and office buildings, and the flight records could be held digitally in any of them.

Craven pulled the car up slowly at the guard hut, and a security guard peered down at them. He wore an Air Corps uniform with the Irish tricolour on his left shoulder. He was in his thirties with a raw shaving rash around his neck and close-set green eyes.

"Good morning, gentlemen," said the guard.

"Good morning to you," replied Kane in his most officious-sounding voice. "I have an appointment this morning for a guided tour of the facility. I am Major Rob Jones from British Intelligence."

Kane sat back in his chair and looked straight ahead. He spoke confidently, just as he had hundreds of times when trying to gain entry to different buildings and facilities over the years.

Rob Jones was a brilliant right-back for Liverpool Football Club back when Kane was young, and it was as good a name as any.

"I'm sorry, Major Jones," said the guard. "We don't seem to have a record of your visit. Who were you supposed to be meeting?"

Kane frowned at the guard. "I don't have the gentleman's name. Administrators at MI6 arranged the meeting on my behalf. Do you think I do these things myself? I need to ensure this place is secure before we arrange a key visit from important British politicians, and perhaps the Prime Minister himself, to discuss the Northern Irish peace treaty."

"Our Commanding Officer is away, sir, and I…"

"Look. Give me your name and rank. I can contact the top brass in your Air Corps and have them order you to let me in. Do you want that? For me to have to go above your head?" Kane paused. The guard licked his lips and rubbed his hands over and over. "This is a national security matter. If you delay me, there will be repercussions. Just arrange for a mid-ranking officer to meet at your main office. I need a ten-minute look around your facilities, that's all."

"Well, sir, I…"

"Do it, man!" Kane raised his voice, giving his best impression of some of the British Army

Officers he had met throughout his career.

The guard swallowed, shook his head, then picked up a landline phone and made the call. Thirty seconds later, Craven and Kane drove beneath the raised barrier.

"You were a bit hard on him, poor lad," ribbed Craven.

"Well, it's not exactly Fort Knox, is it? We'll be out of here in a few minutes."

Craven pulled the car in before a two-storey building beside the main hangar. The airfield was small compared to major airports but larger than some of the strips Kane had landed on in his life. Casement had two runways and hangars large enough to hold multiple planes. The main office building had a small car park, and an Air Corps junior officer came through the front doors to meet them.

"I'm Second Lieutenant Smullin," the young man introduced himself. He had sandy hair beneath a dark beret and smiled warmly. "We don't seem to have a record of your appointment, and our CO is off-base today. How can I help you?"

"That's strange about the appointment," said Kane. "I will take it up with the office back in London. Thank you for accommodating us, Second Lieutenant Smullin. I am Major Jones, and this is Mr Paisley. All we need to do is take a quick look at the facilities here ahead of a potential flight into this airfield by some UK dignitaries."

"That should be fine. I can't let you inside the building without security clearance, which I'm sure you understand. But I can give you a tour of the airfield. We always have schools visiting us for a look around."

"Excellent, lead the way," smiled Kane. He and Craven followed Smullin along a pathway between a recently cut grass verge. He winked at Craven, who frowned and shook his head.

"So, as you can see, we have two runways..." Smullin escorted them around the outside of the hangars and the control tower. He explained how many flights came in and out of the airfield each year and reeled off a list of famous people who had visited. They ranged from Presidents to the Pope, along with ultra-famous celebrities.

"So, have you had many private flights come to the airport this month?" asked Kane.

"Only two, as it happens," Smullin answered as he gestured towards an old biplane on a plinth next to the control tower. Kane and Craven nodded appreciatively at the old machine, and Smullin launched into a well-rehearsed spiel about the airfield's history. He spoke of its founding in 1917 by the British Royal Air Force and how it was originally named Baldonnel Aerodrome but was later renamed in honour of Roger Casement in 1965. Casement was a revered hero of the Irish Republic who was killed by the British in 1916.

Once Smullin's history lesson was over, Kane continued his line of questioning.

"These private landings, were they politicians?"

"We had the Swiss Foreign Minister land here four days ago, and before that, a jet owned by part of the Saudi Royal Family landed here ten days ago."

"And how many passengers were on each aircraft?"

"The Swiss jet had only three, plus the aircraft crew. But the Saudi jet had nine passengers, plus its crew."

"So, you can deal with multiple passenger flights?"

"Of course."

"And do you provide security for the incoming flights?" asked Craven.

"Normally, the Guards would provide any required security of that nature. For the Swiss flight, for example, they provided an armed escort to the Presidential estate in Dublin's Phoenix Park. But for the Saudi jet, they had their own security and had already arranged transport."

"Was the Saudi Royal Family member on the flight?" pressed Kane. Of the two recent flights, that seemed to him to have the most potential of carrying a team capable of pulling off the kidnapping. Nine men or women entering the country on a flight protected by diplomatic immunity. It was the perfect way to enter the country without attracting attention. There was no link between the flight and Annie's kidnapping, but it was a possibility.

"I'm not sure," replied Smullin, "I was off-duty that day."

"We should have a similar sized party to the Saudi arrival. Could you provide the name and number of the person at their embassy who arranged the landing? I would like to talk to them and see if we can mirror their arrangements."

"I don't think so, sir. We aren't supposed to share the personal details of the dignitaries who arrive here."

"Quite right," said Kane, nodding his approval. "And I can see that you are an excellent member of the Irish Air Corps. Your commanding officer should be proud of you."

"Thank you, sir," Smullin smiled and pushed his shoulders back, his chin lifting slightly.

"I don't need any details for any sensitive people, just the person who made the arrangements. They should be a simple administrator. Could you do that for me?"

Their tour brought the three men back to the entrance of the main office building, and Smullin paused. He rubbed his tongue across the bottom teeth beneath his lip, staring at Kane and then at the office.

"I suppose it won't hurt. It's only the administrator."

"If only we had solid, accommodating lads like this in the British forces, eh Paisley?" Kane said, nudging Craven. The big man smiled in solemn appreciation.

"Wait here, sir." Smullin jogged inside the office.

"I can't believe he's actually getting it for you," whispered Craven. "That was like a bloody Jedi mind trick. If we get that number, we can try to find out who was on that plane and why they came to Dublin."

"Exactly," said Kane in a hushed tone. "Then we can either rule it out of our thinking, like the

IRA lead, or it might give us something to go on."

Smullin came striding briskly out of the office doors and handed Kane a white envelope.

"The contact details for the Saudi organiser are inside," he said, flashing another broad smile.

"Thank you, Second Lieutenant Smullin," replied Kane, and he handed the envelope to Craven, who tucked it into his blazer pocket.

Kane and Craven pulled out of the airbase and turned right to rejoin the N7 motorway. Their next stop was to talk to the disgruntled jockey, whose details Fran Doyle had provided. Craven drove, and Kane kept a vigilant eye on the surrounding traffic. The assassin was out there somewhere, and Kane expected her to attack again at any moment. He still had the Glock pistol taken from the IRA, but only two rounds remained. Kane hoped it would be enough.

THIRTY-FOUR

Dickie McHugh lived fifteen minutes away from Casement Aerodrome. The address for the former Kelleher stud jockey said that he lived in Eadestown, a small village between Rathcoole and Naas, the latter being the largest town in Kildare with two racecourses, Naas Racecourse and The Curragh. It was prime horse racing and breeding territory in the heart of Kildare, with sprawling pastures, lush green fields and leafy boughs.

"So, what do we know about Dickie?" asked Kane. Craven kept his eyes on the road. The road to Eadestown was at many points only wide enough for one vehicle, so if a car came in the opposite direction, either he or that vehicle would have to tuck in tight to the verge. The winding roadways took them alongside crop fields and meadows teeming with cows and sheep. Farmhouses butted onto the road, old buildings with sprawling ivy and barns with corrugated roofs.

Some broken-down barns and outbuildings had been transformed along the road into modern architectural houses. Smooth white plastered walls swallowed the old stone and brickwork in box-like structures with too many windows.

"Only what Fran Doyle said. He fell out with John Kelleher a while back and doesn't ride for him anymore. He was one of a list of four jockeys who had left the stud, but the only one to do so under a cloud." Doyle had sent the list of four names and addresses to Craven, but only Dickie McHugh stuck out as a person of interest in the case. The other three had left employment on good terms, either for more money with another horse owner or to go abroad.

"Hang on to that Saudi envelope," said Kane. "We'll call the number later on when we are somewhere quiet."

Craven followed the satellite navigation map built into the rental car's touchscreen. It stood out from the dashboard like a tiny television, and the satnav had picked up Dickie McHugh's address from the Eircode, Ireland's version of the UK postcode address system. Farmers' fields ended, and the road dipped under large oak and beech trees whose eaves blocked the daylight. A red sign beside the road told drivers to watch out for deer, and small clutches of houses appeared as the tarmac widened and fresh white and yellow road markings stood out bright beneath the leafy gloom.

"I noted the way you handed me that envelope at the airfield like I was your fucking valet or personal assistant," muttered Craven. The satnav told him to turn left in fifty metres. He could already make out a housing estate in that direction, a curving collection of seven dormer bungalows, large buildings with lots of garden space.

"I haven't got a jacket on, and I didn't want to stuff the thing in my pocket. We were trying to look like serious officials."

"Aye, well, next time, stick it up your arse instead. Here we are."

"Arrived," announced the satnav's female voice, sounding strangely pleased with itself.

Craven pulled up outside the corner bungalow in a circular cul-de-sac. A man knelt by a motorbike in the driveway, cranking away with a shiny silver wrench. A blue toolbox lay open next to him, and the man turned with a frown to see who had parked outside his house. He stood and wiped the oil from his hands on a dirty cloth and came to meet them.

"Dickie McHugh?" said Craven as he stepped out of the car.

"Who wants to know?" McHugh responded. He was a small, frail man. Which was unsurprising, given that he was a jockey. Dickie had bowlegs and a long, clean-shaven face.

"I'm Frank Craven, a detective with the UK police. If you can spare a few minutes, we'd like to ask you a few questions about your former employer, John Kelleher." Craven supposed it wasn't too much of a stretch to introduce himself as a police detective. He had, after all, been one until recently.

"You got any ID?" said Dickie McHugh. He spoke with a deep voice and an Irish accent Craven couldn't place. It wasn't the more obvious Dublin, Cork, or Belfast accent. Craven assumed it was more familiar to Kildare or the Irish midlands.

Craven fished his wallet from his jacket pocket and flipped it open to show his UK police warrant card and ID. He had left the force quickly without ceremony and had not handed his credentials in on the way out. If someone were to check the details, it would show that Craven was no longer in active service, but it still looked the part.

"I'm Dickie McHugh," the small man nodded

after squinting at the wallet. "What do you want to know?"

"Me and my colleague here," Craven jerked his thumb in Kane's direction, "are looking into the kidnapping of Mr Kelleher's daughter. We are assisting An Garda Síochána and would like to ask you a few questions about the stud."

"Little Annie?" gasped Dickie. He stood straighter, eyes flitting between the two Englishmen. "Kidnapped?" He rocked backwards as though the shock almost knocked him down. "Holy Jaysus. You'd better come in."

THIRTY-FIVE

"Tea or coffee?" asked Dickie McHugh. He led them into his house through a side door and into a kitchen with the style of pine cupboards and chipboard worktops popular a decade ago. The sink overflowed with dirty dishes, and takeaway cartons littered the worktops. A dozen empty beer bottles interspersed with larger whiskey bottles stood in a neat arrangement next to the kettle and toaster. The place smelled like farts and stale ale, and Craven couldn't help but wrinkle his nose.

"Coffee, black," said Craven, not daring to tempt fate and risk drinking out-of-date milk. The man clearly didn't look after himself or his house, and Craven could only imagine the state of his fridge. The place needed a woman's touch, and it didn't take a detective to discern that McHugh was a single man who'd been drinking a lot, likely because of the parting of ways with his employer.

"Tea for me, please," chimed Kane. "Two sugars, if you have any."

"So, what's happened to Annie?" asked McHugh. He picked up the kettle but waited for a response. He seemed genuinely shocked and stared expectantly at Craven.

"Someone took her outside her school, and John Kelleher received a ransom demand," Kane explained.

"Fuck's sake." McHugh ran a hand down his long face. "Such a sweet little girl. What kind of animal would do such a thing?"

"You worked for Mr Kelleher, correct?" asked Craven.

"Aye, I rode for him. I'm past my racing years. I used to be a handy enough flat jockey once upon a time. But I worked at the stud, exercising his horses, taking them out a couple of times daily and putting them through their paces. Keeping the stallions and mares fit."

"How long did you work there for?"

Dickie McHugh shrugged. "Best part of four years. The little girl was always running around the yard. You'd get great craic out of her."

"And why did you leave?"

McHugh's face hardened, his lips peeling back to show a set of brown, stumpy teeth. "I know what you're hinting at. I've got nothing to do with this. John Kelleher is a fucking prick, but I'd never hurt the wee girl." He held Craven's gaze for five seconds, slammed the kettle down and pulled a packet of Marlboro Gold from his pocket. He lit up the cigarette, which took Craven by surprise. It had been years since anyone had smoked in front of him. Back when Craven first joined the police, people smoked at their desks. Then, it had moved to outside only with the smoking ban and by the time of his retirement, smoking had all but disappeared in favour of the ubiquitous vapes.

"I left because he hadn't paid me for two weeks." McHugh lit his cigarette and inhaled deeply before blowing a cloud of foul-smelling smoke towards the ceiling. "The bastard carries on like he's a fucking mega-millionaire, but he's broke as a Dublin busker in the rain."

"Did you confront him about your pay?"

"Eventually, I did, yes. I spent days chasing that fat fucking tool Fran Doyle around but got nowhere, so I went to Kelleher. He ran me out of the place and called me a bum and a loser in front of the other lads."

"So you left?"

McHugh nodded and wagged the forefinger of the hand holding his cigarette at Craven. "It's that fucking dolly bird of a wife who has him broke. She spends money like it's going out of fashion. Everybody in the place knows she likes a drink. Her father's an awful eejit as well. The two of them drove that place into the ground."

"What do you mean?"

McHugh eyed Craven carefully and took a drag of his cigarette. He filled the kettle and turned it on.

"She ran the finances. The wife, that is. Kelleher ran the horses. He knows what he's doing, in all fairness. But Mrs Kelleher always has new cars and is always going here and there on holidays, without her husband, I might add. This last year she was in Dubai, Marbella, Lanzarote, and fucking New York."

"And did they fight about that?"

"Yes, they did. Her father tried to cover up her misspending, but it was so fucking obvious. John Kelleher is a stupid prick for letting his wife ruin his business, but I actually pity the man because he does know his horses."

Craven's phone rang. He had forgotten to put it on silent. The ringtone was a jerky, standard iPhone ringtone. The name popped up as Jim Baldwin and Craven showed it to Kane.

"Answer it," urged Kane.

Craven raised a finger to Dickie McHugh to apologise for answering the call and pressed the green answer button.

"Craven," he said.

"Frank!" came Baldwin's voice. Craven yanked the phone away from his ear. There was a loud banging sound, like fireworks, close to where Baldwin spoke, and his old friend shouted. His shallow breath made it sound like he was running. "Frank, that woman is here again. She is shooting the place up. We need all the help we can get. If you are still in the country, get over here now!"

"What? She's there again?" Craven said and looked up to see Kane dashing out of the room. "Wait!" Craven shouted after him, but Kane was already running. Craven followed him, leaving a dumbfounded McHugh alone with his cigarette.

Kane sprinted full tilt up the driveway and leapt onto McHugh's BMW motorbike. He kicked the engine into gear, and it purred.

"The bike's faster than the car. I'll meet you there. We can't let her get away if we don't want her to follow us to Spain." Kane pulled back his wrist, and the bike's tyre skidded on the driveway's flagstones, leaving a thick black skid mark. The bike slewed to one side, and Kane took off at full speed, the roar of the motorcycle's engine deafening.

THIRTY-SIX

Kane raced out of Dickie McHugh's housing estate, veering to his left at the last minute to avoid a white Kia jeep turning into the cul-de-sac. He punched the throttle, and the bike took off down the country road. The wind hissed and whipped, and his hair flew back from his face. There had been no time to find a helmet or even check if the motorcycle was safe to drive.

The petrol gauge was three-quarters full, and the engine roared as Kane powered along, greenery flitting past him in a blur. He weaved around the handful of cars he met on the road before coming to a crossroads where cars waited patiently to turn left or right. Kane didn't stop or hesitate. He let the bike race to the junction and broke hard to skid the vehicle into a left turn, placing his foot on the ground to brace it.

Kane remembered the way to Kelleher's

stud farm, and he roared the bike along the road between Naas and Kilcullen, passing the Killashee Hotel, skilfully navigating through the vehicles in front of him and away from oncoming cars. As he forced the bike to its top speed, Kane knew he raced towards a fight for his children's future.

Assassins like the woman would never stop coming, not until he could make the trail go cold. Kane simply knew too much. He was a former government black-ops agent who had already provided evidence against his former agency. The things he knew, the people he had killed, and the countries he had operated in were beyond the understanding of laypeople and far too sensitive to be out there in the wind, outside of governmental control.

The global landscape concealed a much darker reality than people realised. Citizens of the UK, USA, and most Western countries were happy to sneer at the governments of China, Russia, North Korea, and other regimes for what they perceived as ambiguous stances on human rights. Meanwhile, they considered their own countries above reproach, which they most certainly were not.

Kane had seen the things that went on in the shadows, the hard choices governments must make to keep their people safe. As he sped along the Irish roads, the motorbike engine roaring in his ears, faces came to Kane from his past. Men he had killed, rival agents, rogue politicians, oligarchs, warlords, and terrorists. Kane wasn't even sure anymore that the people he had killed were legitimate targets. Much like the woman at the stud, Kane had received orders to kill, and he'd followed them to the letter. The agency had trained him to do it, conditioned him to it, and made him an expert. They could never allow details of his actions or what he knew to spill over into the public domain.

The assassin at the stud farm was a symbol of the covert agencies Kane had once been a part of but who now would pursue him relentlessly. He had to strike back just as hard. So, he leant into the motorbike and kept himself low and tight to its smooth frame, becoming one with its power and the roar of its engine.

The gates to Kelleher's stud loomed before him, and Kane sped through them. Gunfire rattled the air as Kane went to meet that danger head-on. The woman had to die.

THIRTY-SEVEN

Condor had marched through the entrance to Kelleher's farm. The gateway was open, and she came dressed in black tactical trousers and a shirt, with an Interceptor body armour vest over the top. She had taken a silenced MP5 submachine gun from the boot of her car, along with a Sig Sauer pistol holstered at her right hip. A pouch around her vest held spare magazines, and she carried fragmentation and flash-bang grenades around her belt.

Her injuries ached, but Condor forced herself to move fluidly without a limp. She was a hard-bitten assassin and wouldn't limp whilst she still had two legs. Condor came in heavy this time. No more subtlety. Last time, she had infiltrated the house and waited for the detective in his room. Now that she knew Kane was there, the gloves were off. She would go in hard, execute the job quickly, and be out of Ireland before the sun went down.

A woman clad in riding jodhpurs came from a building to Condor's right and met her end with a single shot to the head. A bucket fell from her dead hands to spill animal feed onto the grass. Condor kept low, moving quickly. She swept her weapon in wide arcs, eye peering down the sight and ready to destroy anyone who came across her path. Condor cared little for collateral damage; she considered this a war, and people died in wars. Every day of her life had been a battle to survive, endure, and succeed.

Condor crouched and aimed her weapon at an overhead power cable. She followed the black line until she reached a junction box atop a telegraph pole hidden behind a large tree beyond the house's border hedging. She fired three bursts from her weapon, and the junction box sparked and crackled, cutting power to the stud farm. Cutting the electricity had become second nature, though the operation didn't particularly demand stealth. Condor ran five more steps, took a flash-bang grenade from her belt and tossed it through the sitting room window to the right of the main door.

She knelt and braced her weapon. The grenade went off, illuminating the room in a brief but fierce flash of light, followed by an explosion that shook the house. Smoke filled the bay window and coughed out of the broken glass. The front door burst open, and a man emerged holding a pistol and frowning into the driveway. He wore military-type clothing similar to her own and a protective vest. Condor rapidly dropped him with a single shot to the groin, causing him to slump against the doorframe, followed by an immediate shot to the face.

Silence for twenty seconds, nothing but Condor's own slow, controlled breathing. Orders barked from inside, an American voice. Then, more voices. Condor stood and crept towards the house, weapon ready, resolve unwavering.

A gun report cracked from her right, and a bullet fizzed past her head. Condor swept her MP5 around. A man positioned at the corner of the house aimed a rifle at her. Condor fired two shots. They both hit the brickwork, sending a spray of shards into the air and causing the man to shrink back. She ran in his direction, and when the muzzle of his rifle peeked around the corner again, she fired once at close range into his boot, and he fell screaming.

Condor reached him and kicked the rifle out of his hands.

"Who are you, and how many of you are there?" she demanded, pointing her gun at his face.

"Fuck you, lady," he growled. Another American.

Condor shot him beneath his left eye and then again in his forehead. She had to assume that Kane was in the house. The surrounding outbuildings were stables and sheds related to the care and upkeep of the animals. For a strange, fleeting instant, Condor recalled the moment she had shared with a horse upon her last visit. The sense of contentment and closeness returned in a transient spark, only to die as she suppressed it back into the recesses of her consciousness. The dark moments of her life intertwined with the scarce happy ones in that bleak wilderness. Condor had no time for either. She was a killer, a machine trained and honed to complete her missions. There was no place in her life for sentimentality, just brutal efficiency.

Condor decided against an entry through the front door. She had already engaged an enemy there, and if the two men she had already killed were anything to go by, then she could expect the doorway to be heavily guarded. So, Condor swept around towards the rear. As she came about the south-facing gable end, another gunman appeared. He approached carefully around the rear wall, rifle extended in front of him, moving professionally and with the lightness of a cat. Condor shot him once in the shoulder, closed the distance quickly and finished him with another shot to the skull.

Moving around the rear wall, a bullet smacked into the wall next to her, and another thumped into the earth behind. Condor shrank back, caught off guard by the unexpected resistance but poised for action. She breathed carefully, regulating her adrenaline and maintaining her control. Ready to fight, thrilled that there was a worthy opponent to challenge her, she moved away from the house and ran to flank the shooters from around the barn.

Condor dropped the next man with a carefully aimed bullet to the head. The second shooter fled back into the house, and she followed, hungry for the kill.

THIRTY-EIGHT

Kane yanked on the brakes, skidding the motorcycle in a maelstrom of dust and flying stones. A man lay dead in the driveway, one of Leo Franchetti's group, from the look of his gear. Kane stooped, snatched up the fallen man's MP5, looped the strap around his shoulders, and checked the magazine. The assassin was at the stud for one reason – to kill Kane. People were dying, and he had to get to her as soon as possible. Another body lay crumpled in the doorway, and smoke drifted from a broken front window in sputtering clouds.

He revved the engine and took off around the side of the stud farm, the tyres kicking up tiny pebbles from the driveway. A voice shouted something to him from inside the house, but the words drowned beneath the motorcycle's roar. Kane gunned the bike around the gable end of the house, passing another dead body, and then swerved around the building's rear. The outbuilding and stables were on his right, and there, sprinting across the open space between the stables and the house, was a nimble woman clad all in black and armed with a silenced MP5.

She turned, raising her weapon, prompting Kane to let go of the handlebars with his right hand and bring his own weapon to bear. She fired first, a burst of three rounds, and Kane's head shrank into his shoulders in anticipation of the pain to come. The first shot went wide, the second hit the bike's engine with a metallic twang, and the third exploded his rear tyre. The bike wobbled and careened to the left as Kane's left hand tried to maintain control of it. Kane leapt from the bike, pulling the trigger of his MP5 as he dived through the air, knowing that the bullets weren't well aimed but hoping that the gunfire might distract the woman for a vital few seconds. He needed that time to recover, to regain his feet before she sent a parabellum bullet into his brain.

Kane hit the ground, rolling into the fall. His shoulder connected with a grass verge, and he held the rifle close to him, its hard metal edges crushing and jabbing at his ribs and stomach as he turned in the soft grass. He came up in a crouch and fired again. The bullet went wide of the target, and the assassin smiled at him.

Kane's heart sank as the woman stared along her rifle's sight. For people with their level of training, it was a routine shot, a skill honed through countless missions. Hitting the target was second nature. It was their bread and butter. Kane braced himself for the impending shot, the bullet that would snatch his life away in an instant. But instead, the back door to the Kelleher house burst open.

The assassin turned her weapon away from Kane and fired a burst at three men who came running from the back door. More of Franchetti's team. In response, they opened fire on her, transforming the grounds of the stud farm into a war zone of crackling gunfire and chaos.

THIRTY-NINE

The man on the motorbike was Jack Kane, and Condor couldn't help but smile as she stared at him through the sight of her rifle. He knelt on the grass, about to bring his weapon up to fire, but he wasn't fast enough. Her heart leapt as the realisation dawned on his hard face – he was about to die. Despite being as thick as a Dostoyevsky novel, Condor had voraciously absorbed every detail. From the Parachute Regiment of the British Army to the SAS, and then working in the shadows with the Mjolnir agency operating under the codename Lothbrok, he had amassed multiple confirmed kills. His track record was riddled with missions, the key details of which were redacted, making it hard to follow his movements over the last ten years.

Thoughts sped through her mind like cars on a racing track. This kill would make her career.

Who else could have put a bullet in a famous rogue agent like Kane? She would become a living legend. Status in McGovern's freshly crafted agency would be assured, and only the finest missions would come Condor's way. She would have unrestricted access to private jets, unlimited personal funds, weapons, cars, and boats, and a life spent travelling the world protecting the British people. All of that would be hers. She squeezed the trigger, the pressure tense on her forefinger. Her crosshairs rested on Kane's left eye – *aim small, miss small*, just as she had been trained. Condor's heart was steady, and her breathing was slow. One shot, and it would all be over for Jack Kane.

A crash to her right caught the corner of Condor's eye, a threat emerging from the house with shouts and heavy steps. Americans. She cursed under her breath, swung her weapon around and fired a quick burst at the three men, hitting one in the leg and sending the other two running for cover. She swept her rifle back towards Kane, but he was gone. Another crash behind her, glass smashing.

Condor stood and moved. Kneeling still in a gunfight was to die, and she had multiple assailants on all sides. A man had jumped through a window from the main house, and he hurled a grenade at her. The green dome twirled in the air and landed at her feet. Without hesitation, Condor kicked it like a football back towards the house, where it exploded with a brain-shaking crash. A bullet slammed into Condor's chest, sending her sprawling onto the grass. Her vest absorbed the bullet itself, but the impact drove the wind from her.

Condor gasped violently, her chest heaving as she lay on the ground. Her ears rang from the grenade explosion, and the air was thick with its acrid stink. She rolled onto her stomach and fired at the house as she filled her lungs. A strange sensation kindled in her belly, a hollowness which caught fire and burned, causing her heart to race and her cheeks to blush. Fear – the beast she had tried to keep at bay since childhood. Now, it was here again to stymie her mind and cloud her judgement.

She bellowed, trying to suffocate the fear with rage. Her rifle spat out rounds in an arc towards the house, but the exploding grenade shrouded it in a dust cloud. The rifle clicked, and she cursed herself. The magazine was empty. Condor leapt to her feet, grasping for a spare magazine on her belt, but a bullet whipped past her and flew into the swirling dust cloud. Footsteps approached, thudding on the grass, and she turned just in time to see Jack Kane charging her.

Condor dropped her rifle and leapt at him, pushing his right hand wide just as he fired another shot from a handgun. They crashed together like two stags, punches, kicks, knees and elbows flying, but each one blocked or parried, two perfectly trained humans whose movements resembled a well-choreographed ballet dance. Kane caught her with a glancing blow to the temple, and Condor twisted under his arm, trying to throw him. Kane stepped around to evade the throw, and she cracked her elbow off his jaw.

"Get out of the fucking way, Kane!" shouted an American from behind Condor. He wanted a clean shot at her, so Condor pivoted and shifted Kane's body between her and the gunman. He came towards her, moving carefully in quick steps with a submachine gun up at his eye, trying to find a clean shot to rip her life away, but she was difficult to kill. Kane stamped on her foot, and Condor tried to rake his eyes with her fingers. Kane ducked, and she went with him, a bullet whooshing over her head.

Two of the men who had emerged from the back door approached, flanking the lead American who had shouted at Kane to move. More men materialised from the smoke like ghouls, weapons raised and trained on her. Condor wrestled with Kane, but she couldn't see any possibility of killing Kane and surviving to tell the tale. Condor took a step back, trying to drag Kane with her, but he resisted. He twisted in her grip and headbutted Condor full in the face. She let go of him, stars flashing before her eyes and searing pain jabbing into her skull.

Kane pushed her away, and she grabbed a knife from a sheath fastened to her lower leg. Condor slashed wildly but found only air. Fear washed over her again, panic raging in her mind, death as close as a lover. The chance to kill Jack Kane had passed, and all that remained now was the fight to survive, to live, and to fight again. Condor launched herself to one side as bullets spat from silenced weapons and tore up the grass. She rolled, grabbing two flash-bang grenades from her belt. Condor pulled the pins and threw one from each hand. She turned and tucked herself into the damp turf, shielding her ears with her hands.

Once the grenades exploded, Condor ran. Smoke swirled, and men groaned. She couldn't see her attackers; their figures were lost in the haze. Condor ran like a sprinter, arms pumping and thighs driving her away from the carnage. She jumped over Kane's motorbike and then stopped, turning to lift the heavy machine and climb onto the saddle. Condor squeezed the clutch, opened the throttle, and the bike growled into action. The back end flew out wildly, and she remembered the thing had a flat tyre. Condor drove off anyway. She only needed enough time to escape the overwhelming numbers at the stud farm. The bike wobbled beneath her, but it raced around the farmhouse as gunfire erupted over her shoulder. Condor had failed, but she was alive.

FORTY

Kane stumbled, his balance skewed from the flash-bang explosion. His eyes had gone blind momentarily, and as he took shaky steps away from the smoke, dark spots clouded his sight, and his ears rang.

"Fucking find her," said an American voice from somewhere in the darkness. Kane shook his head, forced himself to regain his senses, and set off at a run. He careened towards the house like a drunk man running at a slant. Kane collided with the brickwork and bounced off it, sprinting towards the sound of the motorbike. In a few heartbeats, she would be gone, waiting in the shadows like a lion to pounce on him or his children at any moment. It had to end now so that he could focus on Annie's rescue.

Kane kept on running, his senses clearing with every step. He passed the body at the side of the house and stooped to pick up another MP5 from the dead man's grasp. Kane rounded the house just in time to see the motorbike moving towards the stud's outer gate, its flat back tyre skidding and sliding on the driveway. Kane slowed his run and opened fire, sending six rounds towards the assassin woman. The motorbike toppled over, and the woman fell to the ground. Quickly, she rolled and then came up into a crouch, spotting Kane. At that moment, she bolted.

Leaping over the hedges before Kane could take another shot, she sprinted away with Kane in pursuit. Chasing her, Kane crossed the front garden in twenty long strides and vaulted over the hedgerow. The woman ran ahead of him, though her movements weren't quite fluid. She limped slightly but still covered the ground fast. Kane's body pumped sweat, and his breath was already ragged. He hadn't kept up his fitness regime since leaving active service and paid that price as he forced his legs to keep moving.

The assassin turned sharply, crashing through undergrowth and into a farmer's field. Kane followed her, running through waist-high crops. She deliberately wove in random directions, making it difficult for Kane to get a bead on her with his rifle. He noticed her arm move backwards, and then his muscles clenched as he realised she had thrown another flash-bang grenade at him. He stopped and curled himself into a ball to protect his eyes, covering his ears. The grenade detonated, and Kane paused for ten seconds. When he opened his eyes, he could see clearly. He surged to his feet, and his balance was fine. A flash-bang grenade was designed to disorient, blind, and cause ears to ring, but he had avoided the worst of it.

Kane set off into the lingering smoke, the crops whipping at his calves and knees as he ran. Suddenly, a shape lunged at him through the drifting cloud, and Kane fell backwards as a kick connected with his midriff, the rifle spinning from his hands. He scrambled, hands clawing for purchase in clods of earth, and then she stood over him. A tall woman with fierce eyes and her mouth set into a determined line.

"It's just you and I now, Kane," she uttered, moving into a fighting stance.

"Who sent you?" he said. Kane rose slowly to his feet, and the woman let him.

"Who do you think?"

"Mjolnir is gone. Which agency are you?"

"Mjolnir is gone. But there are many other agencies just like it. Did you really think you could ride off into the sunset just because you killed Odin? What we do is of the highest secrecy. You can't just live out there in the wind after you have provided evidence about your old life."

"But then, where does it end for any of us?"

She shrugged. "We serve and then retire. With our mouths shut. You broke that code."

"And you have come to kill me?"

"And I have come to kill you."

"It doesn't have to be this way."

"You want to beg for your life now? The legend that is Jack Kane on his knees?"

"No. But is this really what you signed up for? Killing one of your own?"

"I do what is necessary to protect our country. You are a traitor, and it's my duty to put you in the fucking ground."

Kane had been like her once. He had killed without remorse. He knew in that moment, by the snarl on her face and the gleam in her eye, that talking was a waste of time. She only understood one thing. Violence. So, he went for her, lashing out with a front kick and driving his outstretched fingers towards her throat. She blocked the kick and swayed away from the jabbing fingers.

The woman was as fast and highly skilled as Kane expected. He had the strength advantage, but she was in her prime and supremely fit.

Kane observed that she favoured her right leg and guessed she had injured herself in the jump from the motorcycle. Seizing the opportunity, he kicked her injured leg, and she yelped in pain. The woman fell to one knee and grimaced up at Kane, eyes flitting to the fallen rifle and then back to him.

"These are the risks we take," Kane said, advancing on her. "You knew what you risked coming here after me. Now that we've met, I can't let you live. I can see it in your eyes. You will never let this go until one of us is dead. They take us and turn us into these monsters when all we wanted was to be the best and serve our country with pride and honour."

The woman winced and clasped a hand to her injured leg. She peered across Kane's shoulder, and he turned to see Leo Franchetti and four of his men clambering into the field. Kane reached for her head to break her neck in a quick, painless twist. At the last moment, she launched herself at him, punching Kane in the groin and crashing her elbow into his knee to send him spinning into the dirt. Then, she was up like a gazelle. She snatched up the rifle and unleashed a ferocious wave of bullets at Franchetti and his men in a blaze of gunfire. They threw themselves to the earth to evade the unexpected attack.

She turned the rifle on Kane, a triumphant

look upon her face, and pulled the trigger. The weapon clicked, its magazine empty. She laughed then, throwing her head back and roaring at the sheer madness of it all. The woman threw the rifle at Kane and loped off across the field, disappearing into the darkness of a forest on its western edge.

Deflated, Kane lay back in the field, surrounded by crushed crop stems and yellow rapeseed flowers bright in the sunshine. She was gone again. The woman had wrought carnage in County Kildare, and there would be a heavy police presence after the explosions and gunfire. Kane sighed. He had resolved nothing. Luck had saved his life. Annie was still missing, and the assassin was on the loose.

"The bitch got away," Franchetti remarked laconically. He reached out a gloved hand and helped Kane to his feet. "She killed three of my men, and two more are badly wounded."

"She'll be back," said Kane.

"She wants you, not Mr Kelleher."

"I know. It's my fault she turned his home into a war zone."

"So come back to the house with us and get patched up. And then get the fuck out of here."

FORTY-ONE

McGovern sat back in the plush leather desk chair and leaned back. It pivoted on its hinge and reclined so that she could stare at the high, white-plastered ceiling. The leather was warm and smooth under her fingers, where they rested on the chair's arms. She rocked forward and adjusted her laptop on the wide oak desk. The wood was old and stained with ink in ancient blobs, and McGovern wondered which office had held the piece of furniture before hers. She closed her eyes and inhaled the aroma of old cigarette smoke and whiskey that emanated from the wood, conjuring images of a bygone era, imagining some powerful MI6 commander or World War II general poring over reports scattered across its top.

The new office was spacious, with an armchair and coffee table in one corner, a television mounted on the wall, and her very own assistant stationed just outside the door. She had made it. This was the office of a senior government mandarin, a position far from some mid-management burnout. She had power and influence, high-level security clearance and the ability and means to send her agents wherever she deemed necessary. While she didn't quite have full budget approval just yet, her next meeting would dot the I of her budget and cross the T of her success.

McGovern smiled at the memory of her years working as a liaison for Odin and his Mjolnir agency. Even its name was antiquated. Odin had been passionate about Norse mythology, and every codename in his operation, including his own, had some link to the Viking world. Her agency would be different. She had a shortlist of names and couldn't decide between Sycamore, Silverbird, or something more exotic like Medusa. She would need a codename, of course. It simply wouldn't do for her team of twenty Secret Service MI6 affiliated agents to know her real name. It would be too much of a risk.

There was a gentle knock at the office door, and her personal assistant, Harry, opened the heavy door and popped his head in.

"Your next appointment is here, ma'am," he said and smiled. He was young and fresh-faced, a former soldier injured in the line of duty, and McGovern simply loved it when he referred to her as ma'am.

"Send him in," she instructed. Harry closed the door, and McGovern straightened her skirt and blouse. She fiddled with the laptop, pen, notebook, and phone on her desk to ensure everything lined up perfectly. This was the final meeting, the icing on the cake. This was where a Chief Intelligence Officer from MI6, not the man at the top, but a head of one the organisation's key branches, would come and give her the keys to the kingdom. He would give her access to a slush fund of millions of pounds siphoned off from the MI6 budget for use at her own discretion.

McGovern stood and forced a smile onto her face, then decided a more serious demeanour was appropriate. She wanted to be taken seriously, as a person to be respected. So, she dropped the smile and relaxed her face. She brushed her bobbed hair away from her face and hardened her mouth.

The door swung open, and a lean man in a black suit strode in. He was of average height and bald, with dark brown eyes and a face that would curdle milk. McGovern held out her hand, and the man stared at it as though it was covered in shit.

"You are due back in with Aziz in three weeks to close his internal investigation into the Mjolnir debacle, are you not?" he spoke in a harsh Scottish accent, making his anger even more poignant.

"I am McGovern. Pleased to meet you," she said. He snorted and sat down in the chair facing her.

"You don't need to know my name. The agency gave you an opportunity to build something, to have a stake in our great nation's national security. And you are fucking about with a clean-up job. How can we give you responsibility for a network of field agents if you can't even sort out one fucking man? One guy." He held up a stubby finger to illustrate his point. "If Aziz gets a sniff that Mjolnir is still in play, that Jack fucking Kane is still running about with all of our operational secrets and history in his head, ready to blab to the world at any moment, he will have a shit fit. It's not just you who'll be fucked – a lot of powerful people will suffer. His investigation will escalate and descend into a fucking spiral that will end our intelligence work as we know it. Do you understand that?"

"I do, and I have my best agent..."

"Your best agent?" he shouted. "You don't have any agents until I say so. This office in which you seem so comfortable isn't even yours yet."

"It's in hand. I'm expecting a call any minute to say the thing is done. Then we can green light my agency and move forward." McGovern winced at the vulnerability in her voice. She hated herself for showing even a chink of weakness. Climbing the greasy pole of governmental office was hard enough, and to do it as a woman was like climbing a mountain in pyjamas.

The man stood and jabbed his sausage finger in her direction. "Get it sorted. Today. Or you'll be back following around junior ministers, taking notes and making coffee."

He marched out of the room, and McGovern waited for the door to close. Each agonising passing second felt like an eternity. The door clicked closed, and she stamped her foot. She banged her fancy desk with two fists and shook her head until her pristine hair fell wildly about her skull.

McGovern snatched up her phone and dialled a secure line. If Condor couldn't get the job done on her own, then she would put out a contract on Jack Kane. Private companies would jump on the job, and investing a substantial sum in this endeavour seemed justified with the money she had coming to her. If Kane lived, McGovern's career was over anyway. She would make the bounty too rich to refuse. Kill squads would descend on Kane like he was a goldfish in a pool of piranhas.

FORTY-TWO

Craven arrived at the Kelleher stud to find it a smoking mess of broken windows and dead bodies. He drove slowly through the entrance gate and left his car in the driveway. An armed member of Franchetti's team came striding towards him, clutching a rifle. He wore black cargo trousers, a long-sleeved black T-shirt, a bulletproof vest, and knee and elbow pads. The man wore shades, even though it wasn't very sunny, and he looked every inch the soldier.

Craven stepped slowly out of the car and raised his hands. Despite his time in Kane's company, guns still made Craven nervous. The American's weapon was a long rifle-type gun with a cylindrical silencer attached to the end. Craven knew little about guns besides what he had picked up on TV or in movies.

"It's just me, Frank Craven," he said nervously. "I'm a friend of Jim Baldwin's, and I know John Kelleher."

"I fucking know who you are," the American retorted. "Wait there." He halted his approach and clicked a radio on the top left of his black bulletproof vest. The American spoke quietly into it, and Craven couldn't pick out the words. The radio crackled, and he lowered his weapon. "You can go inside. Kane, Franchetti, and Baldwin are in the kitchen with Mr Kelleher."

Craven nodded his thanks and skirted quickly around the armed man. He walked past two dead bodies and tried not to let his stomach lurch at the pools of dark blood encircling the corpses. Despite the many police years under his belt, he'd never got used to the blood. The front door was hanging on its hinges, and bullet holes riddled the plaster walls and the door itself. To his right, a shattered window bore witness to the earlier use of explosives.

Craven cautiously stepped inside and deftly avoided the bullet casings strewn across the floor. The place stank like something had burned. It was like scorched rubber but different, a noxious chemical stench that irritated Craven's throat. He moved along the corridor and stepped into the large kitchen space. One of Franchetti's men met him inside the doorway. He cradled a rifle in both hands and nodded to show Craven he could enter. Another of Franchetti's team sat on a dining room chair in the middle of the kitchen. He was stripped to the waist with heavy bandaging around one shoulder, and blood smeared all over his body. His face was as white as a ghost, and he grimaced and rocked slightly back and forth. Craven swallowed as he took in the scene. The overwhelming stink of blood hung in the air like a ferrous haze, and somewhere out of sight, another injured man groaned in pain.

"...the Guards will be here any minute. Will they arrest me?" It was John Kelleher's voice. As Craven came into the seating area proper, Kelleher anxiously paced back and forth with one hand on his forehead. He turned to look at Craven and sighed, continuing his restless fretting in front of his expansive patio windows.

"They won't arrest you. The woman came to your house and attacked you," said Fran Doyle. He sat around a table with Baldwin, Franchetti, and Kane.

"What the fuck happened?" asked Craven.

"That psycho assassin came back looking to kill your friend here. She tore up my house with explosives and gunfire. All of which gets us no closer to getting my daughter back. My house is destroyed. Fucking explosives and bullets have torn the place to shreds," John Kelleher exclaimed, waving a hand in Kane's general direction.

"If the cops are coming," said Leo Franchetti, "then I'd better stash our hardware. The guns might be hard to explain."

"At this point," Kelleher continued, "I want to know exactly where we are regarding the search for my daughter. I've asked the insurance company to expedite the ransom payment ready for the exchange. They await your report, Mr Franchetti." Then, he pointed at Craven and Kane, his bottom lip quivering. "I told you two to back off. Why are you still here? All you are doing is making things worse. I could have died today."

"There's still the risk you might not get her back," Fran Doyle murmured. Kelleher shot him a murderous glance, and Fran looked at the floor.

"Look, Kelleher," Franchetti intoned, pausing on his way out of the back door. "You've had a bunch of amateurs working on this thing until now. Me and my team are ready and able to track these motherfuckers down and get your daughter back. No offence, guys. I'll tell the insurance company that, don't worry." He winked at Craven, Baldwin, and Kane on his way out.

Jim Baldwin pushed his chair away from the

table, got up and moved to stand opposite John Kelleher, looking the worried father straight in the eye.

"John, I've tried to help. I brought Frank and Kane in to move our search forward, but they just haven't been able to make any headway. Maybe whoever it was that took Annie can't be found. Maybe it was just an opportunistic gang who decided to snatch Annie after seeing some of your horses win races. Maybe it's time to admit that we won't find her, pay the ransom, and hope these men stick to their word. If they do, you could have Annie back by the end of the week."

"Hang on a second," said Craven. "The investigation is ongoing, and we still have some solid leads to follow up."

"What leads?" demanded Kelleher. He threw his arms up and strained to keep himself from shouting. "You are supposed to be finished with this blasted thing. Last I heard, you were on your way out of the country. What exactly do you have that can help bring my daughter home?"

Craven shifted uncomfortably in his seat. He looked at Kane, who nodded slightly. "Well, we have some news about the team who took Annie for a start. We know it wasn't the IRA, and by proxy, we know it isn't a local gang. Other than the republicans, there isn't anyone with the know-how or organisation to pull it off."

"I don't want a list of assumptions, Mr Craven," Kelleher barked.

"A team came to Ireland from abroad to do the job. We looked into flight arrivals and have a good lead on a private aircraft that entered Ireland at Casement Aerodrome."

"Is that the one close to Rathcoole?"

"That's the one. It's used by foreign dignitaries and famous people who want to avoid the glare and inconvenience of Dublin airport."

"You know a team came into Casement?" asked Jim Baldwin with a surprised look on his lantern-jawed face. "How did you find that out?"

"Yeah. On a plane registered to a member of the Saudi Royal Family. So, they could have come from any of the danger zones in the Middle East via Saudi Arabia. I was going to call you about it before all this madness kicked off again today. We found that out using investigative methods commonly known as detective work."

"Leave that lead with me. I'll put the feelers out in Dubai and see what I can find out."

"OK, good," said Kelleher. "So, there is finally a solid lead."

"And then there's Dickie McHugh."

"Don't tell me that toerag is involved?" Fran Doyle tutted.

"Not quite," said Craven. He clasped his hands together. The investigation was on the verge of collapse, and it looked as though Baldwin had all but given up. There seemed little point in holding back to protect people's feelings, not when a girl's life was at stake. If they paid the ransom and the kidnappers killed Annie anyway, Craven would never forgive himself. "He made some remarks about your wife, Mr Kelleher, and about how the stud is run."

"Ah, he's just bitter because he left, that's all," Fran Doyle waved his hand dismissively, and Craven held up a finger to stop that train of thought.

"Kane and I have also been through your accounts. The stud is haemorrhaging money, John. Your personal accounts are overdrawn, and it seems like your wife is overspending massively. She lives the life of a celebrity, travelling the world and eating in the finest restaurants. Hundreds of thousands of euros are spent on clothes and beauty every year. It's a hard thing to bring up at a time like this, but there are also her issues with drink and drugs."

"Now, listen here," John Kelleher blustered. His face reddened, his fists clenched.

"No," said Kane. He stood, and Kelleher involuntarily took a step back. "You listen. You have a kidnap and ransom insurance policy. You are as good as broke, and someone has kidnapped your daughter. That's the long and short of it."

Craven let that hang there for a minute. Kelleher's mouth dropped open, and his eyes rapidly swept across each man in the kitchen as he searched for a supporting voice amongst them.

"You aren't suggesting I had anything to do with this, surely?"

"Have either you or Mrs Kelleher taken a trip to the Middle East recently?" asked Craven.

"That's enough, Frank," Jim Baldwin interjected. He moved to stand in between Craven, Kane, and Kelleher. "I think you should both leave. Now."

"If you want our help, we are staying at the Mespil Hotel by the Grand Canal for one more night. Tomorrow, we leave," said Craven. "The threads of this thing are becoming exposed now. A few more pulls, and it will unravel itself. If you are involved, then I'd say the Guards will have it figured out soon. If not, you might need to look closer to home for answers."

Craven turned on his heel and left, with Kane striding beside him. Police sirens blared in the distance, and the Kelleher stud would soon be a hive of blue and white tape, forensics, and questions. Craven drove away from the farm feeling grim about John Kelleher's chance of getting his daughter back without the ransom. The police would jam Kelleher and his people up for days with questions about the gun battle, and they simply did not have time for that.

"You don't think he organised the kidnapping, do you?" asked Kane. His clothes were soiled, and his face was dirty from the fight with the assassin.

"Well, some bastard is behind it," said Craven. He turned right at the gates and drove in the opposite direction of the sirens, wanting to avoid being stopped and detained for questioning. "And who else would think to capture their daughter other than someone who knows the family and knows they can pay?"

"We should look at Mrs Kelleher and her father again. One of the Kellehers must have a link to the Middle East. Maybe they've been there recently, or there's some other connection we can't see."

"They found Baldwin, and he's based in Dubai. So, they must know someone out there."

"I need to wash and change. Let's get back to the hotel. I want to watch the video of the kidnapping. We need to follow up on the jet lead to the Saudis and talk to Mrs Kelleher."

"That killer is still out there. She tore

up Kelleher's place like it was Bin Laden's compound. She won't stop until she finds you again."

Kane was silent on that point, but as Craven drove towards Dublin's city centre, he knew he was getting closer to finding Annie. His detective's gut told him he was on the verge of cracking the case – as if he stood on the edge of a precipice just waiting to fall into the answers.

FORTY-THREE

Condor showered, and the rivulets of water cascading down her skin turned pink as they washed her blood away. She had been so close to executing Kane; he had been in her sights until the Americans had spoiled the party. The stud was off-limits now. The Irish police would be all over it like a rash, and it was unlikely that Kane would stay there anyway after the fight. He would look for somewhere away from the glare of the police investigation and out of Condor's reach. The hotel shower was powerful, and she let the hot jet of water soothe her aching back. She rolled her shoulder joints and moved her face under the steaming stream so that the water massaged her cheeks and forehead.

The cuts on Condor's face and body stung. She stepped out of the shower and gently wrapped a white towel around herself before examining her injuries in the bathroom mirror. The serious wound on her thigh had opened, stitches bursting when she had fallen from the motorbike. Condor had sustained more bruises and gashes on her arms, back, and scalp during the fight with Kane and the Americans. It was proving to be a more arduous assignment than she had expected.

Her phone rang from the bedroom, so she opened the bathroom door and limped to grab it from the bedside table before it rang out. Condor rolled her eyes as she looked at the screen and saw it was McGovern calling from a secure line.

"Yes?" Condor answered the call tersely.

"What sort of horror show are you creating over there?" McGovern hissed down the phone. Condor pictured the career bureaucrat comfortably seated at a desk in an office somewhere, probably sipping expensive takeaway coffee whilst she herself bled for her country in a hotel room in Ireland.

"Things are complicated. I don't know what Kane's up to here, but he's involved with people who have a heavily armed guard. Serious weapons and training. All hell broke loose when I went to finish the job."

"I can bloody well see that. Have you seen the news? Ireland hasn't seen action like that since fucking 1916."

Condor picked up the remote control and went to switch on the hotel television but then thought better of it. She hated TV and already knew what had happened. She had been there. "Things got heated."

"But you haven't called to report your success, agent Condor, so I can assume that Jack Kane is alive."

"He's alive. For now."

"For now is right. All things considered, you have forced me to put a contract out on Kane's head because of your incompetence and inability to carry out a simple kill order. Effective immediately."

"A contract?" Condor frowned, unable to believe what she was hearing.

"Yes, a private contract on Kane's head. The bounty will ensure that there are killers en route to Dublin now to take him out. I want this job done within the next twenty-four hours."

"But I can..."

"No. You can't. Or you would have done it already. You have one last chance, Condor. Kill Kane or return to London to take up a new role more suited to your capability level. I need someone to fetch my sandwiches and type up reports."

Condor hung up the phone. McGovern was rash and out of her depth. She had hit the panic button by putting a bounty on Kane's head. It invited rogue agents, retired or dismissed soldiers, and the infamous private military companies or mercenaries to hunt him. The message would go out across the military community, and they would flock to Dublin in search of an easy prize. Such people usually plied their trade in war zones or countries where the rule of law had collapsed or was nonexistent. This was a simple seek-and-kill mission in a country with abundant CCTV, facial recognition cameras, and phone signal masts everywhere. Or so the mercs would think, yet Condor knew better. While people with the right technological expertise could hack and use the well-serviced cameras in major Irish cities like Dublin and Cork to search for Kane, most of Ireland was rural, with a population smaller than that of Greater Manchester. The stud farm was in the countryside, so the hunt for Kane was not as simple as the private killers might anticipate. Regardless, they were bound to disrupt her hunt, confuse the trail, and get in her way.

Condor was well aware that McGovern could end her field career if she so wished. With a mere few emails, McGovern could easily tether Condor to a desk for the remainder of her career.

That would kill her. Condor wasn't built to stare at four walls, nine-to-five, five days a week. She was a hunter. She imagined herself trapped in an office with the sounds of keyboards tapping and phones ringing, withering and dying like a great cat in a backstreet zoo.

She took another towel and wrapped it around her short hair. Condor checked her phone again and smiled as she watched a green blip move steadily across a map of Dublin. In the scuffle with Kane, Condor had slipped a small tracking device no larger than her thumbnail into his clothing. Once his tracker stopped and she could pinpoint his location, Condor would pounce and finish the job once and for all. McGovern's private killers were making a wasted trip – this kill belonged to her.

FORTY-FOUR

Kane and Craven sat around the small table in Craven's hotel room. The CCTV recording of Annie Kelleher's kidnapping played in grainy black and white footage. A quick shower and a cup of coffee helped Kane feel refreshed. He had more bruises and scrapes to show for his fight with the assassin but was otherwise ready to focus on finding the men responsible for Annie's disappearance. The woman would come for him again, but Kane had to focus on the kidnapping before he worried about his own problems.

"It happened so fast," remarked Craven. The big man sat back in his chair and ate a handful of crisps from a share-size bag. There was no time to eat properly, not with an assassin on Kane's trail and a kidnapped girl to find, so they grabbed crisps and a sandwich from a shop three doors down from the hotel.

"Professionals," said Kane. He paused the laptop video player at the point where the kidnapping team approached in a white van, swiftly emerging from its sliding door. "See how they form a secure perimeter?" he played it again as four men ran to form a square around the au pair's small car. Two other men ran to the vehicle. One secured the au pair herself by pointing a gun in her face, and the second took Annie. They got to the little girl as she walked from the school gates to the car. "If they had waited until Annie and the au pair were in the car, the doors could have been locked, and the whole thing could have gotten messy. They would have had to break windows and force the girl from the vehicle. Taking her on foot makes it simple and quick."

The whole kidnap took less than a minute. The crew were in the van and on the road before any of the parents in and around the school gates even processed what was happening.

"We can try to get a trace on the van?" suggested Craven, but he shrugged as he spoke, knowing that a crew capable of executing a kidnapping with such efficiency wouldn't use a van that could be traced to them via a simple registration plate check.

"Do you still have the envelope from the airfield?" asked Kane.

Craven went to the sliding wardrobe across from his bed and retrieved the envelope from his jacket pocket. He opened it and handed the piece of paper to Kane. It had a Saudi phone number and the name Ahmad Abdallah written in blue biro ink.

"I'll give them a call," nodded Craven. He dialled the number on his mobile phone and placed it on the desk with the speakerphone activated.

"Na'am?" said an Arabic male voice, deep and terse.

"Hello, I'm Detective Inspector Craven with the UK Police. Do you speak English?"

"Yes, I speak English." The man spoke English well, with an Arabic accent.

"Can I take your name, please, sir?"

"Ahmad."

Craven raised his thumb at Kane. "Thanks for taking the call, Ahmad," replied Craven in his most officious-sounding voice. "As I said, I am calling from the UK Police. A flight came into Casement Aerodrome in Ireland recently, arranged by you on behalf of a member of the Saudi Royal Family. Can you confirm you arranged that flight, please?"

"Yes, it was me who arranged the flight. We

use that airbase for diplomatic flights in and out of Ireland."

"Who was on the flight?"

"What is this about?"

"It's just a routine check, nothing to worry about. Were there diplomats or royals on the flight?"

"No, the jet was leant to a friend of the royal family. That friend travelled to Ireland with some associates."

"What was the name of that friend?"

"Let me check my records," the click-clack of a keyboard rattled through the speaker. "Didn't you say you are from the UK?"

"Yes, sir?"

"But this flight went to County Dublin, Ireland? What business is it of yours?"

"We routinely conduct random checks on aircraft that have flown over British airspace, that's all. Nothing to worry about."

"It was loaned to a Mr Baldwin and his associates from Dubai. It will be back with us next week."

"I'm sorry, did you say Baldwin?"

Kane jumped from his chair in surprise.

"Yes, James Baldwin."

Craven thanked the man and hung up the phone.

"Baldwin...the bastard," groaned Craven, wiping a hand down his face. "He brought the team over. So, he must be behind the whole thing?"

"How and why, though?" Kane questioned. "He wouldn't just decide to fly to Ireland and kidnap a girl. Someone has put him on the job. Wait here whilst I get my weapon from my room. We need to get back to Kelleher's stud. Baldwin has got some questions to answer, and Kelleher too."

"Hang on a minute," said Craven. "We have Kelleher's personal and business accounts on the laptop. So, we can check for any flight bookings travelling to the Middle East. It's a long shot, but it's worth a look." Craven navigated his laptop and opened the accounts spreadsheets. "There. Look, a flight booked with Emirates Airlines. It doesn't say where the destination is, but you can bet a pound to a bucket of shit that it's not fucking Bognor Regis. One of the Kellehers flew to the Middle East two months ago. So, we know Baldwin came here on a private jet with a crack team to pull off the kidnap, and we know one of the Kellehers flew out there, likely to meet him. We don't yet understand the connection between the Kellehers and Baldwin, but we've enough to confront them and free Annie. What sort of animals kidnap their own daughter for the ransom insurance money?"

Kane left Craven in his room. Craven was right. It was beyond belief that the Kellehers would put their daughter through such suffering. But then ten million euros is a lot of money, and Kane had seen people do worse things for far less. Something still did not add up, however. Why would John Kelleher, a man visibly distraught and utterly bereft by the kidnapping, put his daughter through such hardship? Why would he involve rough men in abducting her, forcibly restrain her, and threaten her life? He could have simply arranged for Baldwin to take Annie gently and hold her somewhere comfortable.

Kane entered his own room to retrieve his gun, his mind whirring with questions. Why would Baldwin execute the kidnap only to play buddies with John Kelleher? There was undoubtedly more to the puzzle, and Kane was determined to get to the bottom of it before the assassin had time to strike again.

FORTY-FIVE

Craven stalked his room, pacing back and forth with his big hands clenching and softening as he tried to bend his mind around Jim Baldwin's involvement. He had known Jim when they were younger, and they had been good friends. But he and Jim had drifted apart over the years, and Craven knew very little about the man Jim had become. After all, people change, especially over the course of twenty years.

He entered the bathroom, splashing cold water on his face while staring at himself in the mirror. The assassin woman could strike again at any minute. She was lethal and frightening, and Craven couldn't believe how calm Kane was about the whole thing. He had seemed entirely focused on the kidnap since their return to the hotel, as though the raging gun battle in which people had died at the Kelleher stud farm had not taken place.

Being in the company of a man who could be so detached from an incident of extreme violence, an event that would send an ordinary person reeling for months, if not years, was a strange feeling. It calmed Craven, being around Kane. It helped him compartmentalise the brutality of it all, and if Kane didn't want to talk about it, then that suited Craven. The best way forward was to get Annie Kelleher back alive and well and return to Spain in one piece. Barb waited for him there, and he never wanted to see any sort of action again. Craven would be happy drinking coffees and cokes by his pool and enjoying his retirement.

Craven sighed and went back into the bedroom. He sat on the edge of the bed and stared at his phone. Why had Baldwin deceived him? Had he lured Craven there just to throw him into a world of shit? If Baldwin had arranged the kidnapping, why had he asked Craven to fly to Ireland to help him with the investigation? None of it made sense.

"Fuck it," he muttered to himself. Craven picked up his phone and dialled Baldwin's number.

"Frank?" said Baldwin in his Liverpudlian accent as he answered the phone. White noise in the background told Craven that Baldwin was in a car.

"Yes, Jim, it's me."

"Crazy day today, mate, wasn't it? That woman is a fucking nutcase. It's like World War III at the Kelleher stud."

"We are mates, aren't we, Jim?" Craven paced the hotel room, too agitated to sit, afraid of what he would say and how Baldwin would respond.

"Yeah, 'course we are. What's wrong?"

"Do you remember at the stud when I mentioned that I'd been on to Casement Aerodrome and found out that a team landed there on a private jet?"

"I remember," Baldwin spoke confidently, his voice unwavering. Surely, he suspected that Craven was onto him, or maybe not. Either that, or he simply didn't care.

"You said you would follow it up. How did you get on?"

"I didn't get around to it yet, mate, what with all the gunfire and death. I'll do it now and call you back."

"No need, Jim. I've done it myself." Craven paused, waiting to see if Baldwin would come clean or try to come up with a story that would explain why he had flown into Ireland with a team from the Middle East.

"And?" he said after an uncomfortable silence.

"Cut the bollocks. I know it was you, Jim. You came on that plane with a team of professional soldiers from your private security firm, mercenary force, or whatever the fuck it's called, and you kidnapped Annie Kelleher."

"What are you talking about, Frank? We've known each other for years. How could you even think of such a thing?"

"One or both of the Kellehers employed you to do the job. One of them flew out to meet with you in the Middle East, and you planned it all. That poor little girl, Jim. Let her go. The game's up."

Baldwin laughed. "Well done, Frank. I didn't think you had it in you. Mrs Kelleher is here in the car with me. She'd say hello, only she's pissed out of her brain. She thinks you're as much of a fucking waste of time as I do."

"So, it was Mrs Kelleher, then. How could you do that to your own daughter, you disgraceful greedy bitch?" Craven regretted the name-calling the moment the words escaped his lips. It had come out involuntarily, like a nervous reaction. Whenever Craven came across any sort of child cruelty from parents, or any adult for that matter, it enraged him. He immediately thought of the kind of mother Barb would have been had they been fortunate enough to become parents.

Knowing the gratitude and boundless love she would have showered on their child intensified the enduring sorrow within him. Yet people like Mrs Kelleher seemed oblivious to the precious blessings they had.

"Now, now. No need for that. She's upset. Nobody likes doing this kind of thing. Unfortunately, sometimes people have to do the hard thing for the benefit of their family. Do you think Annie Kelleher would be happier as a child of bankrupt parents living on the poverty line or as the daughter of millionaires? We'll be taking off soon, mate. I've had enough of the miserable weather here, anyway."

"Now that we know the Kellehers were involved, the insurance won't pay out. So, you might as well let the girl go." Craven recalled Mrs Kelleher's state when they met at her father's house. She had been distraught, and Craven doubted that was an act – more like the tears of a guilty woman trying to get to grips with what she had done to her own daughter.

"The policy is in Mr Kelleher's name, and he isn't involved. He doesn't know that his wife and I took Annie. So, they'll pay out if you keep your mouth shut."

"How do you know Mrs Kelleher?"

"Through a mutual acquaintance in the horse

racing world. Caitriona put the feelers out in the Middle East racing community that she needed help with a matter that required military precision, expertise, and discretion, and she came to me. Then, when John got in touch with the same contacts looking for help to recover his daughter, he was also directed to me."

"Why did you bother pretending to work with the Kellehers? And why did you bring me here to find Annie if you knew where she was all along?"

"Mr Kelleher doesn't know about his wife and me. It's going to stay that way, Frank."

"This isn't scooby fucking doo, Jim. You wouldn't just tell me the gory details of your plan and hand yourself in quietly. What are you up to?"

"We're getting on the jet in the next few minutes. My team and the girl are waiting for us. Now, you listen here, Frank," Baldwin's voice hardened. It had been jovial up to that point, as if recounting an amusing anecdote at a party. But now there was steely grit to his tone. "If you tell John Kelleher, or the police, or fucking anyone for that matter, the girl dies." Mrs Kelleher shrieked in the background. "Never mind her crocodile tears. I'm in this for my cut of the ten million quid, so I'm not fucking about. I'm leaving the country and will contact John with instructions on how and where to deliver the money. If I get paid, then I'll let the girl go. If not, then I'll send Kelleher's daughter back to him piece by fucking piece." Mrs Kelleher sobbed and wailed, the sound muffled by the hum of the car's engine.

"Why did you bring me into this?" asked Craven, slumping into his chair. He couldn't believe his old friend would stoop so low. Could he really have changed so much since they had been friends?

"I need it to look legit. That's why I agreed to help John Kelleher. I heard on the grapevine that you'd retired, so I called you in. I remember you, Frank. You were a fucking idiot back then, and rumour has it you've never changed. Stumbling from one investigation to the next, living off collars made by others and riding on their coattails. You were just what I needed, a fucking muppet with a former detective's rank to show that we were serious about finding Annie. That's all you were, Frank, a fucking stool pigeon. A joke. Now, remember what I said – don't open your mouth, or I'll cut that little girl into a hundred pieces. If I get my money, then she goes free. Don't fuck this up, Frank. This isn't a game. I'm with serious people these days. I'm out in the Middle East, and I owe money to fellas who would cut a man's balls off, stuff them down his throat, and hang his body off a fucking bridge. So don't test me, Frank; don't test my resolve on this. If you try anything stupid, I will kill the girl. That's a promise. There's too much at stake for me here. My life is on the line. So keep your nose out of it, don't get the police involved and tell your trigger-happy mate to put a lid on it. Just do what I tell you, and everything will work out fine. It's the insurance company's money away, Frank, not Kelleher's, so nobody will suffer if we do this right."

The phone cut off, and Craven dropped it. His heart thumped in his chest. He had thought of Baldwin as a friend, so the cruelty of his words cut like a blade. Baldwin showed no concern for putting Annie through a horrendous, traumatic experience or the potential damage it would do to her psychologically. From the way Jim Baldwin spoke and the trouble he was obviously in, Craven didn't doubt for a second that Baldwin would kill Annie if he had to. An emptiness spread within him, a cavernous hole of uncomfortable realisation. Craven was confronted with how his former colleagues on the force had always viewed him. They had tolerated his surly demeanour and cantankerous ways because they were all laughing at him. That revelation stung, learning his entire career as a police detective had all been one big joke.

Craven stood and stared at himself in the mirror. He took a deep breath, clenched his fists, and shook his head. Maybe he had been a laughingstock once, but he wasn't a policeman anymore. Craven had figured out Baldwin and Caitriona Kelleher's ploy, and now he didn't have to play by the rules. He had Kane on his side, a ruthless, formidable killer, and Craven was determined to reunite Annie Kelleher with her father. With his resolve cemented, Craven looked at his reflection and promised himself that he would show that bastard Jim Baldwin who was the joke after all.

FORTY-SIX

Matius opened the locker using the code sent to him via text message. The lock clicked, and he pulled open the long metallic door. He checked around him to ensure nobody watched and retrieved a gun and knife from the darkness within.

He stifled a yawn, having barely slept on the flight from Rome to Dublin. The message from his employer had come through just as Matius had completed another job in the Eternal City. He had killed a high-ranking member of the Bratva, the Russian mafia. The man had died with Matius' knife in his throat in a restaurant close to the Colosseum. He had been an eminent pakhan, or boss, in the Russian international crime organisation, and his peers had judged that the man had broken the Vorovskoy Zakon, the thieves' code by which they lived and conducted business.

Matius' employer had notified him of the Bratva bounty three days earlier, and the message had come through as he was teaching a silat class to his students. When he was not travelling the world collecting bounties, Matius ran a silat school, where he imparted the teaching of the Southeast Asian martial arts type as a skilled master.

The job in Rome had gone smoothly. His information package included a picture of the target, some frequent destinations, and his home address. Matius had followed the man to the restaurant, where he had waited outside for the big man in the black leather coat to use the smoking area. After fifteen minutes, the Russian had come outside and put a Zippo lighter to a thick cigar. Matius had stepped in behind the man, who stood some six feet two inches by Matius' reckoning and was dwarfed by the Russian's shadow. Matius had slid a wickedly curved blade across the Russian's throat and stepped away as his tattooed fingers clawed at the terrible wound. Black blood spilt onto the ancient flagstones, and the Russian had fallen to lie sprawled between small tables, a second grizzly mouth grinning up from his slashed throat.

Matius had simply walked away. He tossed

the knife down a road drain, hopped onto a Lambretta moped, and sped towards the snarl of Rome's tiny backstreets. This new bounty had arrived minutes after the Russian kill – a new target in Dublin, Ireland. Matius liked to take on clusters of jobs to minimise his time away from home. A short flight from Leonardo da Vinci Airport got Matius to Dublin in a few hours.

He stowed the pistol, a Beretta 92, in his backpack along with the knife. Matius' phone vibrated, and a notification appeared saying he had received his target information pack. Matius opened his employer's secure application and found photographs of Jack Kane. Some of him as a young man in British Army uniform, and others as a slightly older MI6 agent. His known accomplice was a retired British policeman, and there were also photos of him, a heavy-set man with broad shoulders. Credit card payment records and mobile phone usage put the policeman in Dublin and County Kildare, and a note said the policeman was in the company of Kane.

The bounty was worth enough Indonesian Rupiah to keep his school running for another year, and along with the job in Rome, he could afford to take on more students. Matius offered lodging, food, and clothes to his students. Silat was his passion, an ancient form of martial arts integral to Indonesian history and culture, and it was Matius' calling to keep it alive.

Matius scrolled through the app and saw that the most recent location for the policeman was a hotel in Dublin city centre. The information from his employer said it was an open bounty, so other killers were en route to Dublin, and only the hunter with the kill got paid. The journey from the Dublin bus terminal to his target on Mespil Road was across the city, so Matius put three euros and fifty cents into a bicycle rental machine outside the bus station and headed south to hunt his prey.

FORTY-SEVEN

"So that sneaky bastard Baldwin really was behind it all along," Craven explained, hands on his hips and his face red with anger. "The arsehole was behind the whole thing. He only invited me on the job because he thought I was a shit copper. Me being here was intended to gild the lily, to make the whole thing look like a real kidnapping."

"It is a real kidnapping," said Kane. Craven had filled him in on the details of his call with Baldwin, but he was now talking it out, repeating the details to help process it in his mind. "Annie is still missing, and Baldwin will kill the girl if he doesn't get the ransom."

"I never would have thought that he was that kind of bloke. He used to be, well, normal."

"It's been a long time since you were friends. A

lot can happen in that time. If he's been working with the private firms in the Middle East, then he's seen some action. How long did you say he's been out there?"

"Over a decade, at least."

"So, he was out there when the US military was pulling out of Afghanistan. That's when things really started hotting up. The Taliban regained control, and it became dangerous for anyone doing business. Baldwin probably took on work bodyguarding rich guys or making sure goods moved between the Emirates, Syria, Iraq, Iran, and beyond. He's most likely not the man you once knew. Exposure to extreme violence changes a man; over time, you become desensitised to it, like a surgeon who gets used to cutting upon bodies or a doctor who gets used to breaking cancer diagnoses to patients. It becomes normal. If Baldwin has been through half of what I imagine he has, then this isn't a big deal for him."

"And the wife, Mrs fucking Kelleher. Can you believe it? Do you think she and Baldwin are, you know?"

That part of it was also hard to stomach, and Kane just shrugged. He did not know if they were having an affair or if the kidnap was purely a game plan to get the insurance money.

"We need to talk to John Kelleher, Fran Doyle and Franchetti. Share what we know so we can decide what to do next. Instructions for delivery of the ransom should follow soon, and we need to be ready. Kelleher will need all the help he can get."

"We can't meet him at the stud. The Irish police will be all over that place. I wouldn't be surprised if the Guards have taken in Kelleher and Doyle for questioning about the dead men and the gun battle."

"Call Fran Doyle and arrange to meet. But not at the stud and not in Dublin. Maybe at a pub close to the stud. It's getting late in the day, so a pub seems like the best bet for a meeting place. I'll grab my bag from my room and meet you in the hotel lobby."

"You'll get your gun, don't you mean?"

"Yes, if you like. We need to be armed; the assassin is still on the loose. And we can't be sure that Baldwin hasn't left some of his crew in Ireland to stop us from interfering."

Craven nodded and pulled his phone from his pocket. Kane left the room, letting the door close on its heavy hinges before nipping into his own room. The most significant risk Annie Kelleher faced was if the insurance company got wind that the kidnapping was down to her mother. If they did, the policy would be void, making the ransom payment impossible to pay. He doubted that An Garda Síochána had gotten any closer to finding Baldwin's team – after all, they couldn't use the same methods as Kane and Craven. To requisition flight information from Casement and then the details from the Saudis using official channels would take days. After retrieving his gun, he left his room and walked along the corridor until he reached the lift. Kane pressed the lift button, and the little arrow turned green to say one of the two hotel lifts was on its way. Kelleher's insurance company had hired Franchetti, so Kane had to ensure he didn't discover the sordid details behind Annie's disappearance. But John Kelleher deserved to be told about his wife and his loathsome acquaintance, Jim Baldwin.

The lift pinged, and the door slid open. An Asian man in a black T-shirt and black combat trousers stepped out of the lift, and Kane moved aside to let him pass. He was four inches shorter than Kane and nodded his thanks as he marched past, shifting a navy backpack on his shoulder into a more comfortable position. Just as Kane was about to enter the lift, the man turned and stared at him. Kane stared back.

"Jack Kane," said the man in a thick Asian accent. He said the words not as a question but as a statement. He walked back towards Kane and shrugged his pack from his shoulder.

Kane turned away from the lift, and it slid closed behind him to continue on to another floor. The man knew his name and had gotten off the lift on the floor he and Craven were staying on. The man was tracking him. Logic told Kane that somebody had tracked Craven's phone or bank activity. Either way, another hunter had found him.

"I'm Kane," he uttered, shifting his feet, ready to fight.

FORTY-EIGHT

Matius smiled at the sheer luck of it, bumping into his target in a hotel corridor. At first, he hadn't recognised Jack Kane, but then the face processed in his subconscious, and he recognised the average-looking European white man from his information app. Kane wasn't tall for a European, but nor was he small. He was of average build, without the ridiculous muscular physique of some American and European men. Even his face was non-descript, which was perhaps why Matius hadn't recognised him instantly.

Matius let his bag slip down his shoulder so that he held it in his left hand. He moved cautiously towards the target, refraining from unzipping his bag and taking out his gun or knife. Knowing that Kane was highly trained, Matius refrained from unzipping his bag and taking out his gun or knife, as it would take too long. A few seconds window of distraction was all Kane needed to strike out and get the upper hand. No matter. Matius enjoyed the thrill of unarmed combat. It was, after all, his passion. His father had taught him silat from the time he could walk, and Matius savoured any opportunity to use his skills in real-life situations, not just sparring, but in a fight to the death.

Jack Kane set his feet shoulder-width apart and raised his hands. Matius nodded at his target, appreciating that the man didn't run, beg, or try to talk his way out of the situation. Kane's instinct was to stand and fight, which Matius admired. Matius threw his backpack at Kane and followed it up with an explosive flurry of punches, short but powerful strikes aimed at Kane's liver and solar plexus.

Kane batted the backpack aside and tucked his elbows in just in time to block most of Matius' attack, but two of his punches landed, and Kane gasped in pain from a liver punch. Matius aimed a kick at Kane's face, which he dodged, and then Matius attacked with a vicious combination of elbows and knees. He drove Kane against the wall and was surprised at how little fight the ex-SAS man was putting up. Matius focused his attack on Kane's legs and groin, and when his guard lowered, he aimed a kick at Kane's face.

Kane's powerful hand grabbed the back of Matius' head and dragged him into a savage headbutt, sending sharp, searing pain slicing through his left cheekbone. He jerked away, but Kane had caught the foot that Matius had tried to kick with, and Kane's own foot swept Matius' leg from under him. He tumbled onto the hardwearing carpet and flipped over backwards, bellowing in rage that a simple soldier had thrown a silat master to the ground.

Matius flung himself at Kane, ignoring the throbbing pain in his face. He kicked, punched and elbowed the bigger man, roaring with defiance and aggression with each strike. Kane grunted as blows connected with his defending arms, but some of Matius' blows got through. He relaxed into the fight. Kane stumbled backwards, and Matius leapt up, aiming a knee at Kane's face, only to be grabbed mid-air and thrown against the opposite wall. Matius fell to the carpet again and rolled forward like a rubber ball to spring back into the attack.

He came to his knees, the muscles in his legs bunched and ready to drive toward his target once more. Kane's fist cannoned into Matius' nose, and the silat master heard the gristle of his own face crack under the weight of the punch. Blood flowed, the iron taste foul in his mouth, and Matius swung a blind punch at Kane, but Kane caught his hand and wrenched it around, trying to break his arm at the shoulder.

Matius rolled towards the twist and kicked Kane's leg behind the knee. Now, it was the bigger man's turn to drop to the floor, and Matius used the momentary respite to grab his backpack. Kane was good. He'd proven a formidable opponent, enduring Matius' attacks and retaliating with powerful strikes. Matius couldn't afford to take any more chances with the target, and his gun would draw too much attention, so he grabbed the knife. It was a deadly curved blade shaped like a crescent moon with a long handle for balance. He whipped it free and slashed it towards Kane's eyes.

Kane leapt backwards, away from the shining blade, and Matius followed him, slashing and cutting. Kane deftly caught his elbow and pushed the knife-wielding hand aside before driving the fingers of his left hand into Matius' eyes. He shrank back from the pain and dragged his knife blade across Kane's forearm. Droplets of ruby-red blood dripped onto the carpet, and the two men stood apart, eyeing each other. Matius held his knife before him and crouched in a silat stance, poised to strike. Kane glanced at his wounded arm, grimaced, and then fixed Matius with a flat stare. He had dark eyes that resembled empty brown pools, reminiscent of the lifeless eyes of a shark. Kane remained stoic, showing no anger, emitting no cry of pain. He was like a robot.

A pang of fear suddenly curdled inside Matius, something he hadn't felt for years. His stomach lurched, and his mouth was dry. He was supposed to be the superior fighter, the master. He had killed more people than he cared to remember, but this man was something different. Facing him was like battling an inanimate object – a rock or a tree – devoid of feeling and immovable. Jack Kane seemed able to switch between fighting styles, jiu-jitsu, judo, aikido, karate, and boxing.

Matius sprang forward, low and vicious like a viper, and slashed at Kane's leg. But the target ripped a bland painting from the wall and smashed it across Matius' head. He stumbled, and his knife hand scraped across the carpet. Kane kicked Matius in the ribs and leapt upon him, grabbing a wrist and looping his legs around Matius' neck and shoulders.

Kane dropped to the ground, and Matius grimaced as his arm stretched beyond its normal range of motion, his neck constricted between Kane's shin and thigh. Matius wriggled and bucked, but Kane held him fast. In an attempt to break free, Matius tried to turn Kane and force him to relinquish his grip by lifting his hips and working to run his legs along the floor. Yet Kane moved with him, and his legs tightened like a vice, cutting off Matius' airway. He dropped the knife and tried to slip his fingers inside Kane's grip. Seizing the opportunity, Kane let go of Matius' wrist and snatched up the knife. He released his legs from Matius' neck, and suddenly, a surge of pain tore up Matius' leg like fire.

At first, it felt like a punch, but then Matius realised Kane had stabbed the knife into his thigh and ripped it upwards, laying open his leg like a piece of meat on a butcher's slab. The frame of the painting had cracked his skull, and Matius hastily scrambled away from Kane, dragging his useless leg, desperate to buy himself a vital few seconds to recover his senses.

Kane came on. He stamped on Matius' injured leg and slashed the knife blade across his face, slicing open his forehead so that fiery blood washed into his eyes and down his face. An object shifted under his back. The backpack. Matius grabbed it and thrust his hand inside, rejoicing as the cold grip nestled into his palm. He raised the weapon, but Kane was upon him, and he twisted the weapon savagely from Matius' hand.

Matius sagged back against the wall, the sound of a door opening on his left drawing his attention. A deep voice spoke in English. His lifeblood eked out from his wounded leg, and his arms felt like they were made of concrete. He wiped the blood from his eyes on the black of his sleeve and stared up at his target. Kane met his gaze, his vacant eyes now twinkling with the joy of victory through combat. Matius knew it well, and there was no greater feeling on earth. Not the love of a woman nor the thrill of a fast car. Defeating a man who sought to kill you was to soar like an eagle, to feel like a god.

A big man loomed over Matius, his large belly hanging over the belt of his trousers. Matius tried to find some strength, desperate to get back into the fight, but he was dying. He could feel his life energy pulsing out of him. Memories of his parents and childhood played out in his mind, both happy and sad. Kane moved the big man out of the way and knelt beside Matius. He rummaged in the backpack and pulled out a spare magazine for the Beretta and Matius' phone. Matius helplessly watched as Kane unlocked the phone, pressing Matius' limp thumb onto the cold screen. Knowing that the darkness would soon engulf him, Matius glimpsed fleeting images of men he had killed and women he had loved.

Kane sniffed and calmly scrolled through the phone, no doubt reading the information provided on the secure app, which he now accessed using Matius' thumbprint. Matius clenched his teeth and groaned, channelling all his remaining energy, desperate for one last strike at his target, but the well was empty.

Kane's head tilted thoughtfully to one side. He stared into Matius' eyes as though he searched for something, perhaps a glimmer of those last moments, looking for a hint of regret or sorrow at the lives Matius had taken. Killing was their shared trade. They had lived their lives on the shoulder of mortality, and now that the spectre of death came for Matius, he wondered if he could have taken a different path. What might his life have been like had he taken a different fork in the road? At that moment, Kane rammed the knife into Matius' eye so hard that it punched into the back of his skull, like a bolt of lightning carving its way through to send Matius howling into the afterlife.

FORTY-NINE

Craven drove the hire car through the maze of Dublin city. Its one-way system and pedestrian-only roads and pathways meant traffic had to take circuitous routes to navigate the city. Dublin splits into two halves, north and south of the wide River Liffey, and the road system divides into a painfully halting network of traffic lights. Craven stopped at yet another red light at a junction where he would turn right to travel alongside the Dublin canal and out towards the N7 motorway.

He glanced at Kane from the corner of his eye and tore his gaze back to the red light ahead of the line of traffic. The fight in the hotel corridor had been brutal. Even though Craven had seen Kane in action several times since they had first met, the visceral savagery with which Kane fought never failed to horrify him. Kane could kill without hesitation, and it appeared he could do it without regret or concern for his enemies' lives.

Kane scrolled the phone he had taken from the assassin in the hotel, reading through the contract taken out on his own life. He had shown it to Craven already – details of his army career, pictures of Kane as a younger man in an army uniform and a beret, and other pictures of him in desert fatigues with a beard and a rifle. There were numerous files replete with lines and words redacted in thick black lines. What concerned Craven more was the information in the file on himself. His own career, old address, his bank card and phone number. He was now a known associate of Jack Kane, a man wanted by the darker forces within the British government. They had tracked him to Ireland, which meant they also knew his address in Spain. Craven only hoped that the assassins followed him to Dublin through his phone and credit card use and had stayed away from Barb and the children.

It was a sobering thought that Craven was linked to Kane, a killer and former British agent. Kane was more than able to handle himself, but how would Craven fare if assassins like the man in the hotel or the woman from the stud came for him when Kane wasn't around? He knew the answer all too well. Even if he bought a gun when he returned to Spain, he doubted it would make much difference if it came down to a fight between him and a trained killer.

Every time that Craven had seen Kane kill, it had been in an act of self-defence. He just seemed so good at it, which Craven supposed was what had made him an excellent soldier and secret agent. Kane had used medical supplies from his survival tin to patch himself up quickly at the hotel, a sterilised wipe to clean the awful knife wound, and then a needle to stitch the lips of the cut together. Craven couldn't watch the grisly patch-up job – too much blood and gore for his liking. They had fled the hotel just as four An Garda Síochána vehicles screamed to a skidding halt outside the Mespil Hotel, and Craven had raced the hire car away from the bloody corpse and a fresh wave of police involvement in the wake of Kane's violent encounters.

"It's only a matter of time before the Irish police catch up with you," Craven said, breaking the silence, which hung heavy in the car like a fog.

"The man at the hotel was one of many. You know they are after us both now? We should be more concerned with the assassins than the Irish police, Frank."

"So, what do we do about it?"

"I'm thinking about it. We'll be out of Ireland soon enough, though," answered Kane.

"Baldwin's already left with the girl, and we are going after her. If we take Baldwin at his word, the ransom exchange will take John Kelleher out of the country."

"And we go with him?"

"If he needs us, yes. Which he does. His daughter's survival depends completely upon his insurance company delivering the ransom funds. What if they figure out that Mrs Kelleher is behind the kidnap and the whole thing is an insurance fraud? What if they can't provide the funds in time to meet Baldwin's deadline? There are too many opportunities for this to go wrong and for Annie to die."

Craven anxiously bit his lip. Kane was so sure about what would happen next and that he could help recover Annie. Yet he seemed oblivious to the fact that his precarious situation had turned the kidnap investigation into a murderous whirlwind. The highly skilled killers who hunted Kane had found him and turned Ireland into a war zone. It had resulted in the destruction of John Kelleher's stud farm, the death of members of the insurance company's preferred investigation team, Franchetti's Black Eagle Agency, killed in action entirely unrelated to the kidnap, not to mention the brutal death of a contract killer in the corridors of the Mespil Hotel.

Craven turned off the dual carriageway leading out of Dublin's centre and sped onto the N7 motorway. Part of him wondered whether it would be more beneficial for the Kelleher family if he and Kane simply returned to Spain on the next available flight. Once the French air traffic strike concluded, they could leave it to Franchetti to handle the kidnapping. With Kelleher's wife having left him and his life in disarray, Craven believed that the only valuable contribution he and Kane could make to retrieving Annie was if it turned sour and there was a violent confrontation with Baldwin and his men. If it came to that, there was no better man than Kane to go toe to toe with armed mercenaries.

Craven moved into the right-hand motorway lane and sped up towards the pub where they had agreed to meet John Kelleher and Fran Doyle. It was a ten-minute drive south on the motorway, situated on the outskirts of the quaint village of Rathcoole. Craven tried to wrench his mind and force it to focus on the problem at hand – helping John Kelleher retrieve his daughter – but his thoughts persistently returned to the same thing, like a pulled elastic band.

Baldwin's harsh words about Craven's career had washed over him at first. But as the minutes and hours passed, the comments cut deeper, burning like acid dripping onto soft flesh. Craven was past his best; he was overweight, and his eyes struggled to read things close up. He also knew that he had coasted a little in the latter stages of his career. Craven did as he was ordered and dedicated himself to every investigation. But he had become a nine-to-five man – or whichever shift pattern suited him best. When he was younger, Craven had worked whatever hours were necessary to crack a case. He had come out of uniform with hunger and passion, eager to do some good for society and bring down those who would do the public harm.

Craven had always thought of his younger years as successful. He had been involved in serious cases, bringing down major drug lords and dozens of their minions. But as he drove along the motorway, those cases replayed in his memory without the rose-tinted perspective through which he usually viewed those years. Maybe he had ridden on the coattails of better detectives. Perhaps his so-called glory years hadn't been glorious at all. He had just been lucky to work with good coppers in those days, and his involvement had been as a simple cog in a greater wheel. Looking at his life through Baldwin's harsh assessment was more than challenging. It changed the way Craven saw himself. It shook the foundation on which he had built his self-esteem.

"I think the junction is coming up, Frank," said Kane, breaking Craven from his daze. He blinked, having one of those moments where he wondered how he had gotten from the motorway entrance to this point, having been so deep in his thoughts. "Change lanes."

Craven pulled left as the junction for Rathcoole neared towards him. He swallowed and glimpsed himself in the rearview mirror.

"I was in a world of my own there," muttered Craven, slowing down as the exit lane approached.

"Don't let him get to you. Baldwin said what he said to hurt you. Focus on the task at hand. John Kelleher needs our help, and we must tell all we know about Baldwin and Mrs Kelleher."

"Baldwin brought me here because he thinks I'm a joke. I was supposed to be a stooge, just an ex-copper, here to make his investigation look a bit more thorough. He never thought I could piece together the jigsaw of his plan."

"But you did piece it together. Don't let him bother you. It was you who got the info from Dickie McHugh about how things were at the stud, you who figured out about the Saudi jet, and it was you who went through the finances and saw the financial difficulty the Kellehers are in. And If I get my way, you and I will bring Baldwin down. He's the man who ended up as a mercenary out in the desert, and now he's running around kidnapping little girls. You had a career as a police detective and have retired with honour."

Craven sat a little straighter in the driving seat and parked in the pub car park.

FIFTY

An Poitín Stil was one of the oldest pubs in Ireland. The date on the sign said that it had first opened in the eighteenth century, and as Kane walked through the front door, the walls and ceilings dripped with nostalgia. Kane had drunk poitín before with friends in the army. Poitín, a distilled alcoholic drink, was akin to Irish moonshine. The Irish soldiers had told Kane the drink was linked to the Irish famine and Ireland's oppression by Britain over the centuries, and they had laughed when he baulked at its strong taste. Kane had never been a big drinker, and the taste of poitín was like raki, another powerful spirit Kane had had the misfortune of tasting. He could not understand how anyone could enjoy something that tasted like paint stripper.

Copper stills and pots adorned the bar, and distilling tubes hung on the walls and above an old fireplace. During the Irish revolutionary years, they made poitín from a fermented barley mash, and it was illegal to brew. Very much like prohibition times in America, Irishmen had brewed it deep in the country, and it was a symbol of rebellion against the British government.

The Poitín Stil did not sell poitín, which was fortunate, and so Kane ordered a pint of Guinness for himself and Craven. The big man had gone to search through the warren of smaller bars and hidden alcoves within the sprawling pub to look for John Kelleher. Kane took a sip of the Guinness. Its cool, black liquid was thick and luxurious. Craven appeared and waved to Kane, so he picked up Craven's pint and followed him to a long table in a snug corner of the pub, set behind timber stairs which led to a second floor.

John Kelleher sat with Fran Doyle, Franchetti, and, surprisingly, Dave McNamara.

"So, you know about your wife, then?" Kane said to John Kelleher and nodded towards McNamara. If her father was with Kelleher, then Kane assumed the entire plot was out in the open.

"Unfortunately, yes," Kelleher replied bitterly.

He took a long drink of whiskey from a thick glass. "Turns out the bitch and Baldwin are in it together."

"Did you have any inkling of what they were up to?"

"No, I fucking didn't. Do you think I would ever let this happen to my daughter if there was even the remotest suggestion of it?"

"What about you?" Craven asked Dave McNamara.

"I had no idea. Obviously, I knew she had problems with her drinking and the other stuff. I knew she had been out to Dubai and that friends in the horse racing world had put John and Caitriona onto Baldwin. But I can't believe my daughter would do this to Annie and John."

"Any word from either of them?"

"Not yet," said Fran Doyle. "We are expecting a call soon. You said on the phone that Baldwin threatened to hurt Annie?"

"If he doesn't get the money, he'll kill her. He made no bones about it. The fact that Mrs Kelleher is with him makes no difference." Craven spoke with a cold certainty and fixed each man at the table with a long stare to ensure each knew the genuine danger Annie faced.

"Can somebody remind me what the fuck we

are doing here?" John Kelleher hissed. He crossed his arms and curled his lip at Kane. "I've spent the best part of today being grilled by the Guards about the shootout at my farm."

"We are here to offer you our help," said Kane. He raised a finger to quieten John Kelleher just as he was about to speak again. "Baldwin will call with instructions for the ransom drop, which you must deliver as per the specified split. Then, he may let Annie go, or he might kill her, regardless. So, I still believe your best chance is to take Annie back by force. I can do that for you, but I'll need you to share the ransom drop instructions with me."

"Why should I trust you?" asked Kelleher.

"Will the insurance company give you the money?"

"Yes. Well, I think so." Kelleher glanced at Leo Franchetti, who shifted nervously in his seat. "The claim on the policy is not straightforward. They want to take instructions from the Guards and Leo, so it's getting messy."

"What are they saying?"

"The company has a report from me and from An Garda Síochána confirming that we believe that Mrs Kelleher is involved in Annie's kidnapping," said Leo Franchetti.

"For fuck's sake," snapped Craven, slamming his pint down onto the table. "What did you tell them for?"

"Look, I've worked these cases before for the company, and they won't pay out unless they're sure everything is in order. We aren't talking about a few hundred dollars here, guys. It's millions of euros."

"But you get paid by the company whether Annie is recovered or not, right?" asked Kane.

"Correct. And paid well, I might add." Franchetti smiled wolfishly, his ultra-white, spirit-level straight teeth gleaming in the pub's gloom.

"So, your loyalty is to the insurer first." Kane leant forward and made sure that Kelleher gave him his full attention. "I've got two kids of my own, John. I'm not sure what you know about me, and I'm sorry for the trouble I've brought by coming here. But you need me now. Of all the men around this table, I am the only one with the skills and experience to ensure the safe return of your daughter."

"Now back up a bit, pal," Franchetti interrupted, crossing his muscled arms. "I want to do the right thing as much as the next man. Don't paint yourself to be some sort of hero here. I have to be honest with the insurers, and

John understands that. If they hadn't gotten the news on Mrs Kelleher from me, they would have gotten it from the Irish police. What's in it for you, anyway? My team and I are the official team working this case, and we..."

"Wait," said John Kelleher. "Let Kane speak."

"There's nothing in it for me, no money, no employment contract. Mr Kelleher, if you let me, I will get Annie back for you, or I'll die trying. You have my word on that. I'm not getting paid for this, and I don't work for the insurance company. I am here to help you get your daughter back because it's the right thing to do and because I can do it. I am a former member of the SAS and British Intelligence."

A phone rang, and John Kelleher took it out of his jacket pocket. He licked his lips and looked at Kane. He held the phone up to show the call came from a withheld number.

"Answer it," Kane nodded.

"This is John Kelleher," he said, placing the phone on the table in speakerphone mode.

"If you want your daughter back," Jim Baldwin sneered through the black iPhone, "listen very carefully."

FIFTY-ONE

"Have you got the money?" asked Baldwin. He spoke as though he were on a sun lounger by the pool, not like a man making a ransom demand for ten million euros.

"It's going to take more time," Kelleher answered, wringing his hands and leaning forward to speak into the phone. "I have to get the wheels of the insurance company turning. The mechanics of getting the money together could take a few more days."

Kelleher looked up at Kane with bloodshot eyes and every muscle fibre in his neck and face as taut as a ship's sail in a storm. Kelleher was negotiating for his daughter's life, and every day, hour and minute he could buy to give them more time to track Baldwin down was vital.

"I'm a reasonable guy, John," Baldwin responded. "And I know from your pretty little wife that you can't raise the money without the payment and that insurance companies are tighter than a frog's arse. So, I'll extend the deadline. I'm going to give you an extra day. In two days from now, you need to be in the Paris Gare du Nord station with the money. I will call you on this phone with further instructions. If you don't have the money, Annie will die. I have done some terrible things in my life, so don't doubt my resolve. My crew and I have fought and suffered like you wouldn't believe. I've killed women and children for money many times. It's a different world out there in the desert, and I must have that money. Ten million euros to be split, just as I asked before. And don't substitute the Monero crypto for cash, John, or I'll send Annie back to you in pieces. Be in Paris with the money, and I want confirmation of the crypto."

The call ended, and Kelleher grabbed his head, digging his fingers into his scalp. He shook and came up red-faced, lips drawn back from his teeth in desperation.

"The insurance company won't pay out, will they?" said Kane.

"It will be difficult to get the money in two days, given the complications with Mrs Kelleher.

If at all," Franchetti acknowledged.

"Holy shit. My poor Annie," Kelleher sobbed. He covered his mouth at first, trying to stuff the horror back inside himself, but it erupted out of him like a geyser. His whole body creased and contracted, and Kane had never seen so much suffering.

"I'm coming to Paris with you," said Kane, holding Kelleher's shoulder with his hand. "We'll get your Annie back. He's sending you to Europe for ease of access. He can send you from Paris north to Scandinavia, south to Spain or Portugal, or west to Germany, Russia or beyond, all by land. Baldwin and his team will keep tabs on you, and he'll probably make you travel by train."

"How can you be so sure?" demanded Franchetti. "I think we've had enough of your bullshit, Kane. Best to leave this to the professionals."

"Really?" Kane scoffed. "You work for the insurance company, and you've already briefed them on Mrs Kelleher's involvement. So, when they refuse to pay out and stop paying your fees, will you help John get his daughter back? Or will you fly back to wherever the fuck you came from and leave him to deal with it himself?"

"I've lost good men this week because of you. So, I suggest you mind your tongue."

"Is that true?" asked Kelleher. "If they don't pay out, you're gone?"

"I work for the insurer, Mr Kelleher. You know that."

"You should take Kane with you," piped Fran Doyle. He finished the bottom third of his pint of Guinness with one mighty gulp and wiped his mouth clean on the back of his hand. "As much as Leo and his lads are nice fellas, it seems to me you need someone with experience who's solely on your side, John. We've all seen what he can do. I watched him fight that woman on the lawn, and I've seen nothing like it before. So go to Paris and take Kane with you, for Annie's sake. Mr Craven and I will wait here and try to get the money together. If we get it, then you can tell us where to meet you with it."

Doyle rarely spoke, but when he did, he spoke sense. Kane nodded reassuringly at the Irishman, who raised his eyebrows as if to warn Kane to deliver on his recommendation.

"Me and my guys will follow you to Paris, John," said Franchetti in his loud, American drawl. "I'll leave my wounded here in Ireland to get patched up, and I'll help you for as long as I can."

Kane and Craven left the three men in the pub and walked out into the chill evening air. Kane knew in his heart that Kelleher would not get the money together to pay Baldwin for the return of his daughter. He had to find Baldwin and take the girl back.

"So, you're going to Paris, then," Craven remarked.

"Yes, and then wherever else I must go to get this done," said Kane. "Go back inside, Frank and talk to Kelleher. Get his wife's phone number, handset details, bank accounts, credit cards, store cards – anything she has in her purse or on her person. Get all the details and have them ready when I call you."

"Where are you going?"

"I can't leave loose ends behind me. There's a contract on my head, and I need to wipe out those who come to collect it. I'll take your card and phone when I go to Paris. Ditch the cards and phones I took from the IRA – they will just muddy the waters. You can use one of my burners to stay in touch with Barb. I'll take the car. We hired it with your credit card, so the killers will figure that out and follow it soon enough."

"How will you handle assassins coming to claim the bounty on your head? Lure them out? What if they kill you?"

"I am going to kill them all, Frank. And then

I'm going to rescue that frightened little girl."

FIFTY-TWO

Condor limped through the hotel lobby. Her ankle crunched at every step, like a hundred tiny knives jabbing at the swollen joint. Hating the appearance of weakness and wanting to avoid drawing attention to herself, she masked the limp as much as possible. Condor looked straight ahead, smiling at anyone who made eye contact with her. Makeup hid most of the bruising on her face, and her shirt, jacket, and trousers hid the cuts and gashes that crisscrossed her body like she had been bullwhipped.

The tracker in Kane's clothing and Frank Craven's credit card payment had told her that both men were staying at the Mespil Hotel. The bounty was in the ether, and mercenary killers would descend on the hotel like flies on shit – if they hadn't already. Kane was her kill, her prey.

It was about pride now, as much as her job. She was a professional with a reputation for success and efficiency, and Kane had made her look like a fool.

In her smart clothes, Condor looked like a businesswoman. She blended in, even though she was the only woman of colour she had seen in the hotel so far. Two police officers brushed past her, striding through the lobby and overtaking her slower, halting pace. They hurried to the lifts and waited impatiently for one to arrive. Another officer appeared from the office behind the front desk and spoke urgently to the receptionist.

Heat prickled down the back of Condor's neck. A familiar sense of foreboding or warning. There was a heavy police presence at the same hotel in which Jack Kane was staying, Irish police officers with grave faces. It couldn't be a coincidence. Condor only hoped it didn't mean that one of the bounty hunters had beaten her to the kill. She stood behind the police officers, waiting for the lift. One was a middle-aged man, fit with an orange goatee; the second was a petite woman with a blood-red birthmark on her neck. Both wore pale blue uniform shirts beneath navy jackets and heavy belts with nightsticks and handcuffs. They wore navy stab vests with police radios clipped to the shoulder.

The lift dinged, and the doors slid open. Condor followed the officers into the metal box and waited for them to press the floor selection. The policewoman reached floor number seven and then turned to Condor to silently inquire which floor.

"Seven as well," Condor smiled.

"Really?" said the woman in a County Cork lilt, one of Ireland's most recognisable regional accents. "You won't be able to access your room."

"I've been out all day. Has something happened?"

The lift whirred and moved upwards. It was a small space, and Condor was both tall and broad-shouldered. The policewoman shuffled a step backwards to create a little more room.

"The hotel should have notified you. Your entire floor is closed off because of an earlier incident. They'll arrange for your things to be taken to another room."

"Was there a fire or something?"

"Unfortunately, a murder occurred on your floor, and it's closed for forensic examination."

"Oh, that's awful." Condor put her hand to her mouth in feigned shock. The lift stopped at floor number seven, and the door behind Condor slid open. She turned and pretended to gasp at the scene of carnage. The beige walls and sprawling carpet were spattered with carmine horror, and an Asian man's corpse lay in a pool of black blood. The officers shuffled past Condor, and the woman turned and offered a sad smile.

"Please, take the lift back down and speak to the reception staff. They will help you find a new room and move your belongings."

Condor shook her head as though she couldn't believe what she had seen. The policewoman reached inside the lift and pressed a green button for the ground floor. The doors closed, and Condor let her hand fall to her waist, the pretence of shock disappearing to leave a look of frustrated anger on her bruised face.

The dead man must have been the first to come for Kane's head, and he had paid the ultimate price. Kane wouldn't come back to the hotel now, and neither would Craven. They were in the open somewhere, but Craven used his credit card and phone like a man who did not know that he was under surveillance.

All she had to do was wait for him to use his card or make a phone call, and she would pounce.

FIFTY-THREE

Kane parked the hire car in the car park of a small shopping plaza in Saggart, the next village over from Rathcoole and only a short drive away from the Poitín Stil pub. The L-shaped set of one-storey buildings contained a Dunnes grocery store, a barber, a pharmacy and an Insomnia coffee shop.

He tucked his pistol into his waistband and strolled to the coffee shop. Kane ordered a large pot of tea and a muffin. He tapped the payment on Craven's credit card, grabbed a handful of sugar sachets and took a seat in the rear corner of the shop so that he faced the entrance and its large front windows. Kane took out Craven's mobile phone and called Barb in Spain to check on her and the kids.

She answered, and they made small talk for a

few minutes. The children were in bed, but Barb assured him they were fine. They had taken a trip to the beach that day and spent the afternoon playing in the sea and making sandcastles. Kane thanked Barb for her help and then ended the call.

Using Craven's card and phone would act like a magnet to the killers who had come for Kane's head. All he had to do was wait. There were cameras in the store and around the car park, so once he was done, Kane had to get out of the country quickly before An Garda Síochána tracked him down. He felt like the shark in a Jaws movie, a blipping signal stuck to its back as it circled the deep sea. The pursuers thought themselves the hunters and Kane the prey. But they were wrong.

Kane added two sugars to his tea and took a sip. It was a little tart, so he added more milk. The muffin was soft and doughy, and the blueberries were bright blue, like police sirens. Only one other customer was seated in the café, a man in a roll-neck sweater with a small espresso cup in front of him. He typed on a laptop with such speed that Kane thought the thing might shoot sparks if he went any faster. The sound of the large, black coffee machine hummed and ground its beans. Chrome facings gleamed, and the barista lifted a silver milk jug towards the milk frother. Its curved tube coughed, spluttered, and gurgled the milk into a luxurious froth.

He waited, drinking his tea and finishing his muffin. Kane shifted in his seat and tried his utmost to force his mind to think about the Kelleher case or how he would deal with the assassins once they came for him. But downtime was ever his enemy, and his thoughts wandered to his dead wife. Sally had been the love of his life, and he loved her still. The pain of her loss gnawed at his heart with vicious teeth, and she lived in his brain like a tortured prisoner. Her ghost accused him of not being there when she needed him most. What was the use of his skills if he couldn't protect his family?

Danny and Kim, his beautiful children, also forced their way into his wandering daydream. The familiar worry about their welfare and futures nagged at him, telling Kane that he could not care for them properly. How could he keep them safe and make sure they received a stable childhood and a proper education if killers hunted him at every turn? It was a problem that wouldn't go away and one that he couldn't fix with weapons or guile.

After an hour, two men in overcoats and baseball caps walked from the car park and alongside the high, wide coffee shop windows. One was tall with a long beard and coiffed moustache, and the other was short and bulky. The door dinged as it opened, and the two men scanned the premises. They saw the espresso man hammering away at his keyboard and then spotted Kane. He stared back at them, resisting the ridiculous urge to wave. They looked like Americans, with their caps and tan overcoats over tactical trousers and black boots.

The two men glanced at each other and then at Kane. He shifted his feet underneath the table and placed his hands on his knees. The men took four strides forward, eyes shadowed beneath the peaks of their caps, mouths set in hard, unforgiving lines. The tall man wore a New York Yankees cap and reached into his jacket, and the smaller man in a Chicago Cubs hat dropped his hand to his waist.

Just as the assassins reached for their concealed guns, Kane sprang up from his seat. The cup and teapot smashed on the floor, and hot water splashed onto the window. Kane lifted the table as he charged forward, holding its circular top before him like a medieval shield. The barista screamed as she saw the cold metal of the Americans' guns. Kane didn't check, but he hoped she would follow her instincts and duck behind the coffee bar for safety. The espresso man fell from his chair in horror, and Kane was aware of the man's legs scrambling towards the milk and sugar section to his right.

A silenced gunshot spat from a pistol, and the bullet banged into the table, sending reverberations up Kane's arms. With the speed and aggression of a man in a fight for his life, Kane was upon the Americans in a flash. The table crashed into the two men, and Kane drove them backwards towards the doors. The tall man leapt to his right, and Kane brought the table down, smashing its rim into the man's shins, causing him to bellow in pain. Kane turned quickly. He threw the table at the smaller man, and it cannoned into him, sending a bullet careening into the ceiling.

Kane dived on the taller man, securing his gun hand and wrapping his legs around him to secure an arm bar. The American relinquished the weapon, attempting to break out of Kane's grip by spinning his legs. Kane seized the opportunity. He let go of the man's arm, grabbed his gun, and shot the man twice in the face.

Immediately, Kane dodged as the smaller man shot at him. Kane rolled away and back towards the corpse just as two silenced bullets slapped into the dead American's torso. Kane pointed his weapon at his attacker and then sprang to his feet in wary surprise as the smaller man's head exploded in a cloud of red blood and pale flesh before crumpling to the tiled floor, leaving the smear of his head matter on the wall behind him.

Kane trained his gun around to find a tall woman standing behind the coffee counter holding a silenced twelve-gauge shotgun. It was the same assassin from the stud farm, now dressed in business trousers and a blouse.

"You're mine," she growled down the barrel of her gun. "I've fought too hard to let someone else steal my kill."

"You again," tutted Kane. He lowered his gun. "I had hoped that after our last conversation, you might have realised that this is not what you signed up for."

"Do you really want to spend your last moments giving me a lecture?" She moved aside to let the whimpering barista scuttle out of the back door.

"Killing me does not protect our country from its enemies. I was you once, and I..."

Kane fell silent as the coffee shop's front door opened with a ping, revealing four men armed with MP5 rifles. Clad in tracksuits and Nike trainers, they entered, but the woman swiftly shot one of them before he could raise his weapon to fire. The shotgun's power threw him back against the door, cracking its glass, and then the coffee shop turned into a churning nightmare of bullets, blood, and carnage.

FIFTY-FOUR

Kane kicked a table over and hid behind its faux pine top. Bullets smacked against the underside, but he remained calm, in control of his adrenaline, the master of his fear. To his right, the woman fired her last shotgun round, and a man roared in agony as the shell released its deadly spray of tiny balls to rip through skin and bone. She dived to her left without realising that she was moving in Kane's direction.

"Bastard," she hissed at him.

Kane fired his pistol over the table's rim and risked a peek around its edge.

"Two left," he said, "coming around to flank us." The track-suited assassins moved like predators, crouching with their MP5s held at eye level. Gunfire had smashed the coffee shop's windows, and it would only be a matter of minutes before An Garda Síochána arrived at another gun battle in a quiet Irish town.

"There is no us."

"You take the one on the left."

"Fuck you." She snarled but sprang into action, pulling a Sig Sauer pistol from her belt. Kane laughed at the hate in her, at the irony of the woman helping him to survive just so that she could kill him later.

A shot whipped past Kane's face, so close that it stung his eyes, and he rolled away. Gunfire behind him told of the woman's exchange with her target. As Kane assessed the situation, he saw a man in a black tracksuit surge towards him, a bearded man with a scar across his forehead. He was trying to get closer. The numerous missed shots suggested he wasn't a professional, and the urgency to get close indicated his desire to finish the job before more of his men died.

Kane feinted to fire at the man, darted left, and then came back right. The man took the decoy and surged into the space Kane should have been in, and then Kane was upon him. Within arm's reach, he fired his Glock, but the man reacted just in time and batted the weapon aside. Kane punched him in the stomach, and it was like hitting a slab of cement.

The big man fired at him, but the shot fizzed past Kane's midriff. Kane grabbed the man's gun, and the man grabbed his. Kane headbutted him, feeling the crunch of his nose on his forehead, but the man rolled with the blow and threw Kane over his hip. Kane crashed to the tiled floor and spun on his back, driving a foot into the man's chest and twisting the gun from his hand. The man gasped in panic, dark eyes aghast as Kane shot him once in the throat and once in the eye. The track-suited man hung there, propped up by Kane's foot. Thick blood oozed from his throat, and his eye was a black, cavernous hole. Kane peered into it, and for a moment, he thought he could see into the man's soul. He wondered if he was a good man or a bad one, whether he had a family, and if his mother was alive, would she weep for her dead son?

Kane snapped himself out of his momentary daze and pushed the bloody corpse away. He clambered to his feet and turned to face the rest of the assassins. The woman crouched behind the coffee bar, gesturing with her hand to show that the last track-suited killer was on the other side. Kane nodded and ran to the end of the bar, where the barista would hand steaming coffee to waiting customers.

Without pause, Kane manoeuvered around the counter to find the man on his hunkers, sucking in deep breaths and clutching his MP5.

He had come with three colleagues to kill one man, and they must have thought that it would be an easy day's work – simply butcher Jack Kane with rapid fire from their semi-automatic weapons and collect a rich bounty. They would be out of the country that very day. Perhaps they had planned a holiday, basking in the sun before their next job. The man had jet-black hair swept back from his face and a wash of stubble on his cheeks and chin. He was young, in his early twenties, with a life yet to live, and Kane killed him with a bullet through his left ear.

Kane moved in closer and put another shot into the man's forehead. The woman stood from her hiding place, and she and Kane held each other's gaze for a fleeting moment. She had almond-shaped eyes, dark and deep above a full mouth. The woman was tall and graceful, clever, ruthless and relentless. She was beautiful, Kane thought.

Glass crunched to Kane's left, and a man walked in wearing an Irish Garda police uniform. He was muscled and tanned, with the features of a Middle Eastern man. The man stared at Kane, the woman, and the blood-soaked carnage around them. He looked perplexed, like a dog looking for an imaginary stick thrown by its owner. The tanned imposter had a gun in his right hand, but he failed to raise it in time before the woman shot him in the thigh with her pistol.

The man fell, rolling in broken glass, and the woman shot him again in the shoulder so that his gun spun out of his hand.

Kane had to leave before the real police arrived. He jumped onto the counter and skidded across its shining top on his arse. As the woman turned back towards him, gun poised to rip his life away in a triumphant kill, Kane cracked the butt of his weapon across her skull.

The woman crumpled to the floor, unconscious and sleeping like a murderous baby. Kane tucked his weapon into his belt and stalked away from the coffee shop. Terrified eyes peered at him from behind walls and over car bonnets as he walked to his vehicle. Those who had come to kill Kane were dead, which would hopefully buy him some time to help John Kelleher get his daughter back. He wasn't sure why he hadn't killed the woman. Maybe it was her eyes, or maybe he admired her. But he hoped he wouldn't regret that moment of pity.

FIFTY-FIVE

"So, you're a friend of Jack's then?" asked the English voice at the end of the phone. The man's voice was muffled as though he spoke through a curtain.

"Yes, although at this moment in time, I'm not sure if that's a good thing or not," replied Craven, and he glanced at Fran Doyle, whose mouth turned into an upside-down smile of knowing sympathy.

"He's one of a kind," said the voice on the phone. "He saved my life, and I don't normally stick my head up like this. So, you need to follow my instructions carefully. If you deviate, or if I feel like my safety is threatened, I'm gone. Is that clear?"

"Crystal." Kane had left a list of instructions for Craven and Doyle to follow. Craven knew next to nothing about technology, but luckily, Fran Doyle was savvy enough with secure IP addresses, masked DNS, and other tech jargon that completely flew over Craven's head. They needed to connect to the internet securely, in an untraceable way, and Doyle seemed confident in his ability to get them up and running.

Doyle cracked his fingers and opened the sleek black laptop. He changed the blue screen to a black screen with a blinking cursor and typed in some gibberish. The screen flickered and then whizzed into a cascade of blipping screens and prompts, urging Doyle to continue typing.

"It's like the fucking Matrix," Craven marvelled. The man on the phone sighed, and Fran Doyle shook his head. After another few seconds, the screen crackled, and a man in a mask appeared. The mask, pristine white and gleaming like porcelain, startled Craven, jolting his chair back half a metre. "Jesus Christ, I nearly shat myself."

"Alright, Cameron, we have you on screen," said Fran Doyle. He sat back and smiled at his handiwork. Giving Craven a clap on the shoulder, he gestured towards the screen as though he had completed an impressive feat of workmanship. They sat in the office of Doyle's house in Calverstown, a small rural village in County Kildare. An Garda Síochána presence was still heavy at the stud, so Doyle's house seemed like a better location for the two men to set up their technology hub.

"I am sharing my screen via a bouncing network of secure IP addresses," Cameron explained. The mask he wore tilted slightly from side to side as he spoke. One eye was painted black, the other invisible in the recesses of the mask's eyehole, and the mouth was set in a cruel, hard slit without the sense of any human flesh behind it. Kane had warned Craven what to expect from Cameron, but hearing about a man wearing a white mask and actually seeing it were different things. "So, we are totally secure here."

"Same on my end," said Doyle in his Dublin accent. "I followed your instructions to the letter, new laptop, and all the other bits and pieces."

"Good. I've checked your line, and everything seems secure. My understanding is that we have a target to track, and we're looking for any activity that provides a location or series of locations for that target."

"That's right," nodded Craven. "We also need to figure out a way to prove to the kidnappers that we have the cryptocurrency they want as part of the ransom."

"Leave the crypto part of the problem to me. So, what information can you give me on the target?"

Craven pulled a crumpled envelope out of

his jacket pocket. It was the same envelope he had used to take notes since the start of the investigation, and it had addresses, phone numbers, and marks scrawled across it in blue biro ink. Fran Doyle stared at the envelope and up at Craven with a horrified look on his face. Doyle's eyebrows raised so high they almost sprang off his round face.

"I have a system," Craven assured Doyle with a wink. "We have debit and credit card details for Mrs Caitriona Kelleher, some store cards, her mobile phone number, and lots of other numbers for you to try. Then we need to run a check on James Baldwin, a former British police officer and mercenary active in the Middle East."

"What about Mrs Kelleher's passport number?" asked Cameron.

"We have that too. Her husband retrieved it from one of the airline apps on his phone."

"Good. Have Kane and Mr Kelleher left for Paris?"

"They are on their way. We expect a further location to be provided by the kidnappers once they arrive."

"So, the plan is for Kane to intercept the kidnappers before they hand the ransom over?"

"Yes, but to do that, we need to find their

location using your technological wizardry."

"Do we have the money?"

"Bit of a problem there," said Fran Doyle. "The insurance company has confirmed that they won't pay out because Mrs Kelleher is involved with the crime."

"Can Kelleher raise the funds through his assets?"

"He's in debt up to his bollocks. Even if he sold the stud and all of his horses, it would never happen in time to get the money ready by the deadline."

"And what happens to the girl if we don't pay?"

"Your man Baldwin says he will kill Annie and cut her into little pieces."

"Fuck," Cameron sighed. "Give me what you have then, and let's see if we can pin the mother down and determine who this Baldwin really is."

FIFTY-SIX

The pain in her skull was like a knife jabbing through bone and brain with repeated hammer blows. It woke her, and Condor ground her teeth, forcing down the reflex to whimper at the litany of injuries across her battered body. Condor cracked open one eye, and light shot into her head, heightening the pain, twisting the knife in her skull so that she had to close her eyes again. There was motion around her, and a siren was blaring. She tried to move, but a strap across her chest and arms kept her pinned to a bed. Then she remembered Kane, the assassins, and the café. He had evaded her again and left her unconscious with a crushing blow to her head.

Condor's brain told her to lie back and rest. To keep her eyes closed and let the pain subside in the warm embrace of sleep, but then her heart reminded her who she was, what she had been through, and what she wanted. She was a warrior, a fighter who had come from less than nothing to rise and become a skilled and deadly special agent, and she would continue to climb and build her career. To do that, she had to kill Jack Kane. Condor opened her eyes and refused to let the blinding light subdue her. She was in an ambulance, and an Irish Garda officer sat across from her. The siren came from the ambulance, and it rocked and swayed as the driver moved through traffic to transport her to the hospital. Condor had too many injuries to contemplate, but she would not let them slow her.

She still wore the clothes she had worn to the café, a business suit and shirt, and they had taken away her weapons but left her hands uncuffed. That was their first mistake. Perhaps they hadn't realised that she was the shooter involved in the gunfight, or perhaps they failed to understand just how dangerous she was. Condor glanced at the policeman. He carried no firearm that she could see, only a spray and baton. An Garda Síochána officers do not carry firearms. In Ireland, only specially trained firearms units are armed with handguns and automatic weapons. That was their second mistake.

Condor wriggled on the gurney and shifted herself lower inside the strap so that it moved higher up her chest and upper arms. The guard glanced at her and frowned. He was heavyset with a neatly trimmed beard and dark eyes. Condor just stared back at him. His radio crackled imperceptibly. The ambulance felt sterile and stank of disinfectant, like a hospital washroom bleached and scrubbed by diligent cleaners.

"Keep still," said the guard, his voice deep with a strong Irish lilt.

Condor took a deep breath to prepare herself and then exploded into action. She surged down into the strap again, creating enough room to raise her right hand at the elbow and find the clip. She deftly opened the strap, and as the guard's expression changed from annoyance to surprise, Condor braced herself with her left hand and then pivoted on the gurney. Her long legs came around in a whir, and her right foot cracked across his jaw. She kept moving, landing on top of him with her left knee pressed to his chest, and she cannoned the heel of her right hand into the joint where jaw met skull.

Condor rose and took a second to gather herself. The pain in her skull was nauseating, and her ankle was swollen and stung like shattered glass inside her flesh. Myriad cuts, scrapes, and bruises throbbed and pulsed all over her body, adding to her discomfort. Condor sucked up all the pain, using it to steel her resolve even further. She rifled through the various drawers and cabinets in the ambulance and took painkillers, bandages, sterilising wipes and a bottle of water. She put the items into a clear plastic bag from a tear-away roll behind the gurney and drank the water in a series of thirsty gulps.

The ambulance came to a halt, and Condor quickly knelt down, relieving the unconscious guard of his radio on the ambulance floor. Opening the back, sunlight flooded in as she leapt outside, not bothering to wait for her eyes to adjust. Despite her injured ankle, she sprinted away from the ambulance at full speed, refusing to let her injury slow her pace. Shouting erupted behind her, and Condor risked a glance over her shoulder. Three police cars marked in luminous yellow and green had pulled in behind the ambulance, and officers burst from the doors to pursue her. Two of them were firearms officers and came with Heckler & Koch MP7s held high on their chests.

Condor ran to a set of traffic lights, weaving between cars and darting left to where a busy dual carriageway intersection split in four directions. She ran to a line of yellow and blue Dublin Bus double-decker vehicles that sat in a layby and then jumped to the right to conceal herself between two buses. A man with neck tattoos and a topknot hairstyle stared blankly at her from the bus stop. Condor waited, using the rear window of the bus in front of her to watch the corner hospital entrance and the bus behind her to hide from any approach.

An armed officer of medium height with a lean, fit build came sprinting around the corner. He was fast, legs and arms pumping to catch up with Condor, his face set in grim determination. Condor sprang from between the buses and kicked the running officer's legs from under him. He sprawled on the pavement with a grunt, and the tattooed man leapt away in alarm. The guard rolled on the ground and met the heel of Condor's shoe with his cheek. She knelt on his chest, unclipped his MP7 and used the weapon's butt to knock him unconscious. More policemen came hurtling around the bend, and Condor let off a burst of automatic weapon fire. Bullets raked the hedging and pavement, cannoning off granite and brick, sending the pursuing officers scattering for cover.

Condor ripped a spare magazine of ammunition from the fallen officer's vest and tucked it into the back of her trousers. The MP7 could hold either twenty, thirty, or forty rounds, so she hoped it was the larger capacity. Condor ran into the road where traffic had screeched to a panicked halt. She fired another round into the air, ignored the warning shouts from the remaining armed officers, and dragged a bald businessman in a pinstripe suit from a blue BMW 5 Series. He yelped and covered his face with his hands, and Condor pushed him towards the Garda officers hiding behind the cover of two buses.

She sat in the BMW's driving seat, put the automatic gear stick into drive and slammed on the accelerator. Condor sped away from the hospital and the scene of carnage. She pushed the car to its limits, heading along the dual carriageway towards Dublin city centre, where she would lose herself in the crowds and the snarl of backstreets and alleyways.

There was an iPhone and a wallet in the well between the gearstick and the radio controls, and Condor allowed herself a smile. She was free, armed, and ready for the hunt.

FIFTY-SEVEN

Kane bought a cup of coffee and a chocolate croissant from a kiosk inside the huge Paris Gare du Nord train station, one of the largest stations in Europe. In France, they rarely sold drinkable tea, and the coffee in European countries was always too strong for Kane, so he added a dash of milk and poured in three sachets of white sugar. Kelleher ordered an espresso, which he drank in one gulp. They had departed from Ireland early on Thursday afternoon, taking the car ferry from Dublin to Holyhead, Anglesey, using Kelleher's Range Rover as Kane had left Craven's hire vehicle in Ireland.

Kelleher and Kane had until Friday to get to Paris, and it would have been quicker and easier to fly from Dublin to Paris Charles de Gaulle

Airport. They could have made the journey by air in a couple of hours, but Kane expected Baldwin to be watching for Kelleher's travel arrangements. To fly with a bag of money was impossible. It wouldn't pass through the security bag screenings at Dublin Airport, no matter how cunningly concealed. If they were to convince Baldwin that they had the ransom money, they had to make the journey by car.

They had arrived in Holyhead late Thursday evening and then made the six-hour drive from North Wales to Folkestone during the night. Kane and Kelleher took turns at the wheel, driving three hours each so that the other could catch some sleep. Kane had used Craven's credit card at a service station north of London and then again at Folkestone. He wanted to make sure that any further assassins on his tail, or the fearsome woman he had left unconscious in Dublin, followed him rather than try to take down Craven or decide to check out his friend's home in Málaga.

The drive from Folkestone through the Eurotunnel to Paris took another four and a half hours. On the road south from Calais, Kane stopped and used the credit card outside Lens and then again at Senlis to continue the trail of breadcrumbs for any would-be pursuers. They arrived at the Gare du Nord train station just before lunchtime on Friday and spent the afternoon waiting, sitting on white plastic chairs outside the kiosk, Kelleher on tenterhooks.

"Looking at it will not make it ring," said Kane, taking a bite of the croissant he'd purchased minutes earlier as Kelleher checked his phone for the hundredth time that hour. He placed the phone face down on the white table but then glanced at the station's iconic hall clock to check the time again.

"Jesus, Kane. If we get this wrong, my Annie is dead," Kelleher stressed. He had repeated that phrase constantly on the long journey from Dublin to Paris, which was understandable. They carried a leather holdall full of chopped-up paper instead of cash, gambling that Kane could retrieve Annie before Baldwin and his men figured out that Kelleher could not secure the ransom from his insurance policy.

"We won't get it wrong. You should eat something."

"How can I eat when my daughter is on the verge of being murdered and my wife is behind it all?"

Kane couldn't argue with reason. Kelleher wore a half-zip jumper over a blue shirt. Two-day stubble shadowed his jaw and neck. He stared at Kane through puffy eyes ringed with dark circles.

"I understand what you are going through. You can't help worrying, but it won't get Annie back safely any faster."

"How can you possibly understand how it feels to have your daughter put in harm's way by your money-grabbing bitch of a wife?"

Kane glanced up at the high roof. Iron pillars rose into intricately wrought patterns where they met the beams which held up the vast ceiling. Light poured in through a strip of glass that traversed the length of the roof at its apex and from semi-circular windows along the high walls above the different terminal entrances. The air was heady with the rich aroma of roasting coffee and the sickly sweet smell of vapes. A woman with pink hair blew out a monstrous cloud of vape smoke as she marched past their table, talking passionately on her phone in rapid Metropolitan French.

"Someone took my children away from me," Kane spoke wistfully as though it was something that had happened in a dream.

"Really? What happened?"

"I got them back, but many people died." He didn't want to elaborate on the gory and painful details of what had happened to him last spring. He particularly didn't want to talk of Sally and how she had died at the hands of those who came after him. That was a wound that would never heal, a soul-scraping loss which Kane kept under lock and key in the depths of his mind, too painful to explore or try to comprehend.

"Where are your kids now?"

"Safe, in another country. Remember this, John. Your wife might have done the unthinkable here, but I doubt she would stand by and let Baldwin and his men hurt Annie. They want the money, that's all. They'll hold out as long as they believe there's a possibility that we have the cash and the crypto."

"She's ruined me." Kelleher put his head in his hands and raked his fingernails down his forehead. "Even before this bloody debacle, she had bled me dry. Cars, holidays, botox, clothes. I knew she was drinking and snorting that awful stuff, but I turned a blind eye. I loved her. I never thought she would stoop this low."

Kane's burner phone buzzed in his jacket pocket. He wore a navy Hugo Boss suit with a white shirt and black shoes. Kane had brought along three shirts and changed into a fresh one after they had parked the car in Paris. He had given the burner number to Craven and Franchetti, and he hoped it was the former, but it turned out to be the latter.

"It's Franchetti," he said, reading the text

message aloud. "He's arrived here in Paris and is waiting for instructions."

"Do you think the Americans can help get Annie back?"

"They have resources, so hopefully they can help, yes." Kane didn't say that he preferred to work alone and that the Americans would get in his way. He was waiting for Craven to come back to him with the information Cameron had gathered on Mrs Kelleher and Baldwin's whereabouts. Once that came in, he would need to get there and get Annie out before the money drop, so Franchetti could potentially help get Kane to the location. "But he says they need to leave for the US tomorrow, so he doesn't have much time."

"Good of them to help. Their work is done. The insurance company won't pay out on the policy now that they know Cait is involved."

Kane nodded, but he said nothing. Franchetti could and probably should have left once he had found out the truth of the situation for his employers, but Kane knew that Franchetti's crew were on the clock and that the insurance company would pay his costs. Franchetti and his men were ex-military, so any sniff of action would get their blood up. They'd be all in if there was a chance to get their guns off before the paid contract concluded. The men Kane had served with in the SAS were the same. Fighters loved to fight, and there were few chances outside the military. So, any opportunity to ply their trade was like honey to a bear.

Kane finished his croissant and coffee and replied to Franchetti, asking him to be on standby until they heard from Baldwin. Kelleher checked his phone every twenty seconds, and when it eventually rang, he almost dropped it in fearful surprise.

"This is John Kelleher," he said, putting the phone on speaker mode so Kane could hear.

"Are you in Paris, and do you have the money?" Baldwin uttered, his Liverpudlian voice deep and serious.

"Yes. I have the money, and I'm at the Gare du Nord," said Kelleher.

"Good. Take a picture to prove where you are and send it to this number."

Baldwin hung up, and Kelleher swallowed hard. "What if he asks for a picture of the money?"

"He wants confirmation that you are actually here. Baldwin and his men will be paranoid that you are stringing him along whilst the police are closing in on him. Just send him a picture of that sign." Kane gestured to the ceramic tiles above an entranceway, clearly displaying 'Gare Du Nord' in black letters.

Kelleher took the picture and immediately sent it to the number. Seconds later, the phone rang again.

"Now, you are going to follow my instructions and do exactly as I say if you want your daughter back in one piece."

FIFTY-EIGHT

Craven glanced at Fran Doyle and then back at the screen, trying to look like he knew what was going on. Cameron still had his own computer set to screen share, which meant Craven and Doyle could see everything the tech expert clicked and typed on the system at his end.

"She's been smart," Fran Doyle tutted. He stood up from his chair and stretched his back. In doing so, his bulging belly came within a handsbreadth of Craven's face.

"If I wanted a whiff of the cheese in your belly button, I'd bloody ask for it," said Craven, shifting back uncomfortably.

"Sorry about that, buddy. My back gets sore if I sit down for too long."

"Doesn't look like we have anything on Mrs

Kelleher yet, anyway."

"She hasn't used her cards, her phone is off, and she's dropped off the grid. Must be the first time she has bought nothing in twenty-four hours since before she was married."

"Her phone is off, but I can still track her," Cameron spoke up through the tinny laptop speakers.

"I don't understand how you can track her when the thing is turned on, never mind when it's turned off," Craven said. "We are against the clock here. Jack and John will be waiting around in Paris by now, and if this long shot is to have any chance of working, we need Kane to find Annie before Baldwin figures out that we don't have the ransom."

Cameron's screen blinked, and then the moving pieces of data and black-and-white text flickered off to reveal his white mask. Craven frowned at the screen. The mask made him feel like he was talking to a robot or something from a nightmare. Kane had explained that Cameron had suffered unthinkable injuries during his time in the special forces, but it didn't make the mask any easier to look at.

"Your mobile phone can be tracked quite easily based on the signal it sends out, which bounces off the network of phone masts around the world. Network providers can then keep a record of the date and time of any calls, texts, app usage, and user location. I can access those systems and find the information."

"But her phone is off?"

"Most people aren't aware, but they can track your phone even when it's turned off. We first used the technology in the war against Al-Qaeda. Unless the battery has been removed, a phone emits a small residual signal picked up by the telephone signal masts. It used to be that we would need to infect the phone with malware or specific software to make that possible. But not anymore."

"In the interests of time, I won't ask you what malware is. But can you find her?"

"I've found her already, and Baldwin."

"Ah, Jaysus," said Doyle, blowing his out cheeks in frustration, "why didn't you say that in the first place?"

"I've found the Saudi jet that Baldwin's using and tracked that when I couldn't pick up Mrs Kelleher. They've landed at Hans Christian Andersen Airport, and her phone is emitting a residual signal from the countryside to the north of it."

"Hans Christian Andersen, the kids'

storyteller?" asked Craven, becoming increasingly confused the longer Cameron continued to speak.

"Well, yes. But more specifically, an airport that carries his name in Odense, Denmark."

"So, the bastards are in Denmark?"

"Yes. They landed their plane in Odense and then travelled north to a small beachside place called Gyldensteen Strand."

"Cameron, you are a bloody genius!" exclaimed Craven. "We need to let Kane know immediately. He's in Paris now, and he needs to get to Denmark."

"Denmark is bloody miles away from Paris," said Doyle.

"All the more reason he needs to get moving now."

"That's where the jet flew to, and it's where Mrs Kelleher is," Cameron intoned. He leaned forward so that his mask came closer to the screen, making his appearance even eerier. "But we can't say for sure that's where Annie is."

"But it's our best guess, so we have to go with it." Craven glanced at Fran Doyle for confirmation, and the big Irishman dragged a hand down his clean-shaven face and nodded his head. "Now. What about that bloody crypto thing?"

"OK, so this is a bit more complicated. Baldwin wants half of his ransom paid in Monero cryptocurrency, which uses blockchain with enhanced privacy tech to make transactions impossible to trace. That means transactions, history, location, and owner are all secure. It's used on the dark web and by many nefarious organisations to shift money worldwide, for money laundering, and organised crime."

"I don't understand most of what you said, but it's money for bad guys, right?"

"Yeah, sort of. I've created a fake crypto wallet with a convincing logo and balance. Baldwin can try to verify it using several coin market sites, but because he asked for the coin in Monero, the untraceable aspect comes back to bite him."

"What the fuck does that mean?" asked Craven, losing his patience and feeling like a caveman.

"Well, Baldwin wants Monero. If he wanted Bitcoin, for example, he could check the contract address against the official token. He can't do that with Monero, so he will have to assume that the fake wallet I have created is real."

"Which is good, right?"

"Yes, it's good. Now, one more thing," the

timbre of Cameron's voice dropped. "I checked Baldwin out. He's a nasty piece of work. I can trace him and his company to lots of atrocities in Syria, Palestine, and North Africa. Baldwin and his men are killers working for the highest bidder, dictators, military juntas, you name it. So his threat against Annie's life is very real."

"Alright, then. Let's get Kane briefed and see if we can bring Annie home safe and well," said Craven. He didn't know Cameron, but for all the strangeness of his mask and the techy jargon, if Kane trusted him, then that was good enough for him. They had to believe that Cameron's work had been accurate, that the location was reliable, and that the fake crypto wallet would effectively convince Baldwin. If Baldwin got spooked, then Annie was dead. So, Craven took a deep breath and dialled Kane's burner number.

FIFTY-NINE

McGovern paced across the width of her office. Her heels clicked on the tiles and then turned silent as she marched across the plush rug placed beneath her oak desk and the two leather visitors' chairs. The television on the wall hung over expensive, tasteful wallpaper. On the screen, a news presenter stood in front of a small shopping centre in Ireland, her hair whipped by the wind and her vivid red lipstick contrasting starkly with the dour grey buildings behind her. The caption across the yellow scrolling section at the bottom of the screen spoke of carnage and slayings in suburban Ireland.

A twisting, hollow feeling rolled around in McGovern's stomach as she approached her desk. Fumbling through a chaotic assortment of papers and green folders, she hunted for the remote control. After a brief search, she found it beside her laptop case and clicked the power button. It didn't work. She clicked the red button again, but still nothing.

"For Christ's sake," she huffed, pressing the back of her hand to her forehead. Nothing was going right. Condor, usually so dependable, ruthless and efficient, had utterly mishandled the Kane situation. Now, the private contract had backfired. Assassins in a County Dublin coffee shop, multiple gunshots, and uproar. McGovern took a deep breath. She popped open the sliding clip on the back of the remote, took one battery out, shook it, and pushed it back in. She pressed the power button once more, and the television flickered before switching off to leave the screen black and silent and her office peaceful.

McGovern calmly placed the remote control back on the desk and straightened her shirt. She glanced at the blank television screen, catching her reflection, and ran the fingers of her right hand through her hair to straighten it out.

"I can fix this," she said to herself, shadows playing on her cheekbones in the darkness of the blacked-out screen. "This is my time. This is my chance. Focus. Maintain control."

The room with its antique desk still smelled of old MI6, stale cigarette smoke and good whiskey.

McGovern liked it that way and had deliberately tossed out any air fresheners left on the shelves by the cleaners. The atmosphere lent to the historic nature of the job and underscored the challenges she had overcome as a woman to rise to the higher tier of what once was an entirely male-dominated world. A file labelled 'Medusa' rested on the desk. That was going to be her unit, the new Mjolnir. But its very existence teetered on a knife edge, and if she couldn't end Jack Kane, it would die before ever seeing the light of day.

McGovern had such grand plans for the Medusa agency, women in positions of power, more funds than she could possibly spend, international travel, covert operations and a genuine ambition to help influence the world on a global scale. She would right the wrongs of Mjolnir and use her agents to bring stability back to a world gone mad. She could prevent wars and international incidents with a stroke of her pen, take the credit, and work her way upwards until there were no more glass ceilings to shatter.

A rap on the heavy door snapped McGovern from her daydream, and she pushed a stray hair behind her ear.

"Yes," she said loudly and confidently. She was in control; nothing could fluster her.

Harry entered and flashed an upside-down smile. He closed the door and stood with his hands clasped behind him, his military background as evident in his stance as in his high and tight haircut.

"Sorry to disturb you, ma'am," he said in a cockney accent he tried so very hard to soften. He licked his lips, and his blue eyes flicked from her to the floor.

"Yes, what is it?"

"Mr Aziz's secretary called. He wants to come and see you on Monday. Your diary is full, but the secretary was very insistent. So I have moved your ten o'clock and put Mr Aziz there instead."

"Monday," she said wistfully. It wasn't a question, more of a statement to herself.

"Yes, ma'am. Should I grab you a coffee?"

"Coffee? Yes."

He stared at her, his mouth half open as though he wanted to say something else. She returned his gaze and couldn't help the vacant look on her face. McGovern remained still until Harry left the room, the door clicking closed behind him. Only then did she allow her lip to quiver, but only for five heartbeats. Her hands balled into fists, and she clenched her jaw, the muscles behind her cheeks working and shifting with rage.

"Bastards!" she shouted, the reference

encompassing Condor, Aziz, Kane, the MI6 bigwig who had insulted only days earlier and everyone who had ever doubted her. McGovern swiped the papers off the surface of her desk with a sweep of her right arm. She banged her fist on the table and reached for her mobile phone.

It had gone too far. McGovern had to remove Kane from the chessboard immediately – no more of the softly-softly approach. It was time to break out a hammer. She still had access to resources, and the private bounty she had put on Kane's head remained unclaimed. McGovern typed a message, her manicured fingernails tip-tapping furiously on the digital keypad. Condor was finished, and McGovern would turn her loose. Her incompetence would be McGovern's sacrificial offering to the gods of luck and career progression. McGovern could blame the failings to date on Condor and the dying embers of Mjolnir's ineptness. Condor wasn't part of Mjolnir, but McGovern could tar her with that brush. Condor was finished. A desk job beckoned for the once-so-promising agent.

McGovern hit send, and her message winged its way across the secure pathways of digital messaging to an elite ex-military mercenary team. She had used such teams before, back in the days of the war on terror when private ex-special forces teams made fortunes doing the tasks government military operatives could not.

This team was the best, and they would take care of Jack Kane. It all had to be done before Monday so that McGovern could meet Aziz with the case closed and the door of her future wide open.

SIXTY

John Kelleher stared at the phone. He held it upside down, and both he and Kane leaned towards the microphone on its bottom end to hear Baldwin's instructions over the din of the bustling Gare du Nord station.

"If you're at the station," Baldwin spoke slowly and confidently, "you have half of the money with you in cash and the other half ready to go in Monero crypto. First, I am going to need confirmation that you have the crypto ready to transfer, so send me a screenshot of the account with the funds in and ready to transfer. OK?"

Kelleher looked at Kane, and Kane nodded. "Yes, I have that ready," said Kelleher. Kane winced at the nervousness in his voice but hoped that Baldwin would assume it was just fear for his daughter's safety and not suspect any tricks.

"Good boy, John. I must admit, I never thought you had it in you. I thought you'd send someone else to do your dirty work. Is that mug Craven with you?"

"No, Craven isn't here."

"What about Kane, then? He there?"

Kelleher looked up again, unsure what to say, and Kane nodded again – he thought it best not to lie in case Baldwin had someone watching them at the station.

"Yes, Kane is here."

"Tell him to get any funny business ideas out of his head. He can go with you so you don't get fucking robbed on the way, but if he tries anything, I'll send you Annie's head in a box. That clear?"

"Clear."

"Right then, Johnny boy. Send me the confirmation of your crypto wallet, and then I want you to transfer the coin to me before we meet to exchange the cash. You can send it to…"

"You don't get the coin or the cash until we can see Annie in front of us," Kane interjected.

Kelleher shook his head violently, fearing that

Kane might provoke the man who held his daughter's life in his hands.

"You'll do what I fucking tell you. Do you hear me?"

"We'll follow your instructions, but we won't give you anything until Annie is in front of us. We want to hand over the money for her in one go. No separate locations for ransom and exchange."

There was a pause, and beads of sweat broke out on Kelleher's forehead. Kane wouldn't have sent the coin to Baldwin even if they did have it. With that much money, there was nothing to stop Baldwin from forgetting the cash and leaving Annie for dead. But the cat-and-mouse game of ransom demand and payment was irrelevant. They didn't have the money or the coin, so Kane had to string Baldwin along and find enough time to rescue Annie before Baldwin realised that.

"You're not as stupid as you look. Alright, send me the wallet confirmation, and we'll do the transfer when we hand over the cash. You are going to take an Uber from Paris to Fredericia Station in Denmark as soon as we finish the call. The journey will take you just under thirteen hours. You will share your trip status with this number, but I will also send you a text with six different stops, and you are going to call this number and send a picture of each stop when you get there. Clear so far?"

"Yes," replied John Kelleher.

"When you get to Fredericia, you will call this number again and await further instructions. Do you understand?"

"I understand."

"Wait," said Kane. "Will you be at Fredericia with Annie?"

"You'll have to wait and see. For now, do as I say. Send me the picture of the crypto wallet and get in the Uber to Denmark."

Baldwin hung up the phone. Kane reached down to his watch and set a timer to count down to thirteen hours.

"What now?" asked Kelleher.

"You get in the Uber and do as he says, and I've got thirteen hours to find Annie."

Kane's phone buzzed in his pocket, and he answered it.

"Is that you, Frank?" he said.

"It's me. Cameron is a bloody genius. We have the crypto wallet thing all set up and ready to go. Apparently, it's just the job, and Baldwin won't be able to tell there's anything wrong with it."

"Send me the link or the image or whatever you have."

"It's winging its way to you now."

"What about a location for Mrs Kelleher?"

"Cameron pulled it out of the bag again. She and Baldwin flew into Hans Christian Andersen Airport. I know it sounds made up, but it's an actual place in Odense in Denmark. We have a location northwest of there called Gyldensteen Strand. It must be where they're holed up. Cameron reckons he can get satellite imagery of the place soon, so he should be able to give you an idea of the layout. The buildings, how many vehicles they have, and an estimate of personnel. Don't ask me how. Cameron told me, but I had no fucking idea what he was talking about."

"Good. Gyldensteen Strand must be close to Fredericia."

"What's that when it's at home?"

"It's where Baldwin is sending John. A train station in Denmark. I need to get to Gyldensteen, and I've got thirteen hours to get Annie out of there."

"Can you do it?"

"I have to do it. Stay alert, Frank. Thank Cameron for his work. He's a good friend."

"One more thing, Jack. Cameron also ran

some checks on Baldwin, and it turns out he really is a changed man from the bloke I knew on the force. He's involved in some serious shit, a real bad guy. So be careful."

"Will do." Kane ended the call and placed the phone in his jacket pocket.

"I think I know where they are."

Kelleher's face lit up, and for the first time since they had left Dublin, there was hope in John Kelleher's eyes. Kane knelt and pulled a black sports bag from under the white plastic table. The bag was heavy, and he stood, slinging its weight across his shoulders.

A metallic clink came from its contents, and Kelleher stared at the bulging mass. Inside the bag, Kane had a Glock handgun and an MP5k submachine gun, both fitted with silencers and enough ammunition to take over a small country. He had grabbed the weapons in the fight at the café, bought the bag en route from Dublin, and stowed the lot in the boot of John Kelleher's car. Disembarking the ferry at Holyhead, they had driven through a checkpoint which comprised a layby and a corrugated warehouse where customs officers would direct some vehicles over for checks. Most of the vehicles they checked were trucks and vans, and Kelleher's car, along with most of the rest, was waved through without incident. They had passed through the customs checks at Dublin Port and again at Folkestone with no problems.

"Are you going there now?"

"I'm going to their location, and if your daughter's there, I'll get her out. You follow Baldwin's instructions. I have the images he wants to prove that we have the crypto. I'll send them to you shortly so that you can send them on. So get in the Uber, and do as he said. We have thirteen hours, John, and then this will all be over."

"What should I do if something goes wrong?"

"Call me on the number I gave you earlier. I'll keep using this burner until we have Annie back. Good luck, John."

Kelleher nodded, and as Kane turned to walk out of the station, Kelleher took a step towards him.

"Jack," he said tentatively, putting his hands together as though he were about to say a prayer. "Please don't put Annie's life in danger. She's all I have left. She doesn't deserve any of this."

"No, she doesn't. You didn't ask for this, either of you. But it's happening, and we are going to get her back. We are the only chance Annie has, so we have to make this work. Baldwin wants the money badly enough to go to these lengths, so he will see this through. Steel yourself, John. Be strong for Annie."

Kelleher nodded, but his expression was blank, and his eyes were hollow. Kane clapped him on the shoulder to give the man more reassurance. What they were about to undertake was incredibly risky. All Kelleher had was a bag of chopped-up paper and a fake cryptocurrency account to take to a ruthless man and his band of skilled ex-soldiers in exchange for his daughter's life. Everything depended on Kane getting there first and doing what he did best, what he had spent a lifetime doing.

"OK," said Kelleher, and he swallowed hard.

"Don't worry. Just do as he said." Kane left him there and strode through the Gare du Nord concourse and beneath its famous clock. He thought of Annie and how afraid she must be, alone and taken from her home. An image of his wife Sally and his own children crying flashed into his mind, of how scared Sally must have been and how his children had watched her die at the hands of ruthless men.

Kane took his phone out again and dialled one of the few numbers in the contacts.

"Hey Kane, what's going on?" chimed Leo Franchetti in his confident American drawl.

"We have a location for the girl and the

kidnappers. I need your help, if possible, Franchetti."

"Listen. It's like I said before – I might be on the insurer's payroll here, but I want this little girl back home as much as you do. What do you need?"

"Fast transport to Hans Christian Andersen Airport in Denmark."

"No problem, get over to Paris-Le Bourget Airport. We have a jet here."

"Whose jet is it?"

"It's my plane, man, and my company. The work we do pays well. Get over here, and we'll get you there as quickly as possible."

Kane waved at a black Toyota Prius with a glowing 'Taxi Parisien' sign on the roof. The driver, a big man in a leather jacket, hopped out and helped Kane put his bag into the boot. Kane sat in the back and told the driver to head to Paris-Le Bourget. A private jet at a small airport meant basic security checks, and if Franchetti used it, then it was likely that Kane could get his weapons on board without having to pass his bag of weapons through a scanner. The flight to Denmark would take around two hours, and if Franchetti could get them in the air quickly, then it would give Kane plenty of time to find Baldwin's location well before Kelleher arrived in

Fredericia. Everything seemed to be falling into place, and Kane could be back with his own family before the weekend was over.

SIXTY-ONE

The trail Kane had left was too easy to follow. He had ditched the clothing in which Condor had hidden her tracking device. But he had used Frank Craven's credit card at motorway services and shops from Dublin Port all the way to Folkestone and then at a café at the largest train station in Europe. It was as though he was inviting her, daring Condor to follow him. Kane knew she was tracking Craven's accounts. How else could she find him?

Kane could have simply dropped off the grid again and disappeared after their fight in Dublin. He was a former black ops operator in a shadow branch of MI6 and an ex-SAS soldier, so Kane knew how to hide his movements and how to make himself noticed. Why he was travelling to Paris by road was a mystery. All Condor could do was follow him and keep focused on completing her mission. Paris was his last known destination, and that was where she had to be.

Condor had spent the train journey to Paris chewing over Kane's reasons, his motives for leading her, and any other assassins on a merry dance. The only logical conclusion was that Kane wanted to lead them to a specific location, somewhere he felt he could take them on and win. Just as he had in Dublin. What she couldn't understand, however, was why Kane had let her live at the cafe. Had he gone soft, or was there a reason she couldn't quite fathom?

She and Kane had been through similar training. They knew how to go dark, and it could only be pride or his warrior hubris that drove him down this path. That was fine with her. Condor was more than ready for the fight and only hoped that she found him before any of the private contractors McGovern had sent in pursuit of the bounty on Kane's head.

Condor's phone vibrated, and she reached into her bag. It was McGovern again, for the third time in the last hour, but Condor didn't want to talk to anybody in London until the mission was complete. No more threats to her career, no more shouting orders or barking demands. Condor would talk to McGovern when the job was done. Until then, there was nothing to say.

She left the train, took a taxi to the Saint-Ouen district in Paris, and got out beside one of its famous flea markets. Immigrants from North Africa inhabited Saint-Ouen alongside the native Parisiens, and the arrondissement was a mix of vibrant street food, restaurants, and diverse cultures. She winced at the pain in her ankle and stood up straight to stretch the bruises on her torso. The bullet cut on her thigh was sore but healing, and her ripped earlobe scabbed beneath a white plaster. Condor breathed in the smells of roasting lamb and mouthwatering spices and ducked into a shop musty with the smell of old clothes. The place was narrow and made smaller by a selection of open umbrellas, some with bright colours popular in the '60s and '70s. She walked along the aisle and ignored the shop assistant, an old black woman with iron-grey hair and a tired face.

The door to the back room creaked open, and Condor moved a net of draping beads aside with her hand. Inside the room was a small kitchenette, and the back wall was busy with more antiques and secondhand objects. Condor had been here before. It was a way station for British government operatives, and she bent and placed her hand on a metallic-looking pad hidden amongst the bric-à-brac. The scanner flashed beneath her palm, and a locking mechanism worked behind the wall before a door the size of a microwave oven popped open. Condor peered inside and took out a handgun and two stacks of euro notes.

Condor had ditched her stolen vehicle back in Dublin, along with the weapon she had taken from the An Garda Síochána officer en route to the hospital. After quickly stopping at her hotel to retrieve her bag, she boarded the next flight to London from Dublin Airport. She picked up Kane's trail there and followed him to Paris via the Eurostar railway. Condor left the thrift shop and bought a shawarma wrap and a coke.

Just as Condor tucked into her meal, her phone vibrated again. Thankfully, it wasn't another call to avoid; instead, it was a message:

Kane en route to Denmark. Team poised to take him out. Meet them at HCA Airport, Odense, in case of any loose ends. Don't fuck it up, or you are finished. Plane waiting for you at Charles de Gaulle.

Condor swallowed her food, and it went down like sandpaper. She hated McGovern. She hated imagining her, as she always did, sitting in a fancy office, leaning back in her leather chair safe and out of harm's way, casually issuing orders without a care in the world for the agents. Condor finished her meal and flagged down a taxi. She asked the driver to take her to the airport and gave him the gate reference for private plane charters. She would pass through the entry gate and board the plane in minutes with her diplomatic entry card. The MI6 operations team would help pinpoint Kane's location, and then, the hunt was on. Condor would be in Denmark in a matter of hours, and god help Jack Kane because nobody else could.

SIXTY-TWO

Kane breathed a sigh of relief as he saw Leo Franchetti waving at him from the deep black tarmac runway of Paris-Le Bourget Airport. Despite thinking things were beginning to fall into place, Kane had spent the best part of two hours stuck in horrendous traffic on the A1 due to protestors blocking the motorway in both directions. Behind the American mercenary was a Bombardier Challenger 300 private jet. Its long nose and tail were as curved and sleek as a blade. The jet was pure white and spoke of the money Franchetti and his team made working private security operations.

Men Kane had served with in the SAS had also gone into that line of work, bodyguarding the rich and famous or fighting private wars funded by God knows who. Kane also knew a good deal of ex-soldiers who came out of the army and ended up with nothing but nightmares and painkiller addictions. It differed in the Security Services, MI6 or the CIA. Those operatives were lifers – they simply knew too much. Kane had willingly signed his life away when he joined Mjolnir, drawn by the thrill and the prospect of more action. However, once part of the agency, there was no easy way out, and Kane had to become an informant to leave Mjolnir. Then, eventually, they had come for him, and Sally had paid the ultimate price for Kane's choices.

The weather in Paris was overcast, and Kane couldn't see the sun beyond a blanket of iron-grey clouds. Despite the weather, Franchetti wore sunglasses. The wraparound black eyewear matched his black combat trousers, zip-top shirt, and calf-length boots he tucked his trousers into. Kane paid the taxi driver and exited the vehicle. He took his bag from the boot, and the taxi's wheels screeched on the tarmac as it turned and drove away.

"Any security problems?" asked Franchetti as Kane drew closer.

"No, all good, just traffic problems" Kane smiled. "Thanks for this, Leo." Kane had shown Cameron's forged passport at the hangar and had gone through a cursory check with the customs officials, but they hadn't checked his bag. The operator ran the security checks for private planes, and it was much more relaxed than the checks a commercial traveller went through inside the major terminals. Kane had always found that worrying. Anyone with enough money could charter a private jet and, under the right circumstances, transport almost anything on board. While occasional random checks were performed by the respective countries' airline authorities, flying privately was a distinctly different experience from commercial flights.

"No problem, man. We're just waiting on some crew members – seems they've encountered the same delays as you. As soon as they're here, we'll load up our gear and get wheels up ASAP. The flight to Denmark only takes a few hours. You sure the kid is there?"

"I'm sure."

"We need to leave for the States tomorrow, but if you need any help on the ground, just shout, man." Franchetti held out his hand, and Kane took it in a firm handshake.

"I work better alone, but thanks for the offer."

Franchetti excused himself as he had to take a call, prompting Kane to find a seat in a small waiting area next to the nearest hangar. He closed his eyes, deciding to make the most of the opportunity to rest before the impending action.

Almost three hours later, a hand tapped him

on the shoulder, telling him it was time for takeoff. Franchetti's crew were moving boxes of gear from the tarmac into the place, talking and joking all the while. Kane kept hold of his bag and climbed up the steps at the front of the jet. He had often flown in small planes like the Bombardier during his tenure with Mjolnir. The agency had three planes to call upon whenever they needed to quickly insert an agent into a situation. Initially, it had all seemed glamorous to a man used to army life. But like anything, he had soon grown used to the jets, designer suits, hotels, watches, and weapons.

Kane preferred the simple life he had led in Warrington during the witness protection programme. Factory work had been facile and fulfilling. He got to spend time with Danny and Kim and didn't have to kill anyone. The simplicity was happiness, and from a life spent living on the edge, Kane understood that family and honest work were the keys to happiness. That was how Kane liked to remember his time in Warrington, but deep down, he had longed for a return to action and had missed the adrenaline of his old life. They were dark thoughts, and Kane pushed them back to the recesses of his mind.

The cabin of the jet smelled like a new car. Its reclining seats were cream leather, and the wooden floor was a birch wood colour. Kane stowed his bag underneath a clear perspex table between two facing chairs and took a seat halfway down the Bombardier's cabin. Two of Franchetti's operators came up the steps and through the hatch. The first was a big, muscular man with a black bandana tied tight across his head and wraparound sunglasses above a spade-shaped beard. A tall and lean woman followed him with dark hair pulled back into a severe ponytail. She removed her shades, settling into the seat across from Kane, and the big man took the seat behind her.

SIXTY-THREE

"Catching a ride to Denmark, huh?" said the woman across from Kane.

Kane glanced at her, smiled, and nodded. She had a square face and thin lips above a pinched chin.

"Leo says you were with the SAS?" chimed the big man in a slow southern American drawl.

"Yeah, I was with the regiment for a while. You serve?"

"Delta. Two tours in the sand."

"I was recon infantry. Loved it, but the money's better on the outside. Name's Grolski," the woman introduced herself and raised two fingers to her brow in a sort of half salute.

"Kane."

"Schwartz," said the big man.

Another of Franchetti's men barrelled into the jet's cabin. He was younger than the other two. He had narrow shoulders, but huge biceps bulged beneath his khaki half-zip shirt.

"Damn, I need a beer, the new arrival declared. He walked along the cabin and high-fived the bigger man on the way past. He headed to the galley, and the sound of glasses and bottles clinking came from the rear of the plane.

"That's Skud," said Grolski. "Don't mind him, we sure don't."

Kane smiled. He closed his eyes to indicate that he didn't want to talk. He just wanted to get to Denmark as quickly as possible and get the job done. Skud and Schwartz opened their beers, clinked the bottles, and talked loudly about an upcoming American Football game. The final three of Franchetti's men boarded the plane, and Leo himself climbed up the steps, closing the door behind him. He took the seat in front of Kane, his face lighting up with a smile.

"Hey, man, we'll be in the air shortly, brother," said Franchetti. "D'you think it's going to get heavy over there?"

"I hope not," Kane answered with a shrug. "If I can get in and get the girl out with no trouble, I'll be happy."

"Fuck that, man," Skud piped up from behind

Kane. "Ain't no fun if there ain't no shootin'."

"Fuckin A," said another of Franchetti's crew, a Hispanic man with a tattoo of a spider crawling up his neck.

"So, you ever think about going into the private sector?" Franchetti asked.

"Not really," Kane answered, doing his best not to sound bored or irritated. Franchetti was doing him a favour, so he didn't want to seem ungrateful. A flight, even a short one like this, usually offered a chance to relax, but Kane had a feeling that this particular journey might not be as smooth sailing.

"You're missing out, brother," Franchetti waved his arms around the cabin as if to emphasise the benefits. "The lifestyle is great. We get to pick our own work. We do insurance jobs; the money is OK, but the work is easy. Then we pick a few jobs where there's action. Plenty of work in the Middle East, South America and Africa. You should try it, Kane. We fought for our governments and our country, but nobody gave a shit. Even when I was a frogman, I got paid peanuts. When we get out, it's our time to make some green. Know what I mean?"

"Good luck to you, Leo," smiled Kane, doing his utmost to look happy for the American. Maybe Franchetti was right, and Kane had been a fool. Kane's love for his country and the thrill of his regiment and Mjolnir days were undeniable. He had handled equipment worth millions of pounds, working to keep Britain safe from foreign and domestic enemies, and now he was nothing. Just an average Joe. Franchetti had capitalised on his experience and training and made himself a millionaire. He had to be worth millions to buy and run a private jet. Baldwin had gone down the same route as Franchetti, even though he was an ex-policeman and not an elite soldier like the Americans. But that hadn't ended well for Baldwin. He had resorted to kidnapping a child to pay back his debts. Kane reminded himself that there's more to life than money, and he hoped it was true.

The pilot made the usual unintelligible radio announcement as Franchetti's crew buckled into their seats. The jet taxied across the runway, and Kane, relieved by the sudden quiet, leaned back and closed his eyes. The mighty roar of the engines and the thundering motion accompanied the aircraft's acceleration down the runway. Kane felt a slight lurch in his stomach as the jet lifted off. Once the Bombardier reached cruising altitude, Franchetti's crew unfastened their seat belts and headed to the galley for refreshments. Kane sat in silence, thinking about how it might go down in Denmark. He had no intel until he could see the imagery Cameron picked up from satellite pictures, but he knew that Baldwin would have a crew not dissimilar from the ex-servicemen on the Bombardier. They had an asset to protect that was worth ten million euros, and they would keep Annie under close guard.

The flight continued as it had begun, with Franchetti's crew talking loudly and whooping whenever one of them said something they agreed with. Kane tried to tune them out and catch some sleep, but the more bottles of beer they drank, the more boisterous they became. They recounted old war stories and rhapsodised about tricky situations they had been in together, mistakes they had made, and guys they had taken down.

"Come on, man, have a beer," urged Skud, leaning over Kane's chair.

"No thanks, I've got to work on the other side. You enjoy them, though," said Kane.

"Jesus, you Brits are always so fucking serious. Lighten the fuck up, man."

A bleep sounded on one of their electronic devices, and Schwartz climbed from the seat behind Grolski. He lumbered between the seats and crouched down next to Franchetti's chair.

"You might want to see this, boss," he said. He still wore his sunglasses, and his head twitched slightly in Kane's direction and then back to Franchetti.

"Looks too easy," Franchetti remarked, and Schwartz stifled a snort. "Tell them we'll take the job."

Schwartz nodded, gesturing for Skud and another member of Franchetti's crew to come down from the galley and join them near the cockpit. Franchetti headed that way with Schwartz, and the two men engaged in an urgent whispered conversation. Kane assumed it was instructions for their next job, and he leant back again and closed his eyes.

Moments later, Kane felt a presence across from him, and he opened his eyes with a sigh.

"Kane?" Franchetti intoned. He, Schwartz, and Skud stood in the aisle in front of Kane's chair with stern expressions. Kane frowned and, feeling a sudden unease, instinctively glanced behind him, noticing that the rest of Franchetti's crew had closed in. Grolski turned around in her cream leather chair to stare at Kane, her face drawn taut, and her features creased into a frown.

"What is it?" asked Kane.

"Sorry, brother. But it's like this – a contract came in, and it's big money."

Kane shifted in his seat. Franchetti's crew had pressed in close around him, faces like thunder. He could smell the lager on their breath and their stale aftershave. There was more to this, and Kane tensed himself, his senses telling him he should be on his guard.

"And?"

"The target is you, brother," Franchetti raised his hands with his palms open. "It's nothing personal, Jack. It's just business. Don't get any crazy ideas. We don't want to hurt you. So, just let us slip these flex cuffs on you until we land, and then we'll bring you in nice and peaceful."

Schwartz held up a pair of black looped plastic handcuffs, which were like doubled-up cable ties. Kane set his jaw. The contract must have come in from the people who now ran Mjolnir. Their first round of assassins had failed. Kane had dealt with them at the café in Dublin. So, they had upped the ante and now planned to send the entire Black Eagle Agency after him. What luck for Franchetti that Kane was already in his lap and in a closed environment. Franchetti's crew moved in closer so that the jet's cabin became smaller. Their imposing figures loomed over Kane like giants, perhaps underestimating the challenge. Their strategy was clear – they'd overwhelm him in the confined space, using their numbers to subdue and restrain him until the plane landed. Then, it would be a drive into a quiet wood or around the coast somewhere where they could put a bullet in his head, send confirmation to their employer, and then get rid of Kane's body.

Kane glanced at Franchetti, then across at Schwartz and Grolski. They had all killed before and were all battle-hardened. One more death was nothing to them. They would bury his corpse beneath the rotting leaf mulch in a Danish forest, throw his body into crashing waves, or put a rock in his belly and send him to the bottom of a deep fjord. They would leave Danny and Kim without a father or a mother, and he would never see their smiling faces again.

Kane raised his hands with a resigned look on his face. Schwartz gave him a wry smile and shook his head as though he expected more from a man with Kane's CV. Schwartz bent towards Kane's hands, his broad, heavily muscled shoulders filling the gap between the seats.

Kane jabbed his fingers upwards, fast and hard, so that the tips of the middle and forefinger of his right hand drove into Schwartz's eye. He cried out in pain, and Kane grabbed his ear with his left hand, ripping it as hard as he could. Sunglasses fell, and blood spurted over the cream seats. Kane remained undeterred despite being outnumbered seven to one in the confined space. He was a former agent of Her Majesty's Secret Service and an ex-SAS operator. He was a killer, and he had to save a girl from ruthless men who would kill her if they did not get their ransom. So, Kane fought with all the venom and skill in his being.

SIXTY-FOUR

"Son of a bitch," growled Franchetti as Schwartz twisted away, screaming, clutching at his ruined eye and the rag of his ear. Blood had sprayed over the cream leather seat in front of Kane, and he was moving, quick and merciless.

Grolski surged towards him, and Kane headbutted her in the nose, leaving her reeling. He kicked out, connecting with Franchetti's shin, and the American grunted in pain. Rough hands grabbed Kane's neck from behind. He fell to his back in the cabin aisle and kicked upwards so that his toe made contact with the face of the man who had held his neck.

The Bombardier's cabin erupted into a welter of shouting, screaming, and muscled bodies flailing and pushing. They tried to get to Kane, but because the space was so small, they got in each other's way. A knee cracked into the side of his head, but he caught the boot and twisted it savagely so that the ankle cracked audibly. He rose, skilfully ducking a punch, only to take one to the back of his head. Kane punched the man in front of him in the balls and then immediately slammed his elbow into the man's temple, dropping him to his knees.

"Kill that son of a bitch!" came a shout behind Kane, and he turned to see Skud bearing down on him with a knife in his fist. The blade shone in the artificial cabin lighting, and it curved like a lion's tooth as long as Kane's hand. A boot kicked Kane in the back, pushing him off balance towards Skud's knife. Kane veered away, but the knife sliced through his jacket and scored his ribs.

Kane grunted, but he caught Skud's wrist with his left hand. The American was strong, and he locked the joint to stop Kane from twisting the knife out of his grip. Skud dropped the blade, caught it with his free hand, and slashed it across Kane's thigh. It stung as though the knife was made of fire, but Kane was still in the fight, and his heart pounded, blood rushing behind his eyes. The war fury was upon him, the battle-induced frenzy that dulls pain, causing everyone else to move in slow motion while Kane moved with lightning speed.

Kane elbowed Skud in the chest to force him back, and he cannoned into Franchetti, who tried to wrench Skud out of the way. Franchetti's frustration was evident as he desperately tried to get past Skud to attack Kane himself, but the two mercenaries got in each other's way. Kane braced himself between two chairs and kicked out with both feet, thrusting the men backwards and off balance. Kane let himself fall back and elbowed Grolski in the face, prompting her to yelp loudly in pain.

"Put that gun away!" a desperate voice shouted from the rear of the plane. "Are you trying to kill us all?" Franchetti's crew were afraid that a bullet hole in the fuselage would tear the cabin open and suck them all out into oblivion. They had to subdue Kane with their bare hands or melee weapons, and that suited Jack Kane just fine. Grolski squirmed beneath him in her seat, and her fingernails scraped down the back of his skull. Kane twisted around and punched her in the stomach twice. Hands grabbed him, dragging him off her, and threw him hard to the cabin floor. A boot stomped on his back, and Kane wriggled and turned. He kicked the attacker's standing leg so that the man landed on top of him just as Grolski was about to fall upon him with a crazed scream and knife in her hand.

The knife blade plunged into the shoulder of the man who had fallen on top of Kane, and Kane rolled him. He grabbed Grolski's ponytail, smashing her head into the metal housing beneath the chair, and she slumped to the floor. Kane pulled the knife from the fallen man's shoulder and stabbed him twice, two rapid punches into his neck. Blood spurted hot across Kane's hand, and he sprang to his feet, knife at the ready to meet the next attacker.

Skud came on cautiously with his knife held underhand. He muttered inaudibly and jerked his hands up and down like a boxer. Kane held his knife low and used his left hand to guard his face and torso. He waited because to attack him, Skud would have to clamber over the bodies of his fallen comrades, and each step would be a hazard. Skud came on, his tongue darted out like a lizard, and then suddenly, a man leapt upon Kane's back. His weight drove Kane down to his knees, and something hard and metallic cracked off the side of Kane's head.

Lights flashed before his eyes, and the cabin went dark for a heartbeat. He shook his head and realised that it was the man who had brandished a gun but had been warned not to fire. He had used the weapon to smash Kane across the head to knock him unconscious, and it had almost worked.

"Hold him still," growled Skud, and he thrust at Kane with his knife. Kane leant forward, and the gunman cried out as Skud's blade stabbed the arm he had coiled around Kane's neck. "I said keep him still!" Skud bellowed. He stabbed again. This time, Kane couldn't move the man on his back far enough, and the blade thrust into his shoulder. Kane grunted. The adrenaline pulsing through Kane's body made the stabbing feel like a punch. There was no pain in those first moments, but he could already feel the blood soaking his shirt, clinging to his skin.

They had him. With one more swing of his knife, Skud could open Kane's throat, and it would all be over. Kane stabbed down with his own knife, and the blade pierced the leg of the man on his back. He ripped the blade upwards, tearing through flesh and muscle, and the man screamed in agonising pain, releasing his grip. Kane leapt forward from his kneeling position and ducked beneath Skud's thrust. Kane slashed the insides of Skud's thighs in two quick motions. Skud fell back as his legs buckled beneath him, and Kane turned to rip the gun from the hand of the man behind him.

Kane released the safety and shot that man in the eye, the sound like an explosion inside the Bombardier's cabin. He turned and shot Skud twice in the chest and then advanced on Franchetti with the gun held before him. Franchetti raised his hands in surrender, panic etched on his face as he glanced at the gun barrel and then up at Kane's determined expression. Kane knew well that the notion of bullet holes causing planes to explode or suck people out through tiny holes was a myth. The most a bullet could do was create a small hole in the cabin, which could alter the pressure inside the jet. Even so, the aircraft's systems would compensate and re-regulate the cabin pressure. But if a window blew out, that would be a different story.

Schwartz reared up from where he crouched between the seats, his face and neck coloured crimson by the ruin of his eye and where his torn ear had bled profusely. Kane shot him once in the leg, and he fell back to the cabin floor, clutching his wound and grimacing in pain.

"On your knees," said Kane. "Turn around and put your hands behind your back."

Franchetti knelt slowly and did as he was told. Kane snatched a handful of plastic handcuffs from the seat across from where Franchetti had sat and secured the American's wrists. Kane pushed his knee into Franchetti's back so that he fell forward and slipped a pair of the cuffs around his ankles. He did the same to Grolski, Schwartz, and the few surviving members of Franchetti's crew.

Kane moved down the plane and knocked on the door, which separated the cabin from the pilot's space.

"Yeah, what is it?" came an American voice from beyond the door, the pilot's voice clipped and obviously annoyed.

"How much longer until we get to Odense?" asked Kane.

"Forty-five minutes. You guys are having one hell of a party back there. Any chance you could stop all the jumping around?"

"Sorry about that. Some lads got a bit carried away. Can't handle their beer."

Kane turned and winked at Franchetti, who just glared at him. The formerly pristine private jet had become a scene of utter carnage. Blood splattered the plush cream leather seats and pooled on the faux wooden floor. Seven bodies lay between the chairs, three dead and four wounded and secured with plastic handcuffs. Kane sat down on the seat next to where Franchetti lay prone on the cabin floor and slowly took off his jacket. The stab wound in his shoulder was bleeding freely, and now that the fight was over, pain pulsed from it, suddenly making Kane weary.

"Where's your first aid kit on this thing?" Kane said.

"Go fuck yourself," Franchetti snapped.

Kane sighed and shook his head. "You can just

tell me where it is, or I can make you tell me."

"In the galley, asshole."

Kane stood and picked his way through the snarl of bodies to find the first aid kit in the galley. He opened a bottle of water, took a long drink, removed his shirt, and washed the blood away with the rest of its contents. The wound gaped like an open mouth, and Kane unzipped the first aid kit. He ripped open a sterilising wipe and dabbed the wound clean. He opened a large adhesive dressing pad, pressed the lips of the wound together, and placed the dressing over it. Kane grabbed a bottle of whiskey from the galley counter, opened it, and took a swig. It burned his throat but distracted him from the searing pain in his shoulder. He wrapped the dressing with a bandage and gave himself a quick once-over.

The rest of his injuries were just bruises. His head hurt, and there was already a lump where the gun had cracked against his skull, but considering he had just fought a crew of mercenaries in a confined space, he hadn't come out of it too badly. The stitches on his forearm from the knife wound taken at the hotel were red and raw, so he wrapped them in a clean bandage.

Kane returned to the cabin and checked Franchetti's luggage. He found a pair of black combat trousers, some boots, one of the half-zip shirts the Black Eagle operatives wore, and a navy version of the classic woollen British army pullover with patches on the shoulders. He pulled that on, gingerly sliding it over his wound. There was also a combat jacket and the copious weapons amongst Franchetti's crew's belongings and in Kane's bag.

Kane strode down the cabin and sat in the first seat, closest to the cockpit and next to where the door would open to release the steps. Kane leaned back and tried to rest, ignoring the groans and moans of the injured behind him. Franchetti and his crew would have killed Kane without a second thought. They saw a chance at some easy money and had paid the price. Kane closed his eyes and waited for the plane to reach Odense, where the hard work would really begin.

SIXTY-FIVE

"Do you want another cup of tea?" Fran Doyle asked. He paced across his kitchen and grabbed the kettle.

"No, thanks," said Craven. He had drunk four cups of tea whilst they waited for Cameron to call back with news of the satellite imagery of where Baldwin was hiding out in Denmark.

"You sure?" This time, Fran made the drinking tea gesture with his hand.

"Go on, then." Craven stood up from the kitchen chair to stretch his back. Craven wasn't sure why the gesture convinced him he suddenly wanted a cup of tea, but it always seemed to do the trick, and he did not know why. It had been a while since they had last heard from Cameron.

The crypto wallet aspect was handled, as was tracking down Jim Baldwin and Mrs Kelleher to Denmark. Baldwin's chosen location for the ransom handover had bothered Craven all day. "Why Denmark?"

Fran Doyle shrugged. "I suppose it's far enough away from here that nobody would expect it."

"Yeah, that was my thinking, but then why not just do it in Paris? What made Baldwin specifically choose Denmark and not somewhere else in France, Belgium, Germany, or Poland, for that matter?"

"Maybe he likes Denmark. I went to Copenhagen once. It was grand but very expensive. Ten euros for a pint."

"It's fucking expensive here in Ireland, mate, never mind bloody Denmark. I paid eight euros for a pint of Guinness in the hotel bar the other day."

Fran Doyle filled the kettle and clicked it on. He took two mugs from the drawer below the kitchen counter and placed a tea bag in each from a red Barry's Tea box. He turned and stared out of his window as the moon shone on the rolling hills of Calverstown, Kildare, which surrounded his house. Craven, too, glanced over at the picturesque view for a moment.

Craven had found Ireland to be a quiet place. If, of course, he discounted the assassins, gun battles, and ruthless child kidnapping. Dublin was a busy city, but outside of that, Ireland seemed much emptier than England. Certainly, it was far less populated than the northwest of England, where he had grown up and lived for most of his adult life. Craven couldn't even drive to the shop for a bottle of milk without getting stuck in traffic. He liked Spain, but Craven wasn't good at making new friends, mixing with people, or liking people in general. Spain's warm weather had been fantastic for Barb's chest and her condition. She had made friends easily and adapted well to their new lives as expats, but Craven had to admit he had been lonely. He told Barb and himself that he loved the quiet, but a big reason he had taken this job was to have something exciting to do. He'd wanted to mix with people and have the chance to see Jim Baldwin again, whom Craven had still thought of as an old friend before finding out that he was a ruthless criminal scumbag. The idea of it had gotten Craven's heart going. He also liked Kane. Craven thought they made a good team, and he knew Kane was a decent man. Though they were in the shit now, and the mission to retrieve Annie Kelleher was about to come to a head, Craven had secretly enjoyed himself, despite the life-or-death situation.

The kettle clicked off, and Doyle poured the steaming water into the mugs, his brow furrowed.

"I think Baldwin chose Denmark because he knew John could make the journey there and that there would be enough opportunities for him to establish if John was serious and had the money or if the police were involved. Perhaps he has a man watching him. Then there's the small airport in Odense to land and depart from quickly. There's open country to hide out in, and people would expect him to be in France or Germany, but who would suspect Denmark? Perhaps he picked it simply because we wouldn't understand it," the Irishman concluded.

"I'm impressed," Craven smiled.

"With what?"

"With how you came up with that in the time it took the kettle to boil. You aren't as daft as you look, mate."

"I'll take that as a compliment. I think. Do you want a biscuit?"

"Aye, go on then." Craven rubbed his gut and thought he probably shouldn't, but he decided he would anyway.

"I have some in the press here somewhere."

"What's a press when it's at home?"

"This?"

"That's a cupboard."

"That's what I said, the press. Here they are." Fran Doyle grabbed a packet of chocolate digestives and brought them to the table.

"It's nice here, County Kildare."

"It's grand."

Craven wondered if he might be happier living in Ireland rather than Spain. The people were nicer, and the food was the same as in England. Ireland's countryside was quiet, and Craven would be left alone. A town or city was only a half-hour drive away if he wanted to return to the hustle and bustle for a few hours. The air in Ireland was fresh and clean but obviously not as warm as in Spain. He took a biscuit and decided that it was a bad idea. Barb was happy and settled in Spain.

The laptop on the kitchen table let out a sing-song tune, and Fran Doyle took a quick slurp of his tea before opening the lid. The secure video chat link Cameron had set up flashed on the screen, and then Cameron's masked face appeared like the Phantom of the Opera.

"Doyle? Craven?" Cameron said.

"We can hear you. Can you hear us?" asked Doyle.

"Yeah, all good. So the satellite came around, and I have footage of where Baldwin is holding up."

"Great," said Craven. "Can you see the girl?"

Doyle looked at him as though he were a simpleton. Craven shrugged and frowned, unsure of what he'd said that was so stupid.

"No," Cameron replied. "Their location is in a pretty remote area, so all I can see as the satellites pass over is the top of the buildings and their vehicles, and then any of their personnel who are outside."

"Can we see a video of them now?"

"No, Frank. The satellite has passed over, and there won't be another one in range for a while. But I'll have fresh images as soon as one comes around."

"Comes around?"

"The satellites are going around the planet in orbit, so they pass over a location and send a picture for a limited time. Once they move out of range, the picture is gone. But over ten thousand satellites are orbiting the earth, so another should come in range soon. I need to find the ones I can access or find a way to access, and then we have our images."

"Ten thousand sounds a lot. Must be like the

fucking M6 up there."

Doyle laughed and shook his head. "So where are they, Cameron?" he asked.

"Baldwin and Mrs Kelleher are at an old farm on the edge of Gyldensteen Strand. It's a nature reserve in Denmark, basically a lagoon or bay that faces the Kattegat Sea. The buildings are on its edges and set inside a small woodland. It looks like a farmhouse and some outbuildings."

"Can you work out how many men they have in there?"

"Four jeeps are parked outside. They appear to be Range Rovers or something similar."

"So they could have anything from four to sixteen men with them," supposed Craven.

"We know Baldwin is there, obviously. Then Mrs Kelleher and Annie, so that's three. That's one car almost full," said Doyle, counting the numbers off on his fingers.

"Four men snatched Annie outside her school."

"So that's seven and one other full car."

"So, there could be another nine bad guys in the final jeeps?"

"Can't tell for sure," Cameron replied, "but I think there's another vehicle parked under some sort of lean-to or garage by the side of the main building. I can just make out the rear, but it could also be a tractor or trailer. I'll check again when I can get another image. Three men are patrolling the woods around the building. I can't see them fully, but they are there."

"Probably armed as well," said Craven.

"Best to assume so."

"We'll relay all of this to Kane, so that knows what he's up against."

"There aren't many CCTV or other cameras around the nature reserve, but the road cameras are pretty good once you get further out. I've already got access to that network, so if Baldwin and his men leave the farmhouse, I'll be able to monitor them."

"Good work, Cameron," Craven enthused.

"Let's hope it's enough to get the girl out. I'll call back when I get another satellite image and let you know if anything changes."

Cameron switched off his video link, and the laptop screen flickered. It then transitioned to a screensaver of the Irish rugby team celebrating with the Six Nations trophy. Craven closed the laptop and pulled out his phone. The images were on the secure email network Cameron had set up with untraceable IP addresses, which

Craven was now beginning to understand, and he sent the pictures to Kane.

SIXTY-SIX

"Don't you want to know who put the hit out on you?" asked Franchetti, his usually confident voice strained and distorted by his uncomfortable position on the cabin floor.

Kane turned in his seat and stifled a yawn. He checked his watch, and it was 11 P.M. Naturally, it would be dark when he landed in Odense, and Kane would need to make his way from the airport to Baldwin's location in darkness. The jet was only a few minutes from Hans Christian Andersen Airport, and Kane allowed himself a second yawn to help burst the pressure in his ears as the plane descended towards its destination.

"No," he said. The order had to have come from the British government or the remnants of the Mjolnir agency. Mjolnir would surely be in tatters after Kane had killed their leader last spring. The agency had made a complete horror show of trying to tidy up the mess surrounding Kane's re-emergence from witness protection. Alarm bells would ring inside MI6, and the senior top brass figures, referred to as the Ruperts, would put a lid on the covert agency without Kane having to lift a finger.

"Your own government wants you dead. How long do you think you'll last out there with all that heat on you? If the contract came to me, it's gone to other highly skilled and expensive mercenary units. You are a dead man walking, pal."

"Do you have any night vision goggles in your kit?"

"In the baggage."

Kane reached over to Franchetti's luggage and dragged a bag into the aisle. He unzipped it, and inside was a pair of L3Harris night vision goggles with their distinctive three lenses at the front. Also inside the bag was a knife belt, a rucksack, a hip holster for a handgun and a strap for a rifle. Kane took the kit and stowed it in his own bag. He had already packed a Glock handgun and an MP5, plus silencers and spare magazines of ammunition.

"Thanks. The Danish government might not

take too kindly to finding you and your crew on this plane with bags full of weapons and three dead bodies."

"Fuck you, Kane," Franchetti spat. He jerked and struggled against his bonds and then gave up, resting his face against the faux wood floor. "When I get out of this, I'm coming for you, and I'm gonna…"

Kane shushed him and held up a finger, which turned Franchetti's face redder than a glass of merlot. Grolski groaned, and her breath came in ragged gasps. Kane stepped over Franchetti, pulled his knife and cut open the plastic cuffs around her ankles. He helped her to sit upright. She looked pale, and her eyes rolled. Kane went to the galley and opened a bottle of water. He knelt beside her and slowly poured some of the water into her mouth.

Grolski sipped the liquid, and her eyes became lucid. She realised the help came from Kane and instinctively jerked away. Her face was a mess, pulped by Kane's elbows, and she had a hideous gash on her forehead from where he had smashed her skull against the seat frame.

"Drink some more for the headache," Kane advised. He didn't remove the plastic handcuffs from her wrists. Grolski was still dangerous and would kill him if she had the chance. So, he helped her take three more sips of water. She was just a soldier doing her job. That was their profession, their entire world. Kane didn't want her to die, nor did he want Franchetti to die. He barely knew either of them, and in another world or time, they could have been comrades, but fate had decreed that they were adversaries, and Grolski and Franchetti had suffered the repercussions of that roll of the dice.

"Seats for landing," came the pilot's voice over the cabin speakers.

"Good luck in Denmark," Kane said. He left Grolski and took his seat, fastening the belt across his waist. The jet's descent steepened, and the plane tilted in the air. One of Franchetti's men groaned as their bodies shifted in the aisle. Kane peered out of the small window next to his seat. The lights around Odense appeared from beneath the jet as it turned and levelled out. Yellow and orange illumination punctured the deep blackness as they descended towards a Danish city shrouded in darkness.

Tyres hit the tarmac, and the jet bounced a fraction. Kane unclipped his seat, grabbed his bag, and moved to the door. He pulled and twisted the lock, and an alarm sounded in the cabin. Kane leant into the door as the jet sped across the runway, and the sound of whooshing air and the howling alarm inside the cabin drowned out the pilot's static panic over the speakers. The jet lurched as the pilot increased the pressure on the brakes. Kane braced himself in the doorway, the cold air whipping his face and hair. The runway zipped past beneath him, and as it slowed and markings became visible, he kicked his bag out of the open door, counted to three, and jumped out after it.

SIXTY-SEVEN

Kane sprinted through the darkness; the sound of jet engines thundered in his ears. To his right, Hans Christian Andersen Airport was a bright glare in the cloak of darkness. It was a small airport, little more than a runway and tower in a sea of grass. The grass was soft and damp beneath his boots, and Kane reached a stretch of wire fence in thirty strides. He wasn't as fit as he had been during his time in the forces, so he was breathing heavily. The wire fence ran around the airport's perimeter, separating it from the fields and woodland beyond.

Kane threw his bag over the fence and clambered over himself. His shoulder throbbed, and he stopped to catch his breath. The stab wound shifted beneath its dressing. It would need to be treated properly soon to prevent excessive blood loss and infection.

Sirens blared throughout the airport, and Kane hefted his bag and briskly jogged to a cluster of bright lights to the northeast. He cursed as his foot snagged in a divot, but he managed to stay on his feet. Crossing the field, Kane jumped over a verge and onto a stretch of concrete pavement. Kane couldn't help but wonder at the surprise that would register on the airport security officer's faces when they found the scene of carnage inside the Bombardier. Hans Christian Andersen Airport could only handle a handful of flights per day, and the staff were unlikely to have dealt with anything like the unprecedented situation awaiting them inside the jet.

Kane turned left, and an illuminated sign told him the building opposite was a softball club. His phone buzzed. It was a message from Craven with pictures of a farmhouse and surrounding buildings at a place called Gyldensteen Strand. That was Baldwin's location, and Kane took a quick look on his map app. The location was only around twenty-five kilometres away. Baldwin was close, and so was Annie.

The satellite imagery showed a large building with smaller constructions at slanted angles to the main building. Fields spread around the complex, and then woodland to the north and southeast. Further images showed a sparsely populated coast area to the northeast, where a curved bay led out to the Kattegat Sea. Craven's pictures included zoomed-in shots of jeeps beside the main building and blurred pictures of what looked like armed guards in the surrounding fields. Kane tucked his burner phone back into his jacket and jogged across the road towards the handball club. Every time his foot hit the road, it sent a jolt of pain into his shoulder wound. Kane came about the handball club into a car park lit by a flickering yellow lamppost light.

There was a fifteen-year-old Volvo estate car in the car park, and within ten heartbeats, Kane had the motor running. He left the handball club to follow his map towards Gyldensteen Strand. The car radio blared a Danish night radio station playing questionable rock music, so Kane switched it off. Sirens howled in the distance, and as Kane joined the main road to drive northwest, lights flashed blue and red at the airport across distant fields.

Late into the night, few cars travelled on the roads between Hans Christian Andersen Airport and Gyldensteen Strand. Two police cars screamed past Kane, heading towards the airport, and he left the main road to turn down a country track faced on each side by high briars. Eventually, Kane was within one kilometre of the target building, so he switched off the car's headlights and let the vehicle crawl until he reached a set of iron field gates. He pulled the Volvo in towards the gate.

Kane took a drink of water from a bottle he had taken from the jet and checked his gear. He placed the night vision goggles on his head, with the lenses pushed up away from his face. Kane holstered the Glock pistol at his hip and strapped the MP5 to his chest. He wore a knife in a sheath at the small of his back and tactical gloves on each hand. Kane stepped out of the car, threw his rucksack over both shoulders and pulled the straps tight. It contained suppressors and spare magazines for both weapons, which he hoped he wouldn't need.

The night air was cool and crisp, chill enough to leave a dusting of dew on the grass verge. Kane climbed over the iron gate, stalking through the soil furrows towards his target. The sky shifted above him, silver-shadowed clouds drifting on the wind, and every so often, a sliver of the moon would peek through the night. In the distance, a fox howled, and the sound resembled a woman's scream enough to make Kane's shoulders shudder.

The burner phone buzzed in Kane's pocket. It was a text message from John Kelleher. Kelleher was following Baldwin's instructions to the letter. Baldwin had been in touch to confirm the meet-up would take place at Fredericia Station in Jutland at 6 o'clock in the morning. Kane knew that was about an hour's drive west from Gyldensteen Strand. Baldwin and Mrs Kelleher would leave the safe house well before five in the morning. Kane had to get into the house – time was short.

A station was a good choice for the exchange. At that time in the morning, it would be busy with commuters travelling to work in Copenhagen. Baldwin and his team would probably get there early to check for any police involvement, just in case Kelleher had gone to the authorities with the details of the exchange.

Kane replied, telling Kelleher to carry on as planned and that he should go to Fredericia Station unless he heard otherwise from Kane beforehand. Kane was at Baldwin's safe house and hoped to find Annie safe and free her in no time. Once he had Annie in his arms, he would notify Kelleher, and they could safely return to Ireland and put this terrifying episode behind them.

Kane could make out the farmhouse building beyond the field, black against grey and silver in the deep of night. He flipped his night vision lenses down and turned the unit on. Suddenly, the world went green and black. The landscape opened up to reveal a hedgerow between the end of the field and a copse of silver birch and ash bordering the farmhouse. Kane skirted around to the southeast and knelt on the edge of the field. The satellite imagery showed guards patrolling the woods, which meant Baldwin and his crew were professional and cautious, so they would likely have eyes on their perimeter. If this was his old life and Kane wasn't up against the clock, he would have spent the day watching Baldwin's crew beforehand and built up a picture of their movements. He'd observe how they patrolled the buildings and how often they relieved each patrol. He wouldn't move in until he understood how many adversaries he faced and where the target building's key entrance and exit points were.

But this wasn't his old life. No longer a Mjolnir agent or SAS operator, he now found himself as a man on a mission to rescue a girl from heartless kidnappers eyeing a ten-million-euro bounty. The girl's mother, consumed by greed, alcohol, and drugs, had allowed her daughter to be ensnared in a life-or-death situation. Shedding his rucksack, Kane retrieved the tube-like suppressor for his MP5. As he fitted the silencer into place, memories flooded back of Sally's demise in a similar circumstance. Government agents had failed to protect her in a safe house, a farmhouse, much like the one he stood before.

Mjolnir had assaulted the building, and Sally had died trying to protect their children. The pain of her death was still there, raw and full of blame and regret. It would never leave him. Their lives could have been different, and they could have been happier. He could have been a better husband and father. Kane couldn't go back in time and right that wrong, but he could use his skills to right other wrongs. Determined, he slung his pack back over his shoulders, gripped his MP5 in both hands and advanced upon his enemies.

SIXTY-EIGHT

Kane moved through the trees in a low, cautious crouch. With his knees bent and the MP5 held up close to his neck in both hands, he took short, quick steps. Silver birch trees loomed above him, washed light green by Kane's night vision goggles, and the undergrowth shone in shades of grey and black. His boots crunched on the forest floor's rotting leaves and fallen twigs. The slightest snap can sound like a drum in the darkness, and the guards were somewhere on the edge of the thin strip of trees. Kane stopped and brought his weapon up to his goggles. He scanned the perimeter of the target building through the sights. He could make out two of Baldwin's jeeps between the trees in shades of light and dark green. The first third of the building was red brick, and the larger part of the construction was a black and grey slate tiled roof. The roof rose, slanting into two dormer windows and culminated in a high chimney.

Kane panned around the outbuildings, which comprised a barn and a double-door garage. Movement caught his eye through the MP5's scope, and he observed a figure walking along the edge of the treeline. A man in a dark jacket and a woollen beanie hat ambled across the wild grass where the trees ended. He carried a semi-automatic rifle slung low on a strap, keeping his hands tucked into his jacket for warmth.

"Clear," the man said, inclining his head slightly to the right. The accent sounded Middle Eastern. Kane wasn't sure if it was Israeli, Lebanese, or Emirati based on that single word.

Kane exhaled and nestled the stock comfortably into his uninjured shoulder. He tracked the man in the circle of his sight. Kane let the black finger of the MP5's sight rest on the target's chest. Kane set himself and then squeezed the trigger. The suppressed MP5 spat two rounds through the silencer, and Kane followed the shot's direction with the weapon held to his eyes, sweeping around the house as he went in case an enemy heard the guard crash to the floor.

The man twitched and groaned on the grass, so Kane fired another round into his face. There was no room for pity or hesitation. The man was involved with the kidnap and ransom of a child, and he had met the fate he deserved.

Kane knelt and turned the dead man's head to the left. He ignored the gory hole and ruined features as he popped the earpiece out of the dead man's right ear and unclipped the small radio from the man's belt. Kane tucked the earpiece into his own ear and put the radio in his pocket, leaving the coiled wire loose. This setup was familiar to Kane, having used similar earpiece-radio configurations in his fieldwork. The wire ran discreetly behind the ear and beneath the user's clothing, connecting to the radio unit. It was basic equipment but reliable. In his more recent operations before entering the witness protection programme, Kane had used a single earpiece, which also contained the radio functionality, but this version worked just as well, if not a little more clunky to wear.

Kane moved on, still in a low crouch, sweeping the building with his eyes fixed through the MP5's sights. He kept inside the trees for cover, the green-tinted world passing through his scope in snapshots.

"Clear," said a voice in the earpiece.

"Clear," Kane affirmed, keeping his voice deliberately muffled as though he were about to cough. The other guards would expect a response from their opposite number, and Kane didn't want the alarm raised, so he took a risk that the guards would all check in at the same time. He paused, but no further communications came over the radio, so he assumed his gamble had paid off.

A glowing light emerged from behind a barn, and its bright white light dimmed and lowered. It was a man puffing on a cigarette. The glaring smoulder resembled the sun in Kane's night vision, and Kane paused, taking aim. He squeezed the trigger, and the MP5 released a quick burst, which took the smoking guard in the head and chest. Faced with a lack of definitive intel, Kane knew he had to remain on high alert, keeping his wits about him as he advanced in the darkness.

Kane moved quickly to the edge of the barn and followed the damp-smelling wooden frame to where it ended twenty paces from the farmhouse. A light was on inside the house, perhaps the kitchen or the entrance hall. He waited to ensure nobody inside the house had heard the guards falling, but the place was still, and the radio silent. He dashed across the open space and leaned against the farmhouse's red brick wall. Kane moved to the back door and turned the round oak handle. With a gentle push, the door creaked open on its ageing hinges. The sound in the quiet of the night was like the Titanic reeling in the ocean, and Kane winced as he slid through the small space. He left the door ajar, not wanting to risk the creaking hinges waking the entire household.

"Jari?" came a deep voice over the radio. "Is that you?"

Kane ignored the sound and paused beside the opening. He scanned the room, his night vision passing over a utility space of pine cupboards, a sink and a cloakroom. There were two doors off that room, and both were slightly open. Kane cautiously approached the first one with weapons raised, entered, and then edged to the corner. The room opened before him, and he scanned the space.

"Jari, you piss more often than my grandfather," came the voice again. "Are you in the bathroom again?"

Kane ignored the voice in his earpiece and swept his weapon around a large kitchen with worktops, cupboards, an old stove oven and an island in the middle of the room with a pine worktop for preparing food. Suddenly, the door opposite Kane opened, and a man dressed in jeans and a jumper strode into the room. He reached for the light switch and immediately died as Kane shot him twice in the head.

Kane hurried across to the door where the dead man had entered. He strode into an entrance hall with another door to the left. Despite his attempt to ignore it, Kane frowned because he could not. He couldn't leave an unswept room behind him. Kane went for the handle, but jerked his hand back in surprise as the door opened. Kane looked up and saw a big man whose expression mirrored his own. The man's eyes were dark, flat and unyielding, even in the hue of green night vision. They were the eyes of a killer that burned with the intensity of a wolf caught in the headlights.

SIXTY-NINE

The enormous man in the doorframe was almost a foot taller than Kane, with shoulders like footballs. He had a wide face, and his forehead stuck out like a Neanderthal. Kane fired, but the big man moved quickly. He jerked to the side as the bullet whipped past his face, and he grabbed the barrel of Kane's MP5 with one hand and Kane's throat with the other. The pressure around Kane's windpipe was like a vice in the man's bear-paw grip. Thick, strong fingers dug into the fibres of Kane's neck, and the giant drove him backwards so that he slammed into the bannister of the staircase that ascended from the entrance hall to the second floor.

Kane struggled to bring his MP5 around, but his enemy held fast. Desperation set in as Kane grabbed at the iron fist around his throat, but he could not shift it. He couldn't breathe, and panic swamped his senses. Kane's tongue popped out of his mouth as he choked to death. The giant sneered and pressed his face closed as though he wanted to hear Kane die. The repugnant odour of stale cheese and onion crisps emanated from the big man's mouth, hitting Kane with a sharp intensity that jolted him. Kane could not allow himself to succumb to death. Not yet.

Kane closed his eyes, steeling himself. He allowed his mind to remember endless hours of combat training. The years spent on the mat, rolling with other soldiers in the regiment. Kane tried desperately to conjure the variety of martial arts he had mastered. So, he drove his knee up into the man's stomach, but his guts were rock hard, and he didn't even flinch. Kane let go of the MP5 and drove the two fingers of his right hand into the man's eyes. He turned and growled as the blow missed, but Kane jabbed again and plunged the knuckle of his middle finger into the giant's Adam's apple. He coughed, and the grip around Kane's throat gave way slightly.

It was enough for Kane to suck in a slither of air into his dying lungs. Kane grabbed a thick wrist with his left hand and pulled the giant's hand closer to his throat. He thrust upwards with his right arm and turned the big man's elbow. His gigantic frame shifted, and Kane drove the elbow away and down so that his enemy had to release his grip on Kane's throat. He bent over as Kane twisted his arm and tried to use his size and strength to resist, but Kane kicked him savagely in the face. Kane reached for the knife at the small of his back, but the man grabbed Kane's ankles and yanked him from his feet. Kane fell backwards and crashed onto the hallway tiles.

The big man snarled like a boar and loomed above Kane. He raised a mighty boot as though to stamp and crush Kane's skull like a watermelon, but Kane swivelled at the hip, pulled his knife free of its sheath and drove the point through the giant's foot. He yelped in pain as Kane twisted the blade, cutting through flesh and bone inside the man's foot, hot blood gushing over Kane's glove.

The man fell on his side, clutching at his ruined foot, and Kane clambered over his vast body, slapped aside his flailing arms and buried the knife in the man's gullet. His eyes widened, and he clawed at Kane's face, ripping the night vision goggles free. Kane jumped away and left the giant to die on the hallway floor.

It had been a desperate fight, and Kane had thought he would die in that terrible grip. He picked up his MP5 and advanced up the stairs in the darkness. A line of carpet ran along the middle of the timber staircase. Each step creaked under Kane's weight as he went slowly upwards, weapon before him, in case another enemy came to attack. The fight in the entrance hall had been noisy and must have woken everybody in the house, so Kane moved faster. His throat felt like it had been rubbed dry by coarse sandpaper, and he told himself to ignore the pain.

Kane reached the top of the stairs and turned quickly to sweep the landing, but it was clear. He went through the first door and into a small, dark room with a tiled floor. The faint plink-plink sound of dripping water caught his attention, and he turned to see a bone-white porcelain bath standing on iron legs.

Kane recoiled in horror as he discovered Caitriona Kelleher in the tub. Her head hung to the side, and in the dim light, her wide, sorrowful eyes stared through him. Her face was pale and still, and her arm draped over the edge of the bath. Kane turned away, realising that the sound of droplets was not from the bath taps but rather from blood leaking from Mrs Kelleher's slashed wrist.

SEVENTY

Craven and Fran Doyle had tuned in to one of the early morning shopping channels and were watching a man in a bright shirt and dazzling teeth try to sell them a food blender.

"Is there nothing else on?" asked Craven, throwing his hands up in disgust. They had watched the mind-numbing programme for too long while awaiting an update from John Kelleher, Cameron, or Kane. There had been nothing for hours, and they had drunk enough coffee and tea to keep half of Ireland awake for the night.

"Not yet. I have Netflix, though. Shall I put that on?" said Doyle, reaching for the remote control. They sat in Doyle's kitchen watching a TV mounted on a wall bracket close to the dinner table.

"Fucking selling houses in LA or documentaries about prisons in Russia? No thanks." Craven stood up from his seat at the breakfast bar and stretched his legs. The moonlight seeped across the hills in the view from Doyle's kitchen window. It cast a pallid glow upon the heavy cloud covering, and in the dim light, Craven could discern the slow movement of sheep on the high pastures moving slowly across a sloping field.

"I hope Annie's alright," Doyle spoke softly and rubbed two fingers into his tired eyes. They had been up all night, receiving calls and texts and passing messages between the three men, one on a train, another raiding a house in Denmark, and the third a masked tech expert in Newcastle.

"The kid has been through a lot." Craven turned and glanced at Fran Doyle. The big man stared into the distance with a drawn look on his round face. He knew the Kellehers well, so it must have felt like losing one of his own family. "We'll have another coffee, maybe a bit of early breakfast as well. Cheer us up a bit." Craven reached for the kettle, but his phone vibrated on the kitchen table.

Craven rushed over to the table and grabbed his phone. "It's Kane."

Doyle sprang out of his chair and clapped a hand over his mouth.

"Jack?" said Craven as he picked up the phone and clicked into speaker mode.

"I've been through the house and swept the surrounding buildings and land, Frank," intoned Kane, his voice flat and weary. "Annie's not here, neither is Baldwin. Two of the jeeps are gone. They were gone before I arrived. I've taken out a crew of Baldwin's men, but the house is empty."

"Bastard."

"See if you can get Cameron to find out where those vehicles went. They've either left early to scout out the train station ahead of the meet, or Baldwin stayed the night closer to the location. Either way, I'm going to head for Fredericia station, but any intel Cameron can provide will help."

"I'll get in touch with him now."

"So how in God's name are we going to get Annie back before Baldwin figures out that we haven't got a pot to piss in?" Fran Doyle sighed, his hands on his hips and his eyebrows knitted together to create a crease in his forehead.

"We have to get her from Baldwin before the meet," replied Kane.

"Yeah," said Craven. "But Jim Baldwin isn't an idiot. He won't bring the girl to the station and just hand her over. He'll make sure he has the money and the crypto safe in his sweaty paws and give John a location where he can find Annie."

"That's the way these things normally go."

"But that can't work for us, Jack. We don't have the fucking money."

"I know. And we are running out of time, fast. So, we need to persuade Baldwin to bring her to the station. It's the only way."

"What if he doesn't buy it?" asked Doyle. "What if he kills her?"

"Look," said Kane. "Baldwin is desperate. We know he's in deep with some serious guys in the Middle East for a lot of money. Things are so bad that he's willing to kill a young girl to get his hands on the money he needs. So, his own life is at stake here. If we leave it until the right time, we can make demands of our own. Baldwin believes we have the crypto and the money. It's so close he can almost taste it. Just before he is about to get the money in his hands, at the point where he thinks his problems are solved, we get Kelleher to demand that Baldwin give Annie to him at the station. The girl for the cash."

"When you say it, it sounds like it could work," supposed Craven, and he glanced at Doyle, who shrugged and nodded. There was nothing else to try. They were out of options, and at least Kane had a plan.

"Frank, there's one more thing."

"What is it?"

"Mrs Kelleher is dead. I found her in the bath. Looks like she took her own life."

"Oh shit," Fran Doyle gasped. He turned and leaned on the worktop around his sink. Doyle stared out of the window. "She had her troubles and did fierce wrong by Annie. But I wouldn't wish that on anyone's soul. Annie will be heartbroken."

"Don't tell John Kelleher just yet. He needs to stay focused, and whether we tell him now or in a few hours' time won't bring her back. Call me when Cameron has found where those jeeps are, and ask him to send me whatever he can find on Fredericia Station."

"Will do."

"Shit, someone is coming."

Kane hung up the phone, and Craven stared at Fran Doyle. Mrs Kelleher was dead, and Baldwin and Annie were gone. Kane's plan was in tatters, and John Keller was going to meet the man holding his daughter hostage with a bag full of shredded paper instead of ten million euros.

Craven's stomach plummeted. He wished he could jump in the car and help Kane or Kelleher.

But all he could do was get Kane what he needed. So, he sat back down, opened the laptop and video-called Cameron. The clock was racing against them. The meeting time drew nearer, and Kane would have to travel to Fredericia Station. He had to get there and figure out a plan before Baldwin realised that the ransom was all a ruse. Craven knew for sure that his old friend would follow through with his terrible threat.

SEVENTY-ONE

The motorcycle tore along the Danish roads like a rocket. Condor leant into every bend, gunned the accelerator at every stretch of straight road and glared through her helmet visor, willing herself to get to her destination quicker, faster so that she could kill Jack Kane.

Operations had told her that a mercenary team had Kane in their hands on board a flight to Odense in Denmark. Kane had escaped and left that team in bloody ruin, which came as little surprise. Condor had flown immediately to Denmark, hired a motorcycle and dialled into the local police radio. Though her Danish was rudimentary and nowhere near as fluent as her French, German, Spanish, Russian or Italian, Condor understood the gist of the carnage exploding in the quiet single-runway airport.

Other calls of note had come in over the police radio. A car was stolen from outside a local handball club, and there was a disturbance at a farmhouse only a short distance from the airport. Gunshots fired. It had Kane written all over it. Condor leant over the side of the bike, guiding it around a sharp bend and into a narrow laneway. She smiled. The litany of injuries stabbed at her battered body. Aching, bruised ribs, stitches in cuts and slashes pulled at her skin as she moved. But she was almost there now. She could feel it.

The motorcycle's headlight beam shone across a trimmed row of briars on either side of the road, and the bike juddered beneath her as it bounced across potholes and ruts in the road. Condor pulled on the brake, and the back tyre slewed as the bike screeched to a halt. She had found the Volvo reported as stolen from the handball club parked next to an old rusty field gate, and beyond a furrowed field was a farmhouse. Its dark tiled roof poked above a line of trees, and Condor could almost feel Jack Kane close by. They had fought, chased, escaped, and hated each other, and a unique bond had been forged in that conflict. They had even spoken in the café where he had butchered the killers sent to take him out.

Condor raced towards the house. She had to admit a grudging admiration for Kane. It was a pity they had never fought side by side rather than against each other. He was good. Cold, highly trained, and efficient. It would be a shame to kill him, to destroy a previously valuable asset. But he didn't work for MI6 anymore, and Mjolnir was all but dead. He was a target, plain and simple. Condor's pursuit of Kane had begun as her gateway to a better position in the service. Now, he was her last chance to hold on to her job and possibly her life.

She reached the end of the lane and turned into the farmyard. Two Range Rovers were parked in the wide driveway, and a dim light shone in the house. Other than that, it was all quiet. The bike engine growled, and she killed the ignition – no time for stealth. She had tried the scalpel, and it had failed. Now, it was time for the hammer.

Condor drove around the driveway and the stables. She let her headlight beam flash across the surroundings and saw a dead man lying in the brush before a line of silver birch trees and another across from the barn. She stopped the bike and took off her helmet. Condor drew her Sig Sauer pistol, stepped off the motorcycle and strode towards the farmhouse.

She marched with her gun held before her, poised and ready to strike. She wore body armour with spare ammunition magazines and other gear strapped to its front. Condor reached the front door and braced herself beside the frame. She waited for three heartbeats but heard no sound. Condor took a deep breath and kicked the farmhouse door in. It exploded on its hinges, and she stepped away from the doorway. Another three heartbeats. No gunfire came, so she knelt and rolled through the open door and came up poised in a crouch with her weapon ready.

Another dead body sprawled across the entrance hall in a pool of dark blood, a big man who had met a grisly end. She moved cautiously around the body and leant to her right to peer inside an open doorway leading into the kitchen area. The house was dark except for a weak light somewhere in the kitchen area. She pushed the pine door open further with her gun, and it creaked slowly.

Condor was about to advance through into the kitchen when the roar of her motorcycle engine snatched her breath away.

"Kane," she hissed through clenched teeth. Condor ran across the entrance hall tiles and sprang over the dead body. She reached the already kicked-open front door and leapt outside with her weapon raised. A man clad in dark fatigues, carrying a backpack and wearing her helmet, gunned the motorcycle down the farmyard. Condor could not help but scream in hateful frustration.

She fired three shots, although he was already beyond her aim, and then another three high into the dark sky. He had gotten away again, and now she hated him. It was a fiery hate, like iron straight from a blacksmith's forge, searing and almost impossible to bear. She ran to a jeep in the driveway and found its key in the well beside the handbrake and armrest controls. Condor pushed the ignition button and began the chase.

SEVENTY-TWO

Kane pushed the motorcycle to its limit, racing along the Danish roads like a speedway racer. The BMW R1250GS was fast and had excellent wind protection despite its slightly clunky appearance, and the brakes responded well. Time was running out. So Kane wove in and out of the traffic on the E20 Motorway. He eased past a lorry and between two white sprinter vans as the overhead sign told him he was about to pass Staurby.

He hadn't told Kelleher about his wife. That could wait. But Kane also hadn't told John Kelleher that his plan to rescue Annie had failed. Annie had not been at the farmhouse, and the only way to get her back now was to go to the ransom exchange and demand that

Baldwin hand Annie over for the money in one transaction. Face to face. Baldwin wouldn't like it, but he had no choice. Kelleher wouldn't like it either. It was a risk, and his daughter's life was at stake. Kane was out of options. It had to work, or it would all end in unthinkable tragedy.

Kane had taken the helmet left beside the motorcycle and wore the tactical clothing he had taken from Franchetti on the jet. Kane carried the MP5 strapped across his chest beneath his jacket and his Glock holstered at his hip despite being in the middle of steadily building traffic. He had stripped a black body armour vest from a corpse at the farmhouse and wore it beneath his woollen jumper.

The assassin was like a bulldozer. It had been her at the house. There was no mistaking her lean frame and cat-like movements. She just kept on coming, and Kane cursed himself again for not killing her when he had the chance. But there was something about her almond-shaped eyes and the hardness in them. She was a younger, fitter version of him. Making her way within the shadow world of MI6, protecting King and Country. Kane had watched her enter the farmhouse, all litheness and power. He could have put a bullet in her skull before she reached the front door, but he had taken his finger from the trigger. Giving her yet another chance at life, and he wasn't truly sure why.

Kane rechecked his mirror and moved into the left lane to overtake a Volvo XC90. He braked as the bike approached a slow-moving car ahead, and once he passed the Volvo, Kane shifted back into the right-hand lane. He glanced at his mirror again, and a dark shape in the distance caught his eye. It was a big car, a jeep, weaving through traffic at incredible speed. Kane checked his front and then flicked his eyes back to the mirror. The jeep was gaining on him. It was a Range Rover, and it could be the woman again. Kane swore inside his helmet and cursed his weakness. What had stopped him from killing her? Maybe he was going soft in his old age.

Kane accelerated, swiftly passing by a Mercedes-Benz showroom on his left. Soon after, he navigated through the junction of a town with the unfortunate name of Middlefart. In the distance, the imposing supporting towers of a suspension bridge came into view. Kane was nearing the New Little Belt Bridge, stretching across the water between Jutland and the island of Funen, on which lay Odense and Gyldensteen Strand.

The Range Rover hurtled closer, and Kane entered the bridge. He stuck to the middle of the three lanes, and the bridge's structural wires whipped along his peripheral vision in a blur. Denser traffic slowed his speed as Kane wove through the vehicles. He checked his mirror one more time, and his breath caught in his chest. The Range Rover was almost upon him, its engine growling like a bear, and its blacked-out windscreen made it seem inhuman, like a murderous robot from a science fiction movie.

The rear window of the vehicle to the left of Kane exploded, and the car swerved. Kane had to brake quickly to avoid the spinning car, and his tyres screeched on the tarmac. He rose from the seat, and the back wheel came up slightly. Kane sat down again and hit the throttle. It was her again, and she was firing at him. Kane hadn't heard the gunshot with his helmet on, but he was sure the assassin had shot out the car's window. A shadow enveloped him, and Kane had to lurch the bike sideways to avoid the black Range Rover from crashing into him. Kane risked a glance at the jeep. The window was down, and the woman glared at him, her angular face stern and determined. A gun rose in her hand, and Kane hit the brakes hard as gunshots exploded from the barrel. His bike stopped dead, and Kane put his foot down on the road's surface.

Vehicles around him screeched to a halt, horns blared in alarm, and drivers shouted wild protests at the insanity of a vehicle stopping in the middle of a busy motorway. Kane ignored them. He unzipped his jacket and grabbed the MP5. He took aim and pulled the trigger. The Range Rover's windows exploded in a hail of bullets. Its rear passenger tyre blew out, and the vehicle skidded across three lanes, crashing into a white Mercedes Sprinter van. The MP5 magazine clicked empty, so Kane let the gun fall to his chest and hit the motorcycle's throttle. He sped past the Range Rover, which lurched and toppled onto its side amidst an unbearable sound of scraping, scratching metal. Kane pushed the BMW bike to its maximum speed as he raced across the bridge towards Fredericia Station.

SEVENTY-THREE

Kane pulled his bike into a car park across from Fredericia Station and dialled Kelleher's number.

"John?" he said when the ringing stopped.

"Is that you, Kane?"

"It's me. Listen carefully…"

"Wait a minute, do you have her? Have you got Annie? I've been going out of my mind with worry."

"John, Annie wasn't at the house…"

"What? Oh my God, oh my God."

"John, you need to stay calm."

"Calm? This was your plan, and it's gone to shit. Where is my baby? Where is my daughter?"

"I went to the farmhouse, but she had already left. We don't have time for this now. You are due to meet Baldwin in fifteen minutes. Are you inside the station?"

"Yes, I'm here, but…"

"You need to send Baldwin a message. Tell him you won't give him the money unless he hands Annie to you inside the station hall. No Annie, no money. Can you do that?"

"I don't understand. We don't have the money, and what if he says no and just kills her?"

"Trust me, John."

"You said that before. Now look where we are."

"There's no time for this, and you have no choice. Send Baldwin the message now. I'm coming into the station, and I will get Annie back for you."

Kane ended the call, left the bike and ran towards Fredericia Station.

SEVENTY-FOUR

Fredericia Station was a long, low, dark brick building with rectangular windows and an old water tower sticking up from its centre like a chimney. It was dull and functional, like a small version of a prison. Fredericia was a regional rail station, not a sprawling travel hub like Gare du Nord or Waterloo Station in London. It had four platforms, seven tracks, and a central ticketing office with kiosks and benches. Cameron had sent some basic information through to Kane's phone, along with confirmation that Baldwin's two jeeps were at the station.

Cameron had utilised roadside CCTV and cameras on the New Little Belt Bridge to track Baldwin's movements from Gyldensteen. Cameron had sent grainy still shots that showed

Annie, Baldwin, and six of Baldwin's men exiting their Range Rovers close to the station.

Kane quickly scanned the information as he ran across a pedestrian crossing towards the station. The road outside the station was wide, clean, and well-maintained. The building loomed up before him, with hard edges and white-rimmed windows. Kane held his hand on the MP5 beneath his jacket to keep the weapon from banging against his body armour vest. He put the phone away and glanced at his watch. It was almost time.

A bus stopped at a layby outside the station, and a dozen commuters piled out of its sliding doors. They marched quickly towards the station entrance like fast walkers in the Olympics. Kane jogged up behind them to fall into the crowd. He kept his head down and matched their pace. Kane was the grey man – average height and build, with a regular oblong face, brown eyes and indistinct features. He was neither good-looking nor ugly, just an average-looking guy who wouldn't stand out in a crowd. It was one reason he had been a successful SAS operator and a major reason he had gone on to have a distinguished career as a black-ops MI6 agent. Only Kane's scars hinted at his profession, skills, or history.

A tall man in corduroy trousers carrying a

battered leather satchel held the station door open for Kane, and he nodded thanks. Kane's phone buzzed in his pocket, and he answered.

"Kane?" said John Kelleher.

"I'm here, John."

"I did what you said. Baldwin went crazy at first and threatened to kill Annie. I could hear her screaming in the background." Kelleher paused, and his voice cracked as he forced back an anguished sob. "But then he agreed. He wants the money. He's bringing Annie to platform two. He'll be here in five minutes."

"Good. I'll be there. Hold tight, John. Keep it together. It's almost over."

Kane put the phone down and wished he truly felt the confidence he had projected in his voice. He entered the station's concourse, a high roof patterned with brown wood-effect panelling and hung with long teardrop-like lighting. The floor tiles were a stale mix of beige, brown and off-white, and Kane's boots squeaked on their shine as he followed the crowd past the ticket kiosks towards a tunnel that led to the platforms. The man in front of Kane scanned his rail card at a waist-high silver unit. It beeped, and the turnstile opened. Kane kept close and leapt nimbly over the rotating iron tubes. Nobody said anything about his fare evasion, but a short woman with bobbed hair behind Kane in the crowd tutted at him. This was Scandinavia. There were no security guards because people rarely broke the rules, and commuters would certainly not expect any sort of criminal activity in their midst.

A short flight of stairs led into a set of diverging tunnels with white-washed walls, and Kane turned right onto a flight of stairs, which led to platform number two. At the corner of the stairs was a big man wearing trousers, boots and a tight-fitting shirt. He leaned against the wall and stared at the four people approaching from the stairwell. Kane slowed his pace so that he was the last in line and kept his head low. He could feel the big man's eyes upon him, almost sensing the thought process as he drank in Kane's clothing, trying to quickly assess whether he was a threat.

There was no time for hesitation or second-guessing. Annie's life was at stake, and Kane doubted that John Kelleher would survive for long once Baldwin saw that his bag contained shredded paper and not five million euros in cash. Kane feigned a cough and lurched to his right as he hopped up the final few steps.

Kane stamped on the big man's foot and drove his right elbow hard into the man's solar plexus as he was about to yelp in pain. Kane grabbed his head in both hands and twisted with all the strength in his arms and shoulders. There was an audible crack as the big man's neck broke, and Kane eased his body to the cold concrete, resting his head back so that he looked like a drunk sleeping off a hard night.

The big man who had been instructed by Baldwin to watch the entrance had been taken care of, allowing Kane to proceed. He came out of the stairwell and continued onto the railway platform. It was a typical long, concrete strip, partially roofed by corrugated steel and held up at regular intervals by cast-iron pillars. There were information signs, a rail map, and benches along the platform. At one end stood John Kelleher in navy chinos and a crumpled, checked shirt. He clutched a sports bag in two hands and stared towards the platform entrance. Four students were standing around chatting, and two businessmen stood between Kane and Kelleher.

Just as Kane's shoulders came abreast with the platform and he emerged from the stairwell, Jim Baldwin strode along the platform on Kane's left-hand side. Three burly men followed behind him, and one dragged Annie Kelleher along by the hand. She whimpered, and the sound tugged at Kane's chest. The man dragging Annie was short and stocky, like a bulldog. The other two were tall and muscular. Baldwin was a metre or two ahead of Kane and hadn't noticed him entering the platform, so he fell in behind them.

The guard on the stairs was there to protect Baldwin's crew's rear, but he was dead. There were only three men with Baldwin, which meant two more would likely be watching the flanks from somewhere else along the platform. Baldwin's crew knew what they were doing. They were professional and, no doubt, highly paid. But none of that mattered because Jack Kane had come for them.

Kane stepped onto the platform and reached to unzip his jacket, but something pressed into the back of his body armour. A hard, cylindrical tube. A gun.

"Got you now, Kane," said a familiar voice. A woman's voice. "Prepare to die."

SEVENTY-FIVE

Kane gasped in surprise and held his breath. He stopped as the gun barrel jabbed into his spine and watched Baldwin and his mercenaries striding towards John Kelleher. Kane could almost hear a monstrous clock thundering every second as though a giant timepiece counted down the moments to John and Annie's deaths in his head.

The assassin had finally caught up with him. Kane thought the crash on the motorway must have stopped her, that he had bought enough time to rescue Annie, but somehow, the killer had fought on and caught him at the worst possible moment. Her voice was cold and ruthless. There was a tired joy in her words as though she savoured the ultimate victory she had worked so hard to achieve.

"Those men are going to kill that little girl," Kane gestured towards Annie with his head, keeping his arms still. Any sudden movement with a gun barrel nestled in his back was to invite death.

Annie Kelleher still wore her school uniform, dishevelled and misshapen from her time in captivity. A red cardigan, tights and a grey dress. Her long brown hair was tied in a plait, which had become ragged and wild in the days since the kidnap.

"Not my concern," said the assassin.

"Her own mother set up her kidnapping. A drunk and a drug addict who took her own life out of shame. She left Annie in those clothes for days. All she has is her father, and those men are going to kill him, too – a whole family wiped out. We can stop that."

"No, we can't."

Time slowed. The clock ticking in Kane's head creaked as it tried to tick another second. The assassin's finger squeezed the trigger, and Kane was about to die. He would never see Danny or Kim again. They would be alone in the world, bereft of both parents because of brutal violence. Annie and John Kelleher would die, and Kane had failed.

"Daddy!" Annie Kelleher called, and the sound

ripped through Kane's heart like a scythe. She had seen her father, and there was such desperation in that call, such hope, such love.

Kelleher dropped the bag of shredded paper and fell to his knees. He held up his hands and shook his head at Baldwin. Kane suddenly sprang forward and launched into a sprint towards Annie. The assassin's gun fired, and a bullet thundered into his back. The impact threw Kane from his feet, and he felt a rib break under its force. His body armour absorbed the shot, and Kane rolled on the hard concrete to come up running again. Kane dodged to his left and right, weaving between an advertising stand and a tall pillar. The sound of another gunshot boomed around the platform, and the bullet ricocheted from an iron pillar.

"Annie Kelleher!" Kane called, and she turned in the hand of her captor, eyes wincing because of the sound of gunfire. Kane didn't have time to reach for his own weapon. He scooped Annie Kelleher up and drove his head into the nose of the man holding her hand. She screamed, and the stocky man fell away.

Angry shouting tore across the platform, and Kane kept running. Another gunshot thumped into his back, and Kane fell to his knees. Annie shrieked in terror, and Kane pressed her head close to him. More gunfire around him. People screamed and shouted in anger and terror. Kane leapt onto the tracks and placed Annie Kelleher down gently with her back against the platform.

"It's going to be alright," he said. Kane held her face in two hands and stared deep into her frightened eyes. "Stay here."

The gunfire had turned the platform into chaos. Some commuters fled towards the exit stairwells, and others curled up into protective balls on the ground. Kane ran along the sunken railway for ten strides, every breath burning like there was a knife in his back. The vest had stopped the bullets, but the internal damage clawed and stabbed like the talons of an eagle. Kane placed a hand on the platform and vaulted himself up onto the edge. He drew his MP5 and fired a volley at Baldwin and his men.

The assassin came at him with her pistol levelled and ready to fire at close range, so Kane let his MP5 go and dropped to the ground. He spun on his back and kicked her legs out so that she fell on top of him. Kane hooked his left arm around her throat and clamped her tight to him. The stab wound in his shoulder screamed in protest, but he swallowed the pain. She growled in anger, and her long legs flailed as she tried to turn out of Kane's grip, but he hooked his legs around hers and pinned her tight. Kane drew his Glock with his right hand and fired at Baldwin's men.

The brutish crew formed a protective barrier around Baldwin and opened fire with handguns. One man fell as Kane's bullet ripped through his thigh, and Jim Baldwin grabbed John Kelleher. The two of them wrestled at the far end of the platform above the bag of shredded paper, which Baldwin thought contained five million euros. A bullet slammed into a bench an arm's length from where Kane lay, and the assassin thrust her head back to cannon into Kane's jaw.

"Bastard," she spat, bucking and jerking in his grip. "I have to kill you. You must die."

She had hunted him, tried to kill him, and Kane had let her live. He had been wrong about that. She was a cold, feral thing of violence and death, and Kane had to protect Annie Kelleher.

Without a moment's hesitation, Kane raised his Glock and shot her in the side of the head. Blood and scraps of skull splattered across the concrete, and Kane immediately pushed her aside. Her dead, heavy corpse slithered off him, and Kane swiftly rolled around a grey metal bin. He fired off another shot, dropping another of Baldwin's men. The Glock clicked empty. Kane ejected the magazine, grabbed another from his belt and clipped it into the handle.

"Hold your fire, Kane," called Baldwin. Kane

peered around the bin, and Baldwin had John Kelleher at gunpoint. The final visible member of Baldwin's crew tentatively inched towards the train tracks, where Annie cowered beneath the platform. "I'm going to take the money and go. We can all leave her alive. Put your gun down."

Kane stood. "Tell your man to stop right there. I'll put a bullet in Kelleher to get to you, Baldwin. I swear it."

"Stand still," Baldwin growled at the tall man, who was only a few paces away from the train line. There were two more of Baldwin's mercenaries in the station somewhere. They would be armed, and Kane expected their eyes to be upon him at that very moment. "All I want is the money, Kane. You release the crypto to me, I'll take the bag, and we can all walk away alive."

"So, we all drop our guns, then?" asked Kane.

"We all drop our guns and do this like gentlemen."

"A bit late for that, isn't it? You've kidnapped a child, Baldwin."

"Don't come over all sanctimonious with me, Kane. You're the biggest killer of all of us. Everywhere you go, people die. You're like the fucking plague."

"Call out your other men, and let's get

everybody here on this platform. The police will be here in minutes. So, if you want your money, do it quick." With the police on their way, Kane had to hurry Baldwin before he checked the contents of the bag at his feet.

John Kelleher stared at Kane from within Baldwin's grip with fear in his eyes. It was a gamble, a deadly gambit that Baldwin wouldn't check the bag, and Kane's only hope was that it would buy him a few moments to swing the balance in his favour.

"Malik, Omar," Baldwin shouted. "Get over here, sharpish."

Two men appeared on the platform on the other side of the train tracks, both men in the same dark tactical clothing as the rest of Baldwin's crew. They both held handguns and made their way across the tracks and up onto platform two.

"I'm outnumbered here," said Kane. "You drop your guns first, and then I'll drop mine. Kelleher and Annie will walk out of here, and I'll transfer the crypto."

"Fuck off, Kane, don't piss up my back and tell me it's raining," sneered Baldwin in his clipped scouse accent. "Send me the crypto now. Then they can go."

"The police are almost here. Time has run out.

I could leave now and keep the crypto. You'll never get out of this station if we don't do the exchange now. Guns down, and John and Annie go free."

"Fuck!" Baldwin screamed and grabbed his head in his hands. The pressure of his debt, the closeness to his money, and his fear of the wicked men he owed seemed to crush his brain under its weight. "Drop them, lads." Baldwin's men all dropped their weapons, and Baldwin himself pulled one from the waistband of his trousers and dropped it to the concrete. Kane dropped his Glock and moved towards Baldwin as he released his grip on John Kelleher.

"Get Annie," Kane said. John Kelleher stumbled past Kane and hurried to the tracks, where he helped Annie climb back onto the platform. The station had gone as quiet as a church, and the sound of police sirens wailed in the distance as the Danish police raced to stop the bloody gun battle.

Kane took slow steps towards Baldwin and his men. "I'm coming closer to you to transfer the crypto and show you the transaction on my phone."

"Hurry, man. Just do it," barked Baldwin. "You lot come closer in case he tries anything." Baldwin's men huddled around him with stern faces and steely eyes.

Kane glanced at Kelleher. Annie was tight in his arms, and she stared at Kane through her father's embrace. Kane winked at her, and she buried her head in her father's breast to shield herself from the fresh horrors that could unfold before her young eyes. Kane came within a metre of Baldwin, and the three remaining mercenaries loomed over him. The smell of their aftershave and the rank stink of their body odour filled Kane's nose.

"Let's do this. The coppers will be here any minute," Baldwin said, gesturing for Kane to hurry. "Malik, check the bag. I want to see the cash."

Kane blinked and fought against the pain surging through his body. Broken ribs and stab wounds pulsed within him. He was exhausted from the carnage, but it was almost over. His enemies were close about him, gathered like a pride of lions around a wounded deer. They were all big men, bulging muscles and clenched fists, experienced soldiers of fortune so close to ten million euros that they could smell it.

Malik bent to unzip the sports bag, and Kane reached to the small of his back as though he was grabbing his phone. But instead, he grabbed the hilt of his knife and slid it from its leather sheath. Kane lashed out like a viper, and the bright blade flashed across Baldwin's throat in a blur. Baldwin stumbled backwards, clutching at his throat, and Kane kept the knife moving, bringing it around and then down with all his strength. The point slammed into the top of Malik's skull, and Kane yanked the blade free. It was like jabbing a knife into a piece of softwood. Malik dropped dead, dark ruby blood spurting from his head to seep onto the grey concrete.

Kane turned just as one of Baldwin's men punched him in the face. A meaty fist cracked into Kane's jaw, but the man's size and sluggishness worked to Kane's advantage. Kane rolled with the punch and stabbed his knife three times in rapid succession into the man's armpit. With the third stab, he forcefully ripped the blade downward to rend and tear the flesh and muscle.

The man dropped to his knees and sighed, eyes closed tight, knowing that he was about to die. The final mercenary snarled at Kane. He had dark-ringed eyes and a black beard as glossy as an animal's pelt. He set himself in a fighting stance and whipped a knife of his own free from his belt. The blade was long, curved, and wickedly sharp. He grinned, turning the knife so that Kane could fully appreciate its deadly edge. The mercenary slashed high, and Kane went to parry the blow, but the man was quick, and the high strike was a feint. Instead, he struck low, and the knife sliced down Kane's thigh, opening his skin in a long wound.

Kane limped backwards, and the man came on again, his knife moving like a blur. Kane had to use his left forearm to deflect the cuts and slashes, and they tore through his skin like claws. Blood flowed freely from Kane's arm and leg, and he shuffled backwards on his good leg. The man howled in anger and launched himself upon Kane, aiming to drive the tip of his knife into Kane's gullet above the top of his vest. Kane caught him and drove the man to the ground. They rolled, grasping and grunting, each man fighting for his life, stabbing, clawing and scrambling to survive.

The man rolled Kane with his hips and came out on top, kneeling on Kane's stomach, pinning his right hand to the concrete. He grinned, teeth bright white in the black of his beard. But he hadn't noticed that Kane had changed his knife hand, and so Kane thrust upwards with his blood-soaked left hand. The knife went through the soft tissue beneath the man's chin, through his beard and up into his mouth. Razor-sharp steel smashed through his teeth and sliced his tongue in half. The man leapt off Kane and clutched at his ruined mouth.

Jack Kane sucked in an enormous breath of air, and his ribs screamed in protest. He rose slowly, battered, slashed, stabbed, shot, and bruised. Jim

Baldwin lay dead in a pool of his own blood, his windpipe slashed open by Kane's knife. The railway tracks hummed and shook with the song of an approaching train. Kane glanced down the tracks, and a lumbering passenger train rumbled into the station towards platform two, blissfully unaware of the carnage at Fredericia station.

"The police are coming. Tell them everything!" Kane called to John Kelleher. "They'll get you home now."

Kelleher nodded numbly, his gaze shifting between Kane and the bodies strewn across the platform. The train rattled to a halt, and the doors slid open with a smooth, gliding sound. The carriage directly facing Kane was empty, so he stepped inside and clung to a shiny brown pole. Blood leaked from his leg and arm, and Kane had to hold himself up before he fell. The doors closed, and the train eased off slowly as if it were an ordinary day.

Annie turned in her father's embrace and raised a small, pale hand to wave, and Kane waved back. She was safe. The train sped Kane away from the station and carried him away from the police and bloodshed. Despite his wounds, Kane would survive. He had to because his own family was waiting for him, and there were others in need of his help, desperate people who needed a grey man. A killer. Jack Kane.

DAN STONE

AUTHOR NEWSLETTER

Sign up to the Dan Stone author newsletter and receive a FREE novella of short stories featuring characters from the Jack Kane series.

The newsletter will keep you updated on new book releases and offers. No spam, just a monthly update on Dan Stone books.

Sign up to the newsletter at https://mailchi.mp/danstoneauthor/sgno14d1hi for your FREE ebook

Or visit the Dan Stone website at https://danstoneauthor.com

ABOUT THE AUTHOR

Dan Stone

Dan Stone is the pen name of award winning author Peter Gibbons.

Born and raised in Warrington in the North West of England, Peter/Dan wanted to be an author from the age of ten when he first began to write stories.

Since then, Peter/Dan has written many books, including the bestselling Viking Blood and Blade Saga, and the Saxon Warrior Series.

Peter now lives in Kildare, Ireland with his wife and three children.

BOOKS BY THIS AUTHOR

Lethal Target

A former Special Forces soldier and Government Agent is pursued by ruthless and brutal operatives.

Jack Kane is a man on the run... a secret agency wants him dead... and his family are in the firing line.

A violent encounter forces Kane to emerge from a life in hiding, where he had hoped his wife and children would be safe. He must go on the run and fight for the lives of those he holds most dear. The forces out to kill him are skilled, well-armed, and are his former colleagues in the Mjolnir Agency, a black-ops shadow section of MI6.

Kane is pursued by savage gangland members and vicious assassins. Can he survive and save his family in his fast paced adventure packed with action, twists, and unforgettable characters?

Printed in Great Britain
by Amazon

42575488R10261